# Called 1

## David West

Copyright © 2022 David West

ISBN:978-1-915225-07-8

# ACKNOWLEDGMENTS

I would like to thank my wife, Claire and my editor, Debz Hobbs-Wyatt for their valuable input to this book. Debz brought her professional editing and critique, and Claire her encyclopaedic knowledge of the Georgette Heyer and Jane Austen novels. Any remaining errors are entirely my own. I would also like to thank Jacqueline Abromeit for another brilliant cover design.

# PROLOGUE

Matthias's mouth was dry, but his hands were clammy. He'd always wanted it, of course. He had plotted it. His brother, Rudolf, had been clever, but weak. But now it was a reality he, well, he feared it. Part of him wished that Henry IV of France had lived and taken this, his birthright, Holy Roman Emperor. But he hadn't. The Treaty of Augsburg was fracturing. The peace and tolerance that both his father, Maximilian, and brother, Rudolph, had pursued, was failing. Protestantism was expanding beyond the agreed boundaries, like a cancer. He looked up from the parchment on his desk, into Melchior's eyes. They showed no emotion. Bishop Melchior Klesl had been chief advisor to his brother Rudolph. If he had found a better man himself, he wouldn't have taken Melchior as his advisor. But Melchior was a very astute man.

'Your Majesty, have you given any consideration to the problem of cereal prices?'

'Melchior, much as I should like to control the weather, it seems beyond my power. I shall continue to pray for good harvests, and encourage my bishops, although I'm sure they already do.'

'It was the question of subsidy, and building more grain silos, that I was thinking of, Your Majesty.'

'If the cities showed a little more respect, I should consider it. How could I commit investment when I am uncertain of their loyalty? Their stream of demands seems never ending.'

'Your Majesty, concerning the unrest in the cities, and Frankfurt in particular, I recommend that the councillors be required to swear an oath of allegiance. It would be best before your coronation, rather than after it.'

'Yes, Melchior, you are a wise counsellor. Make the arrangements.' As Melchior bowed and turned to leave, Matthias felt the sudden urge to make his own mark. 'Make it clear that if they don't so swear, then they will lose their rights and privileges.'

'Of course, Your Majesty.'

The chamber of the Frankfurt city council had three tiers of benches. They reserved the highest benches for the almost aristocratic city fathers. There were forty-three of them, their positions handed down through the families. In addition, and to show willingness to listen to other views, there were fifteen artisans, hand-picked for their obedience. At this council meeting, there were an unusually large number of men in the public space. Their ringleader was well known to the mayor, Hans Friedrich. He baked the bread and, particularly the gingerbread, the mayor enjoyed so much.

'Very well, Herr Fettmilch, say your piece. But please keep it short. We have important business to conduct.'

'What are you doing about grain prices?'

'We have appealed to the emperor for subsidy and investment in grain silos. We shall have to wait and see what his decision is.'

'The people can't wait. The harvests have been so variable, and the current situation helps nobody. Farmers like Andreas Bauer, here, need to know what prices they are going to get. Don't you, Andreas?' There was a cheer from

Bauer in the row behind Fettmilch.

'Millers like Franz Müller here need to know what they're going to pay for grain.'

'That's right,' yelled the man beside Fettmilch.

'All the bakers, not just me, but Ernst Hartmann and Victor Krause here, and the others who couldn't come today, need to know flour prices. What are you doing about it?'

'As I've already said, we have appealed to the emperor for assistance.'

'Why can't the council do something? You're wealthy enough. You're all here on the council because your rich fathers were, and their fathers before them.'

'Herr Fettmilch, you won't get anywhere with such accusations. The governance of the city has been laid down in the charters for centuries. Now, is there anything else, or can we move on to more important matters?'

'Yes, there is something else. What about this oath of allegiance for the new emperor? What we want to know is what these rights and privileges are, that we're going to lose if we don't swear allegiance.'

'Well, they are all set out in the charters.'

'So read them to us. We have a right to know what they are,' Vincenz Fettmilch demanded, to appreciative murmurs from the surrounding mob. Victor Krause, a younger man with curly red hair, stood beside him and slapped him on the back.

'That's right. Read them to us!' Krause shouted.

'We will do no such thing,' Mayor Friedrich retorted. The councillors and artisans around him nodded.

'Is that because you're taxing us too much, and raking off a cut from the fees, you let the Jews extort from us, when we borrow the money to feed our children?' Fettmilch shouted above the chorus of approval from the mob. 'Expel the Jews!'

'The Jews were granted the right to live in the city by the Holy Roman Emperor. So it is not within our power to expel them, even if we wanted to.'

'The emperor wanted their money, just like you do. You're all the same. Show us the charters!'

'We will not. You cast a vile slur on our integrity. Go back to your homes.'

'We won't, will we, brothers?' Fettmilch turned to the mob for approval. They cheered and waved their fists. 'We'll form a committee. We'll come here for every council meeting, and every trial, until you show us the charters. We demand to know our rights.' Councillor Gottburger whispered in Mayor Friedrich's ear. They both nodded.

'Very well, we will show you the charters. But if we do, then you become as responsible as we are for the governance of the city. If any city property is damaged, you will pay your share of the repair. You will answer to the emperor and the bishop, just as we have to. All of you will have to pay,' Mayor Friedrich said, pointing his finger along the rows of citizens who were suddenly quiet. 'No, I thought not. Now go to your homes.' The crowd dispersed. Vincenz Fettmilch pleaded with them to stay, but as the last one sidled out, he turned back to face the councillors.

'You haven't heard the last of this.' Then he turned and left, too.

# CHAPTER ONE

Bellezza reared at the barking and Antonio reined her in and stroked her mane.

'Don't be silly, it's only Luther. What's the matter, Luther?' he asked as he swung his right leg out of the saddle and climbed down. The German herding dog was still barking and trying to jump over the dry-stone wall. Antonio opened the gate and led Bellezza through, with Luther leaping up at him. Once he'd secured the gate behind him, he stroked Luther. 'What's the problem, Luther?' he asked, as Luther turned and ran to the farmhouse door. Antonio followed him up the track and tied Bellezza to the rail outside. Luther pushed open the kitchen door, which was ajar, and scampered inside. Antonio followed him. Luther was nuzzling at his master's body, crumpled on the floor. 'Niccolo!' Antonio called out as he dropped to his knees beside the body. He felt for a pulse, but from the pallor of the skin, he knew it was pointless. There was dried blood on the side of the head. He looked up at the kitchen table and saw a bloodstain on the corner. On the floor there was a broken bowl and flour spread over the flagstones. There was a smear of butter by

Niccolo's feet. 'I'm sorry, Luther. I'm afraid your master is dead. You should come and stay with us. Papa will tell me what we should do about Niccolo. Come on, you look like you haven't eaten for a day or two,' he said, as he gave Luther a hug and got to his feet. Luther followed him outside. Antonio shut the kitchen door, untethered Bellezza, and led her down to the gate with Luther following them. He shut the gate behind them, climbed into the saddle, and rode back up the lane to the Standen vineyard, with Luther trotting along beside him.

'Papa, Niccolo Rosso is dead,' he called out as he opened the door.

'Dead! How?' His father, Sir Anthony Standen, asked, stroking Luther who had run to his side.

'I was riding back from town and Luther was going berserk. I found Niccolo on the floor of his kitchen. He looked as if he's been dead for at least a day, maybe two. It looked as though he was making bread, dropped the bowl and slipped on the butter, then cracked his head on the corner of the table. Either that or he had a seizure and dropped the bowl. What should we do, Papa?' Anthony got up from his chair.

'Are you sure it wasn't the plague again?'

'I'm sure, Papa.'

'I'll go over and have a look for myself. You should ride into town and report the death to the mayor and the priest.'

'What's happened?' Francesca asked as she came into the kitchen.

'It's Niccolo. He appears to have had a seizure and died, darling. Have we got some beef or lamb for Luther? The poor thing looks half starved.'

'Of course. I can't say I'm surprised. When the plague took his wife and children, it broke his heart. Where are you going?'

'I'm going to have a look myself. I'll make sure the

place is secure. Antonio is going into Frascati to report the death.'

'I'm making a stew, so we can eat when you're both back. William will be pleased. He's been pestering us about getting a dog.'

Anthony opened the door of the Rosso house and stepped inside. Niccolo's body was lying, as Antonio had described it. There was no sign of foul play. He went through into the living room. Against the wall there was a wooden chest. He tried the lid, and it wasn't locked. It was packed with blankets. He took one out, went back to the kitchen and draped it over Niccolo's body. He returned to the living room. Most of the surfaces were covered in dust. Poor Niccolo had obviously given up after his wife, Cecilia and their children, Filippo, Luigi and Anna, had fallen to the plague the summer before last. At the end of the room, by the window, there was a desk. There was a leather-bound book lying closed on the desk. Its spine was split, and stitches had been sown to hold the book together. He opened it. The first page was dated 21st September 1505, almost a hundred and six years ago. Below the date there was a column of the produce harvested, the weights, and the sale value made at the market. Anthony kept turning the pages and found that someone had religiously kept the records right up until the year that scythed the Rosso family. He found they had transformed the farm into a vineyard between 1508 and 1530, maintaining a generous kitchen garden to support the family. One at a time, he opened the desk drawers. There were quills and a dry ink bottle. In the bottom drawer, he found a parchment. His attention was drawn to the signature and wax seal at the bottom. Both were familiar to him. Cardinal Pietro Aldobrandini had signed it.

The sun was slipping towards the horizon when

Anthony heard footsteps approaching the house. He closed the book and got up from the desk. As he stepped into the kitchen from the living room, Antonio led Mayor Neretti and Father Battista in through the kitchen door. The mayor nodded at Anthony and pulled back the blanket from Niccolo's body. Father Battista made the sign of the cross, knelt beside the body, and recited a prayer as he closed Niccolo's eyes.

'It's quite clear that Signor Rosso slipped and struck his head,' Mayor Neretti said.

'I don't think so. There would be more blood,' Anthony said, stroking his beard. 'I think his heart failed, then he fell and struck his head.'

'Yes, I see what you mean. But either way it's natural causes, don't you agree, Anthony, Father Battista?' Anthony and Father Battista both nodded. 'Good, then we can get his body on the cart and Father Battista can make the funeral arrangements.'

'Would you let me know when the funeral will be, Father? I'd like to attend. He was a good neighbour, and I don't think there is anyone else.'

'Of course, Anthony,' Father Battista replied.

'The Aldobrandini family leased the vineyard to Niccolo's great-grandfather. The lease and the vineyard account book are on the desk through there,' Anthony said, pointing. 'Would anybody mind if I took them away with me?'

'I know the cardinal thinks highly of you, Anthony,' Father Battista replied. 'There was that matter of the priest burnings that you cleared up a few years ago. It makes me shudder just thinking about it. Why do you want them?'

'The land adjoins ours…'

'Papa, do you think we could buy it and expand our production?'

'Hold your horses, son. Perhaps, but I'm not promising anything. Cardinal Aldobrandini would have to agree to start with. Then I want to have a closer look at the accounts. We need to be sure it would be profitable.'

'I see no reason why you shouldn't take them with you, Anthony,' Father Battista said. 'The cardinal will have his own copy of the contract. Now let's be going while it's still light.'

William, Anna, and Catherine were already eating when Anthony and Antonio got home. Luther was lying on the floor by William's feet. Francesca appeared from the kitchen with warm plates, and Maria followed her with the pot of stew. Anthony and Antonio hung up their coats. Anthony placed the contract and the record book on the sideboard, and they both sat down at the table. Francesca ladled the food onto their plates and everyone continued eating. When he thought Francesca wasn't looking, William picked pieces of meat from his plate, and slipped them to Luther.

'What is it you need to check in the accounts, Papa? The land adjoins ours and the vines are even more well established than ours. Are you trying to find reasons for getting a better price from Cardinal Aldobrandini?' Antonio asked.

'Not him again,' Francesca exclaimed. 'I hoped I'd heard the last of him after he nearly got you burnt alive. He's not got you involved in something else, has he?'

'No, my dear, he owns the Rosso land. I thought we might try to buy it and expand our vineyard. Perhaps not the house though. Poor Niccolo's let that slip into a bit of disrepair.'

'Of course, the house too. Who else would buy a house with no land? You don't think that Aldobrandini devil is going to let you buy the land and leave him shouldered with a house without land? I hate the man, but he's clever and cunning.'

'You're right, but what would we do with it?'

'It won't be long before Greta finishes her medical studies. When does she graduate, Antonio?' Francesca asked.

'I believe she finishes her studies this summer,' Antonio replied between spoonfuls of stew.

'Well, there you are then. What will she do then? If she starts work in Bologna, or returns to help with her father's practice in Turin, what will you do?'

'I don't know. I enjoy working the vineyard. I'm not sure what else I could do.'

'Why are you worrying Antonio so much, darling? Let him eat his dinner in peace,' Anthony added.

'I'm being practical. If she and Antonio marry, they'll need a place of their own. It'll be perfect for Antonio to work the vineyard, and we'll be nearby.'

'I'm not sure Greta will want to live out here, Mama,' Antonio said. 'The population isn't large enough to support a medical practice.'

'Nonsense. Frascati's growing all the time, and we're only a three-hour ride from Rome. She could work a few days a week in Rome and I'll help with the babies when they come along.'

'I'll discuss it with her when I next visit. Anyway, we got distracted. What was it you wanted to study in the account book, Papa?'

'Well, I want to look at it in more detail, but from what I've seen so far, crop yields were increasing until around 1560, then they started falling.'

'Do you think the nutrients in the land are exhausted?' Antonio asked.

'I don't think so. Yields have risen again, just in the last few years.'

'Well, perhaps things improved from one generation to another,' Antonio suggested.

'I don't think it's that, either. Although yields dropped, the income from the market stayed around the same. That means that prices must have risen, which suggests something more widespread.'

'I can explain that,' Francesca said. 'While your father

was rushing around between Scotland, Constantinople, Spain and Italy, he didn't stay anywhere long enough to notice the seasonal changes. It's true, my grandmother talked of much warmer weather when she was young, and kept complaining about how it seemed to get colder every year. I even remember the Arno freezing over. It was difficult to get food in the markets. We all had to work so hard just to put food on the table. I thank the Lord every day that it's been getting better. But it's still much colder than it used to be. Now that I think about it, you seemed to bring the warmth with you, darling.'

'So now that you've saved the world, Papa, what about buying the land and expanding production?' Antonio asked.

'I don't know? How can we be sure we can sell the extra wine?'

'Why don't you sell further afield?' Maria suggested. 'When I was in town on Monday, Giovani, the tailor, was telling me about his cousin who had just come back from the trade fair in Frankfurt. Apparently it's huge. He said something about it being at the crossroad of trade routes. You can buy and sell anything there, even books. Why don't we take our wine and brandy there? You're always saying how good it is, Papa. You even said it's better than anything that Venetian wine merchant you worked for sold, and he was selling to all the embassies in Paris and the royal palace.'

'That's true, so I did,' Anthony said, stroking his beard. 'It's too far, though, Frankfurt. I'm not as young as I was.'

'You don't have to go. Antonio and I can go. Isn't that right?'

'Yes, and I could visit Greta on the way. I can talk to her about your idea, Mama.'

'Can I come too?' Charlotte asked.

'No, sweetheart. I know you're growing, but you're still only six,' Francesca said. 'And now that you've finished your dinner, it's time for bed, and you, Anna, come along.'

'I don't have to go to bed yet, Mama, do I?' William pleaded.

'Not just yet. You should take Luther outside and let him do his business. Maria, Antonio, can you clear the table while I put Charlotte and Anna to bed, please?'

It was only a few days later that they held the funeral in Frascati's new cathedral. The first mass had been held only a year ago. There were pitifully few people at the funeral, just the Standen family and half a dozen members of the congregation, who Anthony suspected the bishop had asked to remain after mass. The bishop did an excellent job of reminding them how close they were to death, and how vigilant they should be for the devil working in their midst. When they emerged into the daylight again, Anthony kissed each of his children, and then Francesca.

'I'm not sure how long I'll be, Francesca. If Cardinal Aldobrandini is in Rome, I may even be back this evening. But if he's away on business, I shall have to decide whether to wait for him.'

'Well, if you have to wait, why don't you spend the time finding out how many physicians there are in Rome? And whether they're any good?' Francesca suggested.

'Good idea, Mama,' said Antonio.

'All right, I'll do what I can. Antonio, can you get the blacksmith to check the wheel bearings on the cart before you return to the vineyard? If you have to take a load of our best wines and brandy to Frankfurt, I don't want the wheels falling off the cart.'

'I will, Papa.'

Anthony untethered Lightning from the rail and climbed into the saddle. He blew them all a kiss, then turned and set off on the road to Rome.

# CHAPTER TWO

Anthony rode up to the Quirinal Palace in Rome. The senior sentry asked Anthony to wait, while he sent the other sentry to find the sergeant of the guard. A few minutes later, the sentry returned with a man most familiar to Anthony.

'Sir Anthony, we haven't seen you for, it must be five years.'

'Yes, it's good to see you again, Sergeant Hennard. I'd like to see Cardinal Aldobrandini.'

'Come through. You know where the stable block is. Wait for me in the guardroom. I'll tell the cardinal's clerk you'd like to see him.'. Then he turned and marched off. Anthony rode over to the stable block. He dismounted, and the stable boy took Lightning's reins. Anthony stroked Lightning, murmuring reassurance. Lightning was quite happy with the stall they put him in, and began drinking from the trough. Anthony took some carrots from his saddlebags and fed them to Lightning. Then he set off towards the guardroom. He didn't have to wait long before Sergeant Hennard returned. 'The cardinal would be very happy to see you, Sir Anthony. Please follow me.' As they crossed the courtyard, a group of men in gowns were in animated discussion near an ornate doorway.

'What's going on over there?' Anthony asked.

'That's the courtroom. There's a trial on. Tissi, Tosso, something like that. He's an artist, accused of raping another artist.'

'Good Lord!' Hennard led the way through the corridors that were so familiar to Anthony. When they reached Cardinal Aldobrandini's apartments, Hennard knocked and the cardinal's clerk opened the door.

'I'll leave you now then, Sir Anthony.' Anthony reached out, and they shook hands. The clerk led Anthony through to the cardinal's office. Cardinal Aldobrandini was writing at his large desk. He didn't look up, but gestured with his left hand that Anthony should sit in the chair in front of the desk. Anthony sat down. He looked around the room. Aldobrandini had added to his collection. He still had The Entombment by Giorgio Vasari, and The Garden of Gethsemane, also by Vasari. Anthony's eye was drawn to a striking, and remarkably well-executed piece. It depicted a beautiful young woman holding the hair of a screaming, naked, reclining man in her left hand as she slit his throat with a knife in her right hand. The girl's face seemed rather impassive. There was an elderly man beside her holding a cloth in both hands. Perhaps it was to wrap around the head. The scratching of the quill stopped.

'I see you like my latest Caravaggio, Sir Anthony. It is rather splendid, isn't it? It's Judith Beheading Holofernes. I recently acquired it from a Genoese banker. Now, to what do I owe the pleasure of your visit?'

'My neighbour, Niccolo Rosso, has died.'

'Yes, I heard. It's most unfortunate. He was a good tenant.'

'I would like to purchase the farm from you in order to expand our vineyard.'

'Would you? I would rather have you as a tenant.'

'As you know, Your Eminence, I prefer to own my land.

15

I will pay a reasonable price. I think five thousand ducats would be a fair figure.'

'You may think so, but I think twenty thousand would be fairer. I will soon find another tenant, or buyer. Frascati is growing. It's a desirable place.'

'I could never make a return from the land at that price, neither could my son.' Aldobrandini stood up and walked over to a window which overlooked the courtyard. He stared out of the window. 'What is the trial, Your Eminence? Sergeant Hennard said that an artist had raped another artist.'

'That's right, Agostino Tassi. His seascapes are good, but his holiness had commissioned him to paint the quadratura for frescoed figures with Orazio Gentileschi, here in the Sala del Concistoro. Orazio had asked him to teach his daughter Artemisia the art of perspective. Allegedly, he raped her, and now refuses to marry her. Orazio has demanded a trial.' Anthony clenched and unclenched his fists. Sweat ran down his brow and into his eyes. 'The daughter has agreed to torture by thumbscrews, so that her testimony is verified. The inquisitors will set about that tomorrow. I've asked that they stick to her left hand. She is a very fine painter, for a woman.' Anthony wiped his hand across his brow, then held his hands beneath the desk. They were shaking. 'What about fifteen thousand? If you are short of money, I'm sure I could find employment for you. Your skills can be unusually useful. Your King James is unsympathetic to our church. Since his parents were both good Catholics, that is unfortunate. You worked for her, didn't you, Mary Queen of Scots?'

'Yes. When her husband murdered David, her secretary, I saved her life. It would be impossible for me to go back to England. They banished me.'

'Banished, but that wouldn't stop you, a man who can walk through locked doors.'

'So what is it you want me to do?'

'I don't know yet. The doge is leading discussions on

our behalf. It's just a contingency plan. Not even a plan. It's just good to know one has resources one can call upon, if required.'

'Would you take ten thousand? That's all I have.' Aldobrandini stared at him for a while. After what seemed to Anthony to be an eternity, the cardinal spoke.

'Well, if that's all you have, that would be sufficient. It's what I paid for Judith Beheading Holofernes. We have a deal. I will get the contract drawn up. When can you have the money?'

'I will collect it from the Medici bank.'

'Sir Anthony, even a man with your mastery of the martial arts shouldn't carry a sum like that through the streets of Rome. Have the manager draw up a bill of exchange in my name. Hand it to my clerk and he will give you the deeds to the farm.'

'Very well, I'll do that. May I ask another thing?'

'Of course, Sir Anthony.'

'Can you recommend a reputable physician?'

'Why, I hope you are not unwell, Sir Anthony. You look well for a man of your years.'

'Oh, I am well, thank you, Your Eminence. Just a few aches and pains from my injuries. My eldest son wishes to marry. The girl is studying medicine. My wife hopes they will set up home in Frascati, and that she can work in Rome. I am tasked with finding out what her prospects might be.'

'You should start with Giulio Mancini. He is an art collector too. You will find him at the Hospital of Santo Spirito.'

◇ ◇ ◇

It took Anthony half an hour to ride to the Hospital del Santo Spirito. It was due east from the Quirinal and just the other side of the River Tiber. He tied Lightning to a rail and enquired at the porter's lodge where he might find Giulio Mancini. A porter led him through what seemed like endless corridors, past wards of patients. Some screamed in agony, and some screamed at those who were screaming to be quiet. Eventually, the porter led him into a ward. A man who appeared to be in his early fifties was at a bedside discussing a patient's infirmities with a group that Anthony assumed were medical students. The porter waited until the doctor finished speaking.

'Doctor Mancini, there is a gentleman to see you.'

'How can I help you, sir?'

'Cardinal Aldobrandini suggested I speak with you…'

'Aldobrandini, why I hear that he's just bought Judith Beheading Holofernes,' Mancini interrupted. 'Caravaggio is a great friend of mine. He has taste.' He turned to address his students. 'We will adjourn for lunch. Meet me at the dissection room after lunch.' The students left. 'Come, sir, we will have lunch in the staff refectory. I'm sorry, I didn't catch your name.'

'Sir Anthony Standen.'

'English then. Welcome to Rome. Let's talk over lunch. You must call me Giulio. Any friend of a Caravaggio owner is a friend of mine.' Giulio led him along the corridor he had just come down. Then he led the way through a door, and across a courtyard. Then Giulio opened a door into the refectory. He led him to a table with plenty of space. They sat down, and servants soon appeared with bowls of pasta, ragù sauce and flagons of red wine. A servant set two goblets down. Giulio poured the wine. 'Are you an art lover yourself, Sir Anthony?'

'Just Anthony, please. Well, I've been told I have a good hand. I enjoyed sketching as a child, and many years ago I discovered I can sketch a face from memory.'

'Then you are talented. Even Caravaggio needs a model. Perhaps I have discovered a new type of artist. I have a theory that there are four types of painter: Caravaggio, Carracci, Cesari, and the rest. I've started writing a book, which I may call Thoughts on Painting, unless I come up with a catchier title. It will include some advice on how to spot fakes. There are so many of them about these days.' Giulio ate more of his lunch and Anthony used the pause to ask his question.

'Giulio, what I wanted to ask you is what opportunities there are for a medical graduate to find employment here? My eldest son hopes to marry a girl who is soon to graduate in medicine. My wife wants her to come to Frascati.'

'Which university?'

'Bologna.'

'Oh, they're very good. Bologna is just as good as Padua, which is where I studied.'

'I've been to Padua. It was to interview Galileo.'

'Remarkable man. Well, what can I tell you? Rome is the centre of the world. It attracts wealthy people. Wealthy men have wives, so a female doctor, a good one, should build up a sizeable practice. There aren't very many female doctors around. The opportunities for dissection were poor in Padua, whereas here, corpses abound. It's a junior doctor's paradise. Of course, it would be better if she'd trained in law. Lawyers seem to get all the best jobs. The pope always seems to have jobs for lawyers, but it's difficult to become the pope's physician. That aside, if it's medicine that interests her, then this is the place to be. There's good money to be made from advising the courts. I did very well advising on a case of poisoning, not long ago.'

'How many doctors are there, per head of the population?' Anthony asked.

'The last figures I read were that we have a hundred doctors here. The population is around a hundred thousand. We have convent hospitals, as well as monastery hospitals, so the girl can complete her training in one of those.' Giulio finished his lunch and drained his wine goblet. 'Talking of students, I'd better get back to mine. It's been a pleasure to talk with you, Anthony.'

'You've been very helpful, Giulio. I have just one more question. Is there another doctor I can speak with?'

'A second opinion, eh?'

'I can't take any chances with the love of my son's life.'

'You should speak with Johannes Faber. That's him at the next table. I'll introduce you.'

Johannes Faber was a younger man, in his early thirties. He had been born in Bavaria and educated at Würzburg. He had been in Rome for around ten years. Like Giulio, he collected art.

'When you come from such a divided country as Germany, it is a relief to live and work in the centre of the Catholic world, Sir Anthony.'

'I know, I too am an exile from the land of my birth.'

'Of course, I do what I can to help my fellow countrymen of the true faith. I have become a conduit between Rome and my brothers, helping them when I can.'

'Do you agree Rome would be a good place for my son's fiancée to work as a doctor?'

'Well, it's better than anywhere else I know.'

'For a female doctor, though. Are you sure that a female doctor would do well here?'

'Yes, I think so. Most doctors are men, but there are a few women, and they're good. Men prefer male doctors, but I think it works the other way around too.'

'They wouldn't be prejudiced, believing that the woman doctor wouldn't be as good?'

'No, they are good. Where is your son's fiancée studying?'

'Bologna.'

'An excellent university and school of medicine. I expect she already knows, but Bologna's professor of medicine in the late fourteenth century was a woman, Dorotea Bucca.'

'Good heavens, a professor.'

'You shouldn't be so surprised, Sir Anthony. A female Greek physician by the name of Metrodora wrote one of the earliest textbooks on gynaecology. It dates from around 300 A.D.'

'Where did you learn that?'

'At the Academia Lincei. I have recently been inducted into the Lincei. It's a significant source of learning.'

'Lincei? I haven't heard of it.'

'It was founded in only 1603, as an academy, it's based at the Palazzo Corsini. They inducted Galileo last year. Federico Cesi is the founder. His great interest is botany, which fascinates me too. I think physicians and apothecaries have a lot to learn from each other.'

'We all have a lot to learn from each other. Would you be willing to help my son's fiancée?'

'Sir Anthony, I'd be happy to make introductions and pass on what I've learnt.'

Anthony rode from the hospital to the Medici bank. After a brief wait, he was ushered in to see the manager. The manager wrote out the bill of exchange, and Anthony returned to the Quirinal Palace. The cardinal's clerk examined it and handed Anthony the deeds to the farm. As he was leaving the palace, he passed a group of people leaving the courtroom. One of them was a young woman. She was around the same age as Maria. Anthony imagined the thumbscrews being tightened, turn by turn. He shuddered and hurried to the stable.

# CHAPTER THREE

It was four days later that Anthony returned to the vineyard. Luther's excited barking and wagging tail alerted them to his return. Francesca poured a jug of beer for him from the cask in the kitchen and handed it to him as he came through the door. He put it to his lips and took a long draught.

'Thank you, darling. I needed that after a long ride.' He put the jug on the table and was just hanging his coat up, when Maria and Antonio came in from the fields. 'You were quick!'

'We saw you riding up the track. Well, did you see him?' Antonio asked.

'Yes, I did.'

'Well, is he going to sell us the land or not?'

'No, Antonio, he isn't.' Anthony saw his son's face drop. Maria and Francesca also looked disappointed. 'He already has. I've bought the land and the house.'

'I thought we were going to go to Frankfurt first, and see if we can find new customers.'

'No, son, you're going to Frankfurt to find new customers who will pay more. Aldobrandini said he wasn't prepared to wait. His initial price was extortionate. I managed to negotiate the price down to half of his asking price. That still seemed to be too high to me. Then I thought about how disappointed you'd be, and your mother seemed set on the house as well. So I accepted it. When I saw your faces just now, I knew I had done the right thing. It's only money, after all. What's money anyway?'

'How much has it cost us?' Francesca asked.

'Well, let's just say that we have little left in reserve. It's cost me everything I had left from the priest burnings, and three quarters of the money from Marie de Medici. He made it clear that he might find a new job for me, if I needed more money.'

'Aargh, that devil! I'll burn for him if you work for him again, and I lose you.'

'Let's hope it doesn't come to that. So, Antonio, Maria, we'd better plan your journey to Frankfurt. Did you get the blacksmith to look over the cart?'

'Yes, Papa. He's replaced both bearings and put new rims on the wheels. I've also had some gallon oak casks made, and been selecting our best wines and brandy to fill them. We could be ready to go tomorrow.'

'I had a look at our maps, and have planned a route,' Maria added. 'I thought about sailing Maia as far as Genoa, then buying a cart to go overland from there. It would save several days if the winds were with us. But I don't like the idea of leaving Maia in Genoa. Then there's the cost of another cart.'

'Well, it was good thinking, but you're right. I think the land route is best. If you find buyers oversea, then using Maia for delivery voyages is an interesting idea, depending on where they are, of course.'

'What about the doctors in Rome, Anthony? How many are there, and are they any good?' Francesca asked.

'Oh, yes, Aldobrandini gave me introductions to two prominent physicians. The first was Giulio Mancini. He was a fascinating man, very interested in art, and building up quite an impressive collection. The second was a Bavarian named Johannes Faber. They're both doing very well for themselves in Rome. They said that although the universities of Padua and Bologna are excellent on the academic side, Rome has much more going for it in terms of practical learning. There are plenty of corpses to learn anatomy from. The city is well provided with hospitals, and they are in great demand for conducting autopsies and doing expert witness work in the courts. Mancini has been involved in some high-profile poisoning cases. But I think if Greta wants a mentor, Faber would be the better man. Mancini seemed more interested in gaining political influence. He kept going on about people with law degrees getting all the best jobs in the papal bureaucracy and the noble households.'

'So how many physicians are there in Rome?' Francesca repeated

'Around a hundred, for a population of about a hundred thousand. So physicians are always in demand. They said that it's becoming dominated by men, but there are convent hospitals, so female physicians are still popular. I'm sure Greta already knows this, but Bologna's professor of medicine in the late 14th century was a woman, Dorotea Bucca. I think that was her name. Faber told me that a woman, a Greek physician called Metrodora, wrote an early medical text. I didn't know that, did you?'

'No, of course I didn't.'

'Neither did I,' Maria added. 'There's no reason a woman can't be every bit as good a physician as a man. You'll have a lot to tell Greta when we get to Bologna, Antonio. When you've finished kissing her, of course.' She winked.

They loaded the cart with the wine and brandy casks, covered by a tarpaulin, which was lashed down to cleats on the wagon sides. They harnessed Bellezza and Allegro to the cart. Maria and Antonio hugged their younger siblings.

William was holding Luther, who seemed disturbed by the farewells. Francesca pulled Maria and Antonio close to her breast.

'I know you can both look after yourselves, but make sure you do. Give my love to Greta, and don't forget to tell her about the house, and how good Rome is for physicians. Where's your father gone?'

'Here he comes, Mama,' Antonio said, as Anthony approached, carrying one of the rifle cases. Anthony climbed up to the driving seat and placed the case behind the seat. 'I've put two flintlock rifles and two pistols in there, together with plenty of gunpowder, spare flints, and projectiles. Maria knows how much more accurate the rifles are than muskets. When I was a messenger in Spain, poor people desperate for food attacked me several times. It was worse in the mountains. Don't look so worried, darling. It's better to be prepared. I'm sure they'll be fine. Now I know what I said about being low on reserves, but don't make false economies on inns along the way. Make sure there's somewhere secure to park the wagon overnight. Better spending an extra scudo or two than have someone drive off with all our wine.'

'Yes, Papa. Can we get going now?' Maria asked. 'The sooner we go, the sooner we'll be back.' They exchanged further hugs, then Antonio and Maria climbed up onto the driving seat. Maria flicked the reins, and the wagon trundled down the track. Antonio looked around as they reached the main road and waved, then they disappeared from sight.

'They've gone now. Go inside, William, Anna, Charlotte,' Francesca said. When they had gone, she looked at Anthony. 'What is it, Anthony? Something is troubling you. Are your old wounds hurting you? The doctors you saw, did they see something in you?'

'No, nothing's wrong with me, not physically.'

'Then what is it? Your shoulders are down, there's something different about your walk. Tell me!'

'There was a trial in progress in Rome. An artist had

raped the daughter of an artist he was working with. I can't stop thinking that if I hadn't left Florence, and you, then it wouldn't have happened.'

'Oh, my love, you had to leave. You knew that the duke's brother had poisoned him. It was too dangerous for you to stay.'

'Yes, but I could have taken you with me.'

'You wanted to, but I wouldn't go.'

'We could have come here, or gone to Rome. I was forever seeking my fortune when my true treasures were in Florence. Maria was working at that wash house with that damned boy. If I'd only stayed. I'm sure I could have kept out of the duke's brother's way.'

'If you had stayed, I'm sure we would have had more mouths to feed. Maria and Antonio would still have had to work.'

'But I would have been here to teach them. They might have had better jobs. She would have been able to fight.'

'It cost you a lot, your trip to Rome,' Francesca whispered, putting her arms around him, pulling him close to her.

'The money, well, the same as the cardinal paid for a painting. It is a very fine painting. It's of a young woman beheading a man. Perhaps I could have been a painter. Oh, what's money anyway? It was silver coins, then for a few hours it was a piece of paper. Now it's that land over there. We work the land, grow crops, mine gold and silver. Then we place some value on the gold and silver, but really it's only land and labour.'

'Yes, and your silver is now that land. Our children will turn the land, the rain, the sun, and the vines into wine. They've gone to Frankfurt to find someone to pay more for the wine. You've invested in their future.'

'Well, we have set a plan in motion for Antonio's future. What can we do for Maria?' Anthony asked.

'I don't know. She has to follow her heart wherever it may take her. She won't have it any other way.'

# CHAPTER FOUR

It took them nine days to reach Bologna. In the large towns or cities, they took their father's advice and stayed at inns where the wagon was secure, and the horses looked after by the stable boy. When they couldn't reach a town by nightfall, such as between Florence and Bologna, they slept under the wagon. They tethered the horses on a long line to the nearest tree. They were quite tired and unkempt when they drove into Bologna.

'I suppose you want to find Greta straight away?'

'No, Maria. She'll be having dinner in the refectory with her student friends. The last thing she'll want is for me to show up looking, and smelling, like this. Let's go to the inn we stayed in last time, then I'll be well rested and bathed. We can have a decent breakfast and see her at lunchtime tomorrow.'

'Why wait until lunchtime?'

'Because she'll be in lectures, or dissecting cadavers, or something. First thing in the morning, I'll go to the porter's lodge and put a note in her pigeonhole to tell her we're here and what our plans are.'

'Sounds like a plan.'

They found the inn they had stayed at four years ago. The owner remembered them and had a tin bath and hot water carried up to their room. Then they ate the fine food that Bologna was famous for.

'It seems so strange, Maria, to be eating again in the room where I first saw Greta.'

'Yes, and what would have become of it if I hadn't convinced you she fancied you?'

'Nothing, I guess. I'll always owe you that.'

The following day, after breakfast, Antonio left a note at the porter's lodge, then he and Maria explored the city, whiling away the time until lunch. When the bell towers tolled twelve, they entered through the porter's lodge, crossed the stone-tiled quadrangle and opened the refectory door. Greta saw them immediately, having taken a bench that was near, and facing the door. She got up, rushed over to him, and flung her arms around his neck. Other students began whistling, and Greta led him by the hand, back out through the door. They left Maria standing in the refectory with students staring at her.

'You must be Maria,' said a young man who had walked up to her as she watched Greta leading Antonio outside. He was tall and slim, with dark hair. 'My name is Joseph Solomon Delmedigo. Please come and sit with us. Greta told us you were coming. We have saved spaces at our table.'

'Thank you,' Maria said, and followed him. Joseph let her sit, before sitting down himself next to her. 'Are you a medical student too?'

'Yes, but I am only visiting Bologna. I'm a student at Padua. We do some student exchanges from time to time. There are some specialisms in which each university excels. I met Greta when she came to Padua for a course last year.'

'If you're a student at Padua, you must know Galileo.'

'Yes, of course. He's teaching me mathematics and astronomy. My interests are wider than medicine.'

'My father says he's very intelligent, but his theory of the tides is completely wrong.'

'I find that hard to believe. Who is your father, and how does he know Galileo?'

'Sir Anthony Standen. He was investigating some murders which appeared to be connected to the theory of heliocentrism. He interviewed Galileo and some of his students. Galileo appears to believe that the moon has nothing to do with tides. I can't vouch for that, as I haven't yet sailed outside of the Mediterranean, but my father has.'

'I shall have to ask Galileo when I get back. Ah, here come the lovebirds.' Greta and Antonio sat down, side by side, opposite Maria and Joseph.

'Antonio, this is my friend Joseph,' Greta said.

'Hello, Antonio, Greta's told me so much about you.' They shook hands across the table. A waiter arrived with plates of roast lamb. Another waiter placed bowls of vegetables on the table.

'So are you a student here too, Joseph?' Antonio asked.

'Not really. I'm studying at Padua. I've come here for a special course, and to see Greta. She's a good friend. We're both in our final year. It's helpful to test each other before our final exams.' There was silence. Maria helped herself to some peas and turnips.

'It was a lovely surprise to get your note, Antonio. Are you staying long?' Greta asked.

'No, we'll be on our way tomorrow. We're on our way to Frankfurt,' Antonio replied.

'Frankfurt! That's a long way. What are you going to Frankfurt for?' Greta asked.

'There's a trade fair there. We need to find some more, and better paying, customers for our wine.'

'I thought you were doing well already.'

'We are, but our neighbour just died and Father bought his vineyard and house. So we need more customers for the extra wine. Mother wants us to get married and for you to come and live with me in the house.'

'Your mother wants me to marry you.'

'Yes. When Father went to Rome to buy the vineyard, she asked him to find out how many physicians there were in Rome. He spoke to two very eminent doctors and there are a thousand people for every physician. Also, they said that Rome is an excellent city to train in. There are plenty of bodies to dissect.'

'That's true. Rome would be an excellent place to complete your training and establish a practice,' Joseph added.

'Well, my father hopes that I'll take over his practice in Turin when I graduate,' Greta replied, staring at her plate.

'It couldn't possibly be as good training as Rome, nor as profitable,' Joseph added.

'You keep out of this, Joseph,' Greta said.

'Mother said she'll help look after the babies…'

'Oh, well that's fine then,' Greta shouted, pushing her plate away and standing up. 'As long as your mother gets her grandchildren and has you with her. It doesn't matter what my mother wants. How many babies does she want me to have, by the way? Good luck in Frankfurt. If you set off now, you'll reach Crevalcore by nightfall. I've got some bodies to dissect,' Greta said as she stormed off.

'This is all your fault, isn't it, Joseph?' Antonio said. 'How long have you been seeing Greta? What have you been getting up to with her?'

'We met on a course last year. She's a good friend. That's all.'

'You expect me to believe that?'

'Yes. Look, I'm a Jew. If I were looking for a wife, which I'm not, I'd be looking for a good Jewish girl, not a Christian. Besides, I was arguing your case. Rome would be an excellent place to complete her training in the hospitals.'

'Come on, Maria. She's right, we could get to Crevalcore by nightfall.' Antonio stood up and walked towards the refectory door.

They drove north out of Bologna on the road to Crevalcore. Antonio was silent, scowling. Maria studied his face.

'You can be such a fool sometimes.'

'Me? You think it was my fault?'

'Of course.'

'I don't believe a word that Jew said. He might not intend to marry her, but they seem too close to be just friends to me.'

'Hello, green-eyed monster, I don't believe we've met.'

'What are you talking about?'

'Jealousy. It doesn't become you, you know.'

'Jealous, me?'

'And stupid. Really stupid.'

'I suppose you would take the girl's side.'

'I struggle to believe you're my twin sometimes. In some ways, it's not fair that I got all the brains.'

'In your dreams.'

'You don't get it, do you? You do not know what you did back there.'

'I know I asked Greta to marry me, and she refused. It's that Jew, it has to be. He's turned her head.'

'No you didn't.'

'I didn't what?'

'You didn't ask her to marry you.'

'Yes I did.'

'No, you absolutely did not. You told her that Mother wanted you to marry. That she wanted Greta to move to Frascati, work in Rome, and have babies that Mother would look after.'

'Well, she does.'

'But you didn't once tell her what you wanted. More to the point, you didn't ask what she wanted.'

'Isn't it obvious what I want?'

'No, and it wasn't a very romantic proposal. It wasn't even a proposal at all. There was no engagement ring. There was no dinner in the moonlight. There was no getting down on bended knee. If I'd known what you intended, I'd have given you some coaching.'

'So you do think it was my fault, then? You're not just taking Greta's side?'

'Yes, it was absolutely your fault.'

'I really love her, you know.'

'I know you do. And Greta loves you, which is why you hurt her.'

'Should we turn back? I could buy a ring, book a moonlit dinner.'

'I think it's best if you let things calm down. We have a job to do. Mother's dreams will come to nothing if we don't find a wealthy wine merchant or two. I think Joseph may calm her down and persuade her that Rome would be good for her.'

'I hate the idea of that Jew hanging around her.'

'Joseph seemed like a very pleasant young man to me. Highly intelligent, charming, quite handsome, really.'

'You're not helping.'

'I think I'll call you Gem,' Maria said. Antonio looked puzzled. 'Green-Eyed Monster.'

'Maria, do you think we could visit Greta's parents near Turin on the way? Perhaps I could persuade them that Greta would be better off in Rome and Frascati.'

'I know you want to do something, but Turin would be a diversion of around two hundred miles. Do you think that going behind Greta's back would improve matters? Besides, we would miss the fair. Then what would have been the point?'

'I suppose you're right, as always.'

They continued north via Milan, across the Alps, via the Saint Gotthard pass to Zurich. They found an inn and after settling in, they took a table in the dining room. The innkeeper came to their table.

'What would you recommend for a couple of starving

travellers?' Maria asked.

'The raclette is a traditional dish of melted cheese, with pickled vegetables. We serve it with bread and wine, as much bread and wine as you can eat and drink.'

'That will be perfect, thank you,' Maria replied.

'Have you travelled far?'

'Yes, we're making our way from Rome to Frankfurt for the trade fair,' Maria explained.

'I don't suppose you would be interested in a sample of our wine?' Antonio asked. 'The Sangiovese grape is exceptionally good and travels well.'

'Thank you, but my cousin has a vineyard and supplies our wine. You're lucky you're doing the journey now and not ten years ago.' Maria and Antonio both looked quizzical. 'Your route is the Spanish road. They marched armies from the Duchy of Milan to the Netherlands along it. Since the peace of 1609, they haven't needed to. But when they were, a wagon of wine and such an attractive young lady as yourself would have been irresistible to those beasts.'

'We're well armed, and can look after ourselves. But an army, well, I'm glad to hear about the peace,' Maria replied. The innkeeper smiled and headed for the kitchen. 'Papa probably doesn't know about the peace. Perhaps that's why he gave us the rifles.'

'No, I think it was just bandits. If he'd expected us to be meeting armies, we wouldn't be travelling at all.' They finished their meal and Antonio put his knife and fork down. 'Maria, I've been thinking about what you said about me not asking Greta what she wanted. It struck me that I don't know what you want.'

'Well I'm not looking for a man, if that's what you mean.'

'I know you say you want to make your fortune and have adventures, but surely you don't want to be alone all your life. What's the point of having a fortune, and adventure, if you can't share it?'

'I'm sharing this adventure with you, my twin brother.'

'Yes, but this is so that I can expand the vineyard. I won't be able to go on every adventure with you, nor will Papa. He made his fortune so that he could buy a big house and marry Mama, eventually.'

'Can we just drop the subject. I don't think there's a man alive that I could love like that.'

'Why not?'

'Just leave it, Antonio. I'd have to be struck by lightening before that happens.'

Despite what she had said, Maria had a fitful night's sleep. When she did dream, she saw herself as a lonely old woman in a large house, counting her money. She wasn't sure that she liked what she saw.

From Zurich, they continued their journey north and reached Stuttgart after five tiring days. They were initially very impressed with the city. There was an imposing palace and a fountain in the main square, where citizens were filling their wooden buckets with fresh water. They stopped to quench their thirst, and one woman filling buckets explained that Duke Christoph had a tunnel a mile long built, from the Pffaf lake in the hills to the city. She had to repeat herself several times, because of the hammering of carpenters who were erecting a large stage next to the fountain. Feeling refreshed, they found an inn and reserved a room.

'Have you come for the witch trial?' The landlord asked.

'No. What's a witch trial?' Antonio asked.

'Lord above, where are you from? What's a witch trial, indeed!'

'We're from Frascati, near Rome. We're on our way to Frankfurt for the trade fair.'

'Don't you have a church in Frascati?'

'Yes, a cathedral,' Antonio replied, exchanging puzzled

glances with Maria.

'Well, what are the priests in Frascati doing to restore the normal balance of God's glorious creation?'

'We're sorry, sir, but we're still not quite following you,' Maria replied.

'Perhaps Frascati hasn't suffered the cold summers, freezing winters, and crop failures then. You're lucky. The Lord must be happy with you. Perhaps the witches haven't reached Frascati yet. They will in time. You shouldn't miss it, it starts tomorrow morning. It won't be as big as the Fulda or Eichstatt trials, but we have three witches. Well suspected witches anyway. One of them has a third nipple, and another killed Schmidt's sow just by looking at it. He loved that sow, he'd had it for donkey's years. I'm not sure what the third one did. With luck, they'll get confessions and get them to name the other witches in the coven. Where have I left the register? Perhaps I left it in the kitchen. I'll only be a minute.'

'Do you think we should find another inn, Maria? This fellow seems insane.'

'The inn seems clean enough, and if there is this witch trial, then my guess is that it will be the talk of all the innkeepers. It might bring in the crowds, so we should take a room while there's one going. I suppose that must be what the stage is for. I hope they finish work on it before bedtime.'

Despite being tired from their journey, they had trouble getting to sleep. The workmen continued work on the stage long into the night. Flickering light danced across the ceiling. Maria got out of bed and opened the window shutters. The carpenters were working in the light of several bonfires around the square. She closed the shutters and went back to bed.

It was mid-morning when they awoke, the sun was already high. Maria got up first and opened the shutters. There was a large crowd gathered around the stage. They tied three women to chairs on the stage, and a man in a cloak with an enormous hat was strutting around. Maria couldn't hear what he was saying above the braying of the crowd. She went over to Antonio's bed and shook his shoulder.

'Wake up! We've overslept.'

Antonio groaned, then opened his eyes. 'Uh. Will they still be serving breakfast?'

'There's one way to find out,' Maria said, pulling on her clothes.

The dining room was being cleared when they got downstairs, but the landlord's wife agreed to get them some water with bread and cheese. They ate their makeshift breakfast.

'How much longer do you think it will take us to get to Frankfurt, Maria?'

'I'd thought four more days. But we won't get over fifteen miles today. Not after the late start we're going to have today. So five days.'

'We'd better get going then. I want to get this thing over so that I can smooth things over with Greta.'

'I know you do. Come on then.'

They collected their bag from their room, paid the landlord, and went to the inn's stable. They hitched Belleza and Allegro to the cart and climbed aboard. The stable boy handed them a bag of carrots before opening the stable doors for them. Antonio flicked the reins, and they trundled out into the square. The crowd was seven or eight deep around the stage. The sound of their wheels on the cobblestones must have attracted the attention of a woman at the back of the crowd. She turned and shouted to them. Antonio reined in the horses to stop the cart.

'What did you say?' he called out.

'Aren't you going to watch the trial? There's only one left.' She shouted up to them. They looked at the stage. There was indeed only one woman left on stage, tied to a chair. The other chairs were empty. The man with the hat was standing beside a child, no older than their sister Charlotte.

'Tell us what you saw, child,' the inquisitor said.

'I saw her sticking pins in a doll.'

'I was repairing my child's doll,' said the woman tied to the chair.

'Continue, Anna. It is Anna, isn't it?' the inquisitor asked the child.

'Yes, sir. Then when I went outside, I saw Herr Ritter lying on the ground.'

'He'd been complaining of chest pains for weeks,' yelled the woman on trial.

'Hear how she screams, see the guilty rage in her eyes,' retorted the inquisitor.

'I see terror in her eyes,' Antonio whispered to Maria. 'Is there anything we can do about this? It's a travesty.'

'I'd like to, brother, believe me. But what can we do? If we argue with him, they'll put us on trial too. It's a dangerous thing to be strangers. I'd like to shoot him, but we wouldn't get ten yards. I'm afraid we'll have to get going and let injustice take its course on this occasion.' As Antonio cracked the reins, the woman who had called up to them turned and called up again.

'Aren't you going to stay and watch? It'll soon be over and then there are the burnings.'

Antonio flicked the reins again and urged the horses into a trot.

In each of the towns and cities on their journey northwards, there was talk of the witch trial that had been held, or was due to be held. As the walled city of Frankfurt came into view, they could see the wide river running east to west on the far side. There was a queue of carts leading to the South Gate. By the time they joined the queue, they were eighth in line. They climbed down to stretch their legs.

'What are you selling?' Maria asked the man on the cart

in front of them.

'Silks, and you?'

'Wine and brandy.'

Antonio climbed back onto the cart as the queue moved. Maria walked along the line. There were shoemakers, silversmiths, furriers, cheesemakers, and a party of minstrels and jugglers. When Maria arrived at the gate, two guards were inspecting the goods on each cart before letting it in. When the silk merchant was let through, and Antonio drew up at the gate, one sentry untied the tarpaulin at the rear of their cart while the other spoke to Maria.

'Where have you come from, miss?'

'Frascati, sir.'

'Where's that?'

'Near Rome, sir.'

'What are you selling?'

'Wine and brandy, sir.'

'We'll have to check. You could have anything in those casks, gunpowder even.'

'They do smell of wine, sergeant,' said the youngest of the sentries. The sergeant climbed onto the cart and selected a cask. He handed it down to his sentry.

'Break this one open.'

'No, please don't break it,' Antonio asked. 'I'll drill it and insert a tap. It won't take a minute,' he said as he reached behind the seat and brought out a hand drill and a wooden tap. He jumped down, laid the cask on its side, and drilled a hole in it. When the drill broke through, some red wine spilled out and he pushed the tap into the hole. 'There, as you see, it's wine.'

'Get my cup, Heinrich,' the sergeant ordered. The sentry went into the gatehouse and reappeared with a wooden cup, which he handed to the sergeant. The sergeant handed it to Antonio, who filled the cup and passed it to the sergeant, who took several large draughts. 'Good wine, you should do well. Your German is very good for Italians.'

'Our father is a master linguist. He taught us many languages.'

'So it seems. On your way.'

Antonio and Maria climbed back onto the cart and drove through the gate into the city. The streets were busy. There were stalls on either side of the street with merchants advertising their wares. The buildings were four, five, even six stories high, and brightly coloured in green, yellow, red, and brown. They gazed through the open doors and windows as they drove past. Most of the buildings seemed to have shops on the ground floor. The window shutters folded down to become tables, on which a range of products were displayed. As they rode further into the centre of the town, the houses became even grander. They saw openings into courtyards, with the shutter tables displaying goods, and further stalls in the centre of the courtyard. Eventually, they reached what appeared to be the main market square.

'What do we do now?' Antonio asked.

'I don't know,' Maria replied.

Antonio noticed a tall young man of about thirty, who was staring intently at Maria. He nudged her.

'You appear to have an admirer,' he whispered. Maria turned her head to look at the man. She felt as though a punch had knocked the wind from her. She couldn't take her eyes off the most beautiful man she had ever seen. His hose and doublet were plain, but beautifully tailored. He had an aquiline nose, blue eyes, fair hair, and a broad, admiring smile. She smiled back, she couldn't stop herself.

'Can I help you? You look lost,' said the man. 'I'm Doctor Manuel Nuñez, at your service.'

'I'm Maria, and this is my twin brother, Antonio.'

'My mother's name is Maria. She's also a famously-beautiful woman. How can I be of assistance?'

'We've come to find buyers for our wine. How do we go about getting a stall?' Maria asked.

'You need to see the Marktmeister. His office is in the

Rathaus, the council building. I'll show you the way. May I climb up beside you?' Maria held out her hand. Manuel took it, as he placed his left foot on a spoke of the wheel, and climbed up to sit beside Maria. She felt the warmth of his body next to her.

'Straight ahead.' Antonio flicked the reins, and they trundled forwards. 'Have you come far?'

'Our vineyard is in Frascati, near Rome. Do you live here, or are you just here for the fair?' Maria enquired.

'I live here. I'm a physician. My clinic is finished for the day, and I decided to have a look around the fair. I'm glad I did.' Antonio saw Maria blush. He'd seen Greta blush, but never Maria.

It was only a few hundred yards to the imposing council building, the Rathaus. Manuel climbed down and held out his hand to help Maria down. She took it, looking directly at him.

'Can I suggest you let me speak with Marktmeister Schultz? I set his son's leg last year. I'm sure I can get you a good price for the best pitch.'

'I'll come with you, Manuel. Antonio can look after the cart, can't you, Antonio?'

'Certainly Maria,' Antonio smiled.

Manuel led Maria into the foyer. The floor was tiled with marble. Paintings hung on the walls. Maria assumed they depicted the growth of the city through the centuries. Manuel led her to an office in the corner. He knocked on the door. A grey-haired man with a thick grey beard stood up and opened the door.

'Manuel, how good to see you, you look well,' the man said, getting up from his desk.

'Thank you, Herman. How is little Tomas?'

'Very well, running about all the time, thanks to you. Who is your young lady friend?'

'May I introduce Maria? Sorry, I don't know your full name.'

'Standen,' Maria answered.

'Fräulein Standen and her brother have a vineyard. They need your best pitch, with a secure store for their wine. What can you do for us?'

'For you, Manuel, I know just the place. My cousin and his family have gone to visit the family in Koblenz. They'll be away until the autumn. He has a fine house, on Wienerstraße. Your friends can have it for two thalers a week.'

'I didn't know you'd taken to robbery, Herman. You can do better than that.'

'For you, one thaler a week,' Herman Schultz replied.

'A thaler a fortnight, and we have a deal.'

'All right, I'll get the keys.' Herman took a bunch of keys from a hook on the wall and led the way out outside. 'Is this your brother, Fräulein?' Herman asked, smiling up at Antonio on the cart.

'Yes, Antonio, this is Herman Schulz. His cousin is away, and Manuel has got us a wonderful deal on his house.'

'I'll walk in front of you. It's only a hundred yards.' Maria and Manuel walked beside Herman as he led them across the market square. Wienerstraße joined the market square at the far side. There was a four-storey house on the corner. Herman opened the door. 'Just give me a moment. I'll open the stable door.' He walked off down the hallway. Two minutes later, they heard a bolt being drawn. They went back outside as Herman pulled open the stable door. 'There, you can keep your horses and cart in here. There's plenty of straw, and the door at the back leads into a paddock. It's only small, this is a city, but the grass has grown a lot since my cousin went to Koblenz. I should get back to the office. You should find everything you need,' Herman said, handing Maria the keys. 'You'll need to sign a rental agreement, and have it registered at the mayor's office. It's just a formality. Could you come to the council house tomorrow morning?'

'Yes, of course. Thank you, Herman. Do you have a

thaler in your purse, Antonio?' Maria asked. Antonio looked in his purse and took out a silver thaler coin. He jumped down and handed it to Herman. They all shook hands and Herman walked across the square towards the Rathaus.

'I'll leave you to sort yourselves out. I look forward to trying your wine. May I come round to see how you're getting on tomorrow, after clinic?' Manuel asked, gazing into Maria's eyes. 'Or perhaps I could come back a little later and give you a tour of the city?'

'Please do,' Maria replied. Manuel bowed, reached out for Maria's hand and kissed it. He shook hands with Antonio, turned, and walked back the way they had come.

Maria and Antonio had just finished cleaning and unpacking when there was knock at the door. Maria opened it, and smiled. Manuel held out a bunch of flowers to her. She took them.

'Thank you, Manuel, they're lovely. Come in, I'll put them in some water.' Manuel followed Maria to the kitchen. She took a vase down from a cupboard, and put some water in it from a jug. She put the vase in the middle of the kitchen table. 'Antonio, Manuel is here. Are you coming?' she called out. Antonio entered the kitchen a few moments later. He and Manuel shook hands. 'Right, shall we go then? Lead on Manuel. You've got the key, haven't you, Antonio?' Antonio locked up and Manuel showed them around the square and the roads leaving off it.

'This is the grocer and bakery that the mayor gets his gingerbread from. He says it's the best gingerbread you can get,' Manuel said, smiling. 'I often wonder why we doctors bother. He complains to me about his gout, but won't take any of my advice.'

'I've heard of gout, but I'm not sure what it is,' Maria said.

'It's a very painful joint condition, most often in the big toe. It's caused by too much alcohol, cheese, and fatty meat.

But in the mayor's case the pain seems preferable to the diet,' Maria laughed. Antonio looked at her, trying to remember the last time he'd heard her laugh. She probably had, but it didn't happen often. Manuel continued the tour. He pointed out the tailor he used, the blacksmiths, then a butcher's shop.

'Those sausages look good,' Maria exclaimed.

'If I were you I'd avoid the pork sausages,' Manuel advised. 'If you knew how many cases of tapeworm I've had to treat, you wouldn't touch them.'

'Yes I've heard about them. Is there a treatment?'

'There are a number of anti-parasitic remedies. Garlic, cloves and pumpkin seeds are the most effective.'

'What's a pumpkin?' Maria asked.

'A large, round, yellowy-orange vegetable from the central americas. Christopher Columbus brought it to Europe. That large house with the white and red walls, is Heinrich's surgery. He's the second best physician in Frankfurt.'

'I suppose you're the best, then. Where is your surgery?' Maria asked.

'It's just down that street,' he said pointing.

'Can we have a look around?'

'Ah, no, it wouldn't be convenient.'

'Why not?'

'I've, er, I've got decorators in. The walls were getting a little shabby. This shop belongs to the best basket maker you will find anywhere.' Manuel continued the tour. 'This is one of the guard towers, set in the city walls.'

'What's that street? There seem to be slogans painted on the walls,' Maria asked.

'Yes, that's Judengasse. It's where the Jews have to live. I'd better be getting back now, to see how the decorators are getting on.' Manuel led them back to the main square and their rented house on Wienerstraße. 'I look forward to seeing you tomorrow.' He reached for Maria's hand, and kissed it. He shook hands with Antonio and walked back towards his surgery.

# CHAPTER FIVE

Antonio and Maria were up at dawn the next day. Antonio collected some logs from the log store he had discovered at the rear of the stable the night before. He took them to the kitchen and fed them into the range, blowing on the embers to get the fire going. Maria was removing the dust sheets from the furniture. Antonio then went out and lowered the window shutters to form the tables on which they could set out their samples.

'Shall I go to the council house and sign this rental agreement, or do you want to do it?' Antonio asked.

'This is all for you and the vineyard, so you do it. I'll get the samples ready and do some shopping.'

'Right, see you later,' Antonio said. He walked back to the council building and found Herman in his office.

'Ah, it's good to see you, Herr Standen. I hope you and your sister find everything to your satisfaction?'

'Yes, Herr Schulz. The house is just right, and the location seems perfect.'

'Excellent. I have the rental agreement ready. We need to sign it with the mayor adding his signature.' Herman led Antonio to the mayor's office. They entered the outer office where the clerk worked. 'Good morning, Karl.' Herman addressed a grey-haired man behind a desk. 'We have a rental agreement for the mayor to sign.'

'I'm afraid he has a deputation with him at the moment,' the clerk replied. Seconds later, the door of the mayor's office opened and three burley men came out. One of them turned back to the open door.

'You haven't heard the last of this. We demand our rights, and the expulsion of that filth. Your days are numbered. We will have fair elections.' They barged past Antonio and Herman and slammed the door behind them. Antonio turned back to see a man standing at the door of the mayor's office. His face was a little red.

'Mayor Friedrich, there is a rental agreement to be approved,' Karl, the clerk, said.

'Yes, very well, come in.' Herman let Antonio go in first, then closed the door behind them. The mayor sat down and indicated they sit in the chairs in front of his desk. Herman passed the rental agreement across to the mayor. He read it. 'I assume you're here for the trade fair. What are you selling?'

'Wine, sir. We have a vineyard in Frascati.'

'I could do with a glass of wine, early as it is. Yes, that all looks in order.' The mayor picked a quill from a stand, dipped it in the inkpot, and signed the agreement. Then he handed the quill and agreement to Herman, who signed, and handed it to Antonio, pointing at where Antonio should sign. 'Leave the agreement with Karl on the way out. He'll keep it in the files.'

Maria didn't know how long Antonio would be, so she did some cleaning . When she was satisfied with the state of the house, she went off to find some food. She bought some cured sausage at a butcher's shop. Then she found a cheese stall and tried some samples. She bought some white, creamy cheese. Then she went off in search of bread. She wanted it to be fresh. Her nose guided her to a shop in the market square. It was a three-storey building with walls painted red. There was a display of vegetables outside the shop, and more inside. There were also shelves laden with loaves of bread behind the counter, where a plump woman, in her early thirties, was serving a slim young woman holding the hand of a young, fair-haired boy. The young woman had a wicker shopping basket in her right hand. Maria stood behind her. There was an open doorway behind the counter, and Maria could feel the heat from the oven radiating out.

'Could I have a large rye loaf please, Hilda?'

'I'm sorry, Ingrid. I'm out of rye. Vincenz has had to pop out for half an hour. He should be back soon, if you can wait.'

'I don't know, Hilda. Perhaps I'll take a wheat loaf instead.'

'Wait, I see him coming.' A large man with a bushy beard entered the shop. 'Vincenz, I need a large rye loaf.'

'Yes, I left some cooling before I went to my meeting. Didn't I tell you?'

'No, you didn't,' Hilda replied.

'Ingrid, and little Tomas. Wait a moment,' the baker said, as he went behind the counter and into the bakery. Moments later, he reappeared carrying a loaf of bread. It was a large loaf, but it looked small in the baker's huge hand. He had donned an apron which was encrusted with dough. In his other hand, he had two gingerbread men. He leant over the counter and handed them to the boy.

'You're too kind, Vincenz. What do you say, Tomas?'

'Thank you, Herr Fettmilch.'

'You're welcome, Tomas. Look how you've grown. How old is he now?'

'He's just turned five. How is Ursula? She's getting married soon, isn't she?' Ingrid asked.

'Yes, she's sixteen now. How the years fly by. I don't know how we'll pay for the wedding, but we'll have to somehow. I might have to go to that filthy moneylender again, unless I can think of something else. Sorry, Ingrid. I must get back to the oven. It's lovely to see you and Tomas,' Vincenz Fettmilch said, smiling and returning to the bakery. Ingrid paid for the loaf and left. Maria bought a wheat loaf and left. She returned to Wienerstraße. Antonio had brought several casks to their stall and had placed some chairs from the dining room for potential customers to sit whilst tasting the wine. When Maria returned, they sat by the stall and devoured the bread, sausages, and cheese.

'What we've forgotten are drinking cups,' Maria said between mouthfuls. 'There are half a dozen in the kitchen, but they're quite ornate. It would be a shame to break them. The stalls are setting up so I'll see if I can buy some after breakfast.'

'Good idea. Manuel seems very taken with you.'

'He's just being polite.'

'If you ask me, he's smitten, and what's more, you seem equally smitten with him,' Antonio smiled and Maria blushed.

'Don't be stupid. I've only met him twice.'

'It doesn't take long, as you very well know. Look at Greta and I. On reflection, maybe that's not the best example. He's coming back tonight, which seems keen to me.'

'Oh shut up, Antonio. You know nothing of how either of us feel.' They finished their breakfast in silence.

'Right, that's better. I'll be off now,' Maria said, pushing her chair back and standing up.

'It would be interesting to know what other winemakers there are at the fair. See what you can find out, Maria.'

Maria went into the kitchen and collected the hessian shopping bag she had noticed hanging on a hook. The market square was getting busier by the minute. She found a stall selling ceramics and bought two dozen small drinking vessels. She continued wandering through the market.

Vendors were calling out to her, trying to entice her to their stalls. There was such an array of produce. The colours, aromas and sounds assaulted her senses. She found three other winemakers and sampled their wines. When the winemaker at the third stall went to get another cask, she whispered to the others, who were also sampling the wines.

'There's much better wine over at the corner of Wienerstraße,' then she drained her cup and left. As she made her way back to join Antonio, she noticed several shoppers who had yellow fabric rings sown around the sleeve of their coats. When she got back to Wienerstraße, Antonio had two customers tasting their wine. Maria set out the new drinking vessels on the table and cleared away the ornate ones of their absent host.

'Thank you, Maria. I've had about a dozen people tasting. They all liked the wine. Some said they'll return and bring a flask to fill. So we're making sales, but I haven't found the big wine merchant that we need yet.'

'Well, I'll tell you this. Our wine is head and shoulders above the other wines I've sampled. Why don't you let me look after the stall while you assess the competition for yourself?'

Antonio took up Maria's offer. She was quite right. They attracted more and more customers to their stall, and sold wine, but in small quantities. From the conversations she overheard, people were discussing handouts they had been given. It was mid-afternoon when Manuel arrived.

'Well, you seem to be attracting attention,' he said, smiling, as he took Maria's hand again and kissed it.

'Yes, but not the attention we're seeking. We need wine merchants, not casual customers. It's excellent wine, try some.' Maria replied, pouring him some. Manuel took the cup and sipped the wine.

'You're right, it is excellent. One of my patients, Franz Schröder, is a wine merchant. He specialises in French wines, but he'll know his competition. Would it help if I took you to meet him?'

'I'm sure it would, wouldn't it, Antonio?' Maria replied, dragging her gaze away from Manuel's blue eyes.

'Yes. That would be immensely helpful of you, Manuel. When would be the best time?' Antonio asked, noting the body language between his twin and Manuel, and trying to suppress a smile.

'You're clearly busy here, and the fair is a busy time for Franz, too. How about if I see him now, and arrange a time?'

'Thank you, Manuel. You're very kind,' Maria smiled. 'Manuel sounds more Spanish than German. Were you born in Frankfurt?'

'No, I was born in Amsterdam. My mother is Spanish, but she emigrated to the Netherlands with her family twenty years ago. She met my father, Francisco, there.'

'Did you study medicine in Amsterdam? My, er, I have a friend who is finishing medical studies in Bologna,' Antonio asked.

'No, I studied at the University of Tübingen, just south of Stuttgart. You will have passed close by on your journey. Leiden would have been closer to home, but it is quite newly established. Bologna is an excellent university.'

'I'm trying hard to forget Stuttgart,' Maria muttered.

'Why?' Manuel asked.

'They had some alleged witches on trial. I say trial, travesty is more like it. It was barbaric.'

'Well, you won't come across any witch trials here.'

'What is the matter with people, Manuel? Why do they have to torture innocent people?'

'If you have time, I could give you my theory. But not in public. Can we go inside?'

'You can look after the stall, Antonio, can't you?'

'Yes, Maria,' Antonio replied, smiling to himself at the way Manuel had managed to get Maria to himself. Maria led Manuel inside. They sat at the kitchen table, near the range. Maria poured them both a cup of wine.

'My theory is that the climate has been changing, and

crops have been failing. Vineyards have been hit badly too. I really think you will do well here. This wine is excellent. Have you heard of Johannes Kepler?'

'Yes, our father has spoken about him. I think Galileo told him about Kepler.'

'Quite possibly he did. Modern science and reason have been probing the secrets of God's creation. Everywhere they find exquisite harmony and order. Planets dance to a mathematical pattern. Artists, musicians, architects and poets perceive strict laws of harmony and structure that please us, and God. God has created an ordered, organised universe. Therefore, something like crop failure must be the result of someone disturbing God's order. A German bishop by the name of Peter Binsfeld decided that the cause must be witchcraft. He wrote a book about it in 1590 and became a witch finder.'

'I see. But you said that we wouldn't see any witch trials here in Frankfurt. Why is that?'

'They don't need witches to blame. They have another group to carry that burden, the Jews. Anyway, I'd better go and see Franz,' Manuel said, draining his cup. 'I'll look forward to seeing you later.' He and Maria stood up, and she held out her hand, which he bowed and kissed. He turned at the front door and smiled. Maria smiled back.

The shadows were lengthening when Manuel returned. People were returning to their homes. Their last customer was just paying for a flagon of wine, and Antonio was taking the cups to the kitchen.

'Manuel, you're back quickly,' Maria said. 'Thank you,' she said to the last customer, and put the coins in the wooden money box on the table as he left.

'Of course. I've spoken to Franz, and he'd like to meet you both, and try some of your wine, if he may?'

'Of course. When can he meet us?'

'I'll take you both there now, if it's convenient?'

'Yes, just give us a minute,' she said, picking up the money box and taking it inside. Antonio and Maria then took the chairs inside, whilst Manuel put the shutter table back up. Antonio locked the door, and they walked with Manuel to the wine merchant's house, Antonio carrying a flagon of their wine. It wasn't far. It was on a street just off the opposite side of the market square. It was a four-storey timber and brick house. The brickwork was painted green, and the timbers were painted white. There was a large shop window, six panes high by eight panes wide. Manuel rapped the brass knocker on the heavy oak door three times. Antonio and Maria peered through the window. The thick panes distorted their view, but they could make out barrels stacked against the far wall. The door creaked open. A bald man with a grey beard smiled at them.

'Come in, come in! You must be Maria and Antonio.' They all shook hands. 'You didn't exaggerate her beauty, Manuel. Please take a seat around the table. I'll get some glasses,' Franz said, going through to a room behind the shop. He reappeared with eight glasses and set them down on the table.

'Drinking glasses,' Antonio exclaimed. 'I've heard of them, of course. You must do very well, Herr..., I'm sorry.'

'Just call me Franz. It's Schröder, but Franz is fine. Yes, I don't do so badly, and I think wine tastes better from a glass.' He then selected a flagon from a shelf and walked over to one of his barrels. He bent to turn the tap, and filled the flagon, which he brought back to the table, and placed it next to the Standen's flagon. 'I always think a comparison is helpful. We shall start with your wine. Would you like to pour?' he asked, looking at Antonio.

'Certainly.' Antonio uncorked his flagon and filled four of the glasses.' Franz picked up the glass nearest him and examined it in the light of the oil lamp on the table. He took a draught of wine and rolled it around his mouth before swallowing it.

'It has a good colour. The oak isn't overpowering and

the strawberry notes shine through, with a hint of cherry, too. This is a Sangiovese, and a fine one, at that. Not too much acidity.' The others followed his example.

'It's the best wine that I've drunk for many years.' Manuel smiled.

'Manuel, that's because you always buy my good value flagons, rather than the exceptional wines,' Franz retorted. 'Now try this.' He said, pouring his own wine into the remaining four clean glasses. They all took a draught of Franz's wine, rolling it around their mouths, before swallowing.

'It's very good,' Antonio said. 'I can taste cherries in this too, raspberries and perhaps blackberries. Is it a Pinot Noir?'

'You know your wine, young man. A Pinot Noir from Burgundy. It is the finest I have, but I must confess that your Sangiovese is up to it. I would be happy to stock your wine,' Franz said.

'Really? That's marvellous,' Antonio said, thinking. 'How many barrels could you take a year?'

'You are from Frascati, yes? Near Rome.' Antonio nodded. 'Sadly, not more than one barrel a year. There is nothing wrong with your wine, far from it. But since the reformation, the vast majority of my customers are Lutheran. Rome, they do not like. I have a few discerning customers who are not so prejudiced, but not enough.' He saw Antonio's face drop. 'However, I know an English wine merchant who always comes to the fair. He might be interested. He doesn't have my scruples, I'm sure he'd be happy to sell it to the English as a French wine.'

'Is he here, in Frankfurt, now?' Antonio asked.

'I haven't seen him yet. But I'm sure he'll be here in a week or so,' Franz replied. 'His name is Thomas Berry. He always comes to see me when he arrives. He wants to know what's new. I won't have any trouble getting him to taste your wine. He'll love it, believe me. What would you charge?' Franz asked. Antonio thought for a while.

'Well, I think I could sell it for twenty-five ducats a hogshead barrel, but that wouldn't include delivery.'

'We could use Maia to sail through the Straits of Gibraltar and onwards to London,' Maria added.

'Thomas knows people in shipping. He'll be able to factor in delivery. Don't worry, let's enjoy these wines. I'll get some bread, and fine French brie.'

They sat around talking, eating and drinking, until they'd finished the Standen flagon, and two of Franz's. Manuel got unsteadily to his feet.

'I think I'd better go home, or I won't be much help at the clinic tomorrow.'

'Yes, we'd better go too. Thank you for a wonderful evening, and thank you for your help, Franz.' Antonio said, as he and Maria stood up too. Franz opened the door for them and they shook hands.

'I'm this way,' Manuel said, pointing up the street, away from the market square. 'Can I see you again, the day after tomorrow perhaps, after the clinic?' he asked, looking at Maria, bowing, and reaching for Maria's hand to kiss. As he took her hand, she pulled him to her and lifted his chin with her other hand. Then she kissed him on the lips.

'Yes, you can, Manuel.'

As Maria and Antonio walked back to Wienerstraße, Antonio whispered, 'Now tell me you don't like him.'

The next day Maria was shopping for cheese and bread, which seemed to be consumed almost as quickly as their wine. The first cheese shop she visited didn't have the cheese she wanted, but the owner gave her directions to another shop. As she made her way there, she saw a familiar figure ahead of her. He was walking in the same direction she was, so he had his back to her, but she was sure it was Manuel. Ahead of Manuel there were men working on the roof of a house. She quickened her pace. She was about thirty yards behind him when she heard a shout. She looked up and saw a roof tile sliding down the pitched roof of the building. It hit the gutter, then did a somersault and plunged vertically. Time seemed to slow down. She watched it fall. She gasped as it struck the head of a boy, just ahead of Manuel. The boy was about the same age as her brother William. Nothing seemed to happen for a second, then the boy's legs crumpled, and he fell to the ground.

Maria sprinted the last few yards. Manuel was on his knees, feeling the boy's head with his fingers. She thought she could see the boy's chest move, and hoped he was alive.

'Manuel, is there anything I can do?' He didn't appear to notice her.

'Breathing is shallow and irregular. His pupils appear to be the same size. There's a small depression where the tile struck. He has a depressed fracture of the skull. I need to get this boy to the hospital fast.' Manuel looked up. 'Maria?'

'Yes, is there anything I can do?' Manuel looked around. Workmen were climbing down a ladder from the roof. The door of the house was open, there was work going on inside as well as on the roof. He could see a door lying on its side in the hallway.

'Fetch that door, we'll use it to carry him on.' Maria saw the direction he was looking and rushed into the house. When she got back, dragging the door behind her, there were four workmen standing behind Manuel, staring at the boy. 'Have you got a cart?'

'Yes, sir,' one of the workmen replied.

'Then fetch it. You others help me to lift the boy onto the door, you too, Maria. I'm going to hold his head still. On the count of three. One, two, three, lift!' Manuel climbed up on to the cart, holding the boy's head. 'You'd all better come with me to help carry him inside the hospital.' Maria was given a helping hand onto the cart by one of the workmen. Then the foreman climbed into the driving seat and they rattled their way over the cobblestones to the hospital.

◇ ◇ ◇

Antonio was clearing up when Maria got back.

'You've been a long time looking for cheese. Everyone's gone now. I was worried about you. Where have you been?'

'I was on my way to the shop when a tile fell from a roof and hit a young boy on the head. It fractured his skull.'

'My God, what did you do?'

'Not much. Manuel was there. I'd seen him in front of me, and I was just hurrying to catch up with him, when I saw the tile fall. He was magnificent. He organised the workmen and me, to lift the boy onto a door, then put it on a cart. I helped him hold the boy's head still on the journey. He would have to operate, to set the piece of skull back in place, and screw a metal plate over it, to keep it in position. I hope I see him tomorrow.'

'Is the boy going to live?'

'Manuel hopes he will. They rushed him into the hospital, and I came back here'

There was a group of neighbours sitting around their stall, tasting their wine, when a boy of around thirteen or fourteen approached Maria.

'Excuse me. Are you Fräulein Maria?'

'Yes, who are you?'

'I have a message for you,' he said, handing a folded sheet of paper to her. She unfolded it and read it. It was from Manuel, explaining that he needed to keep a close eye on the boy for a while. He would also assist with further surgical procedures in the hospital. It wouldn't be possible for him to get away either today or tomorrow. He suggested Sunday. As the market would be closed, they could go for a picnic by the river. Manuel would bring the food, and she and Antonio could bring the wine. 'Will there be a reply, Fräulein Maria?'

'Yes, tell him that would be lovely, thank you.' Maria crumpled the note in her right hand. The messenger left, and Maria turned back to the stall. The group of neighbours were laughing at a joke one of them had told.

'Are you alright, Maria? You look cross,' Antonio said.

'Not cross, not really, just disappointed.'

'Let me guess. Is it Manuel?'

'Yes. He's going to be stuck at the hospital for a while. He's suggested a picnic on Sunday, down by the river. You're invited.'

'Well, that's not so bad. The market will be closed anyway. It'll give us something to do, although I suspect that if it were just me, I wouldn't get the invitation. We could use a rest after the journey,' Antonio smiled. Maria turned away, her fist crushing the note. An elderly man and woman were facing her. They were neatly dressed, but they each had the yellow bands sown around their sleeves, that they had seen before, as they rode into the city.

'Can we try your wine, please?' the man asked.

'Yes, of course, help yourselves,' Maria replied. Antonio poured the couple a cup of wine each and indicated two vacant chairs. The group of neighbours finished their wine, replaced their cups on the table, got up, and left. A few of them cast disapproving looks at the elderly couple.

'Oh, we're very sorry, we should leave,' the man with the yellow armband said.

'Leave? You've only just arrived. Try the wine. It's very good, if I say so myself,' Antonio said.

'But we've scared off your customers,' the woman said.

'Oh! You don't have the plague, do you? Is that what the armbands mean?' Antonio asked, backing away.

'Well, only in a manner of speaking.' The man smiled. 'We don't have the plague, as you know it. The city council insists we wear the armbands, because we are Jews. To them, we are a plague. They tell us where we must live. The emperor and the pope tell us what we can do, and what we can't do, which is a much longer list.'

'I don't suppose wine merchant is on the first list, is it?' Antonio enquired.

'No, nor any kind of craft or shop keeper except for

pawnshops.'

'That's appalling. Of course you're welcome to try our wine. Do sit down, please.' The couple lowered themselves into the chairs.

'You are a good man, and you, Fräulein. This is my wife, Edith, and I'm Daniel Bamberger.'

'So what do you do for a living?' Maria asked, sitting down beside them and pouring herself a large cup of wine.

'I have a pawnshop. I was a lawyer in Flanders, years ago. We fled here when the war started. I still do some legal work, loans, bills of exchange, mortgages, that sort of thing.'

'Our father fought in Flanders many years ago. He started fighting with the Sea Beggars, then became a spy working for William of Orange. Papa said he was the finest man he'd met. He insisted on religious tolerance,' Maria said.

'That's true. He was a good man. There are too few of them. Some think they are righteous, and good, but they are not,' Daniel replied. 'You have heard of Martin Luther, I take it?'

'We recently inherited a dog called Luther. But I can't say I've heard of Martin Luther. Is he a wine merchant?' Antonio asked. Daniel and Edith both laughed, almost choking on their wine. It took some coughing and slaps on the back before Daniel could speak again.

'Oh, that was funny. Martin Luther has been dead for more than sixty years. He was a priest, who split from the Catholic Church and was a leader of the Protestant reformation. Luther came here to Frankfurt. We suffered, and he saw it. I read what he wrote. "They are compelled to wear yellow rings on their coats. They have no houses of their own, only furniture. They can only lend money at great hazard." That is what he wrote.'

'So he was sympathetic to the Jews,' Antonio said.

'Briefly. He was trying to convert us to Lutheranism, and when we wouldn't reject the faith of our fathers and mothers, this is what he said: "Burn the synagogues and the Jewish ghettoes!" He was no William of Orange.'

'Maria, we should think of a new name for the dog.'

'If he'll answer to it,' Maria said. 'Why is there this intolerance of Jews, Daniel? And why don't you move somewhere else? You must have a homeland. I thought the Jews came from Judea.'

'Yes, we had a homeland, and it was the Kingdom of Judah. But then the Muslims, invaded, followed by the crusaders. As refugees, we were driven to flee our homeland. We settled all over Europe, but the masses did not welcome us. We had our uses. Jews are considered to be excellent organisers, physicians, financiers, and lawyers, so we have been useful to kings and emperors.'

'So why are the masses intolerant?'

'Because of the masses,' Daniel said, smiling. Maria and Antonio looked puzzled. 'Forgive me, you don't have a monopoly on jokes. Masses as in Catholic mass. The gospels didn't give the Jews a sympathetic account concerning the crucifixion. Well, not the gospels that got included in your bible, anyway. It's a bit much coming from the Roman Catholics, don't you think? Roman soldiers arrested Christ, who was a Jew, by the way. It was Roman soldiers who nailed him to the cross. Does anyone think the Rabbis had as much say in events as those who had conquered our land?' He paused, but Maria and Antonio didn't know what to say. Edith spoke.

'Your wine is wonderful. Is your vineyard near here?'

'No. It's in Frascati,' Antonio replied.

'Where is that?' Edith asked.

'It's, er, it's about twenty miles from Rome.'

On Sunday morning Manuel arrived with a basket of food and a blanket. Maria had already packed a wicker basket with three wooden drinking goblets, and a flagon of their wine.

'Good morning, Maria, how are you today?' Manuel asked.

'Good morning, Manuel, I'm very well,' she replied, blushing at the memory of their last but one meeting.

'I'm so sorry about being tied up at the hospital. I hope you can forgive me for letting you down?'

'Think nothing of it. How is the boy?'

'He's doing quite well. It was a very risky operation. His chances weren't good. I'm unusually particular about cleaning my instruments. The other physicians laugh at me, but my success rate is better than theirs. Once the bone heals, I'll have to operate again to remove the gold plate.'

'Gold! Were his parents able to afford it?'

'No. When the boy regained consciousness, we were able to send a messenger to fetch them. They're poor people.'

'So who paid for the gold, and the operation?'

'I did. I'll be able to clean the plate and screws and use them again.'

'Nevertheless, that's very generous of you.'

'I took an oath.'

'Where is the best place for a picnic, Manuel?' Maria asked.

'Near to the eastern city gate, there's a meadow on a bend in the river. There are fine views up and down the river.'

'That sounds perfect. Hurry up, Antonio! Manuel is here.'

Antonio came downstairs and greeted Manuel, noting that he and Maria both looked flushed. Then he locked up, and the three of them set off. Manuel nodded at the guards by the gate as they left the city. It only took them ten minutes to reach the meadow. Upstream there was a good view of a bridge, which connected the main part of the city to a smaller, walled section on the north bank. Ships were moored on both banks. Downstream there were fields, with a few scattered villages. Manuel spread the blanket on the ground. He sat down and took out wooden plates, some bread, a cooked sausage, and a knife. Maria sat beside him, and Antonio sat on the other side of Maria. Antonio poured some wine and handed out the goblets. Manuel passed round plates of food, and they ate and drank in silence for a while.

'How did the other operations go yesterday, Manuel?' Maria asked.

'Very well. It was an amputation of the right leg, below the knee. A man was run over by a cart, and it was crushed beyond healing. He should recover well.'

'I think you must be an excellent physician.' Maria smiled at him. 'How long did it take you to train?'

'I was in medical school for five years. It was intense, but fascinating.'

'I think I'll go for a walk along the river bank,' Antonio said, draining his goblet, and putting down his empty plate, then standing up. Manuel and Maria smiled at him before he turned and walked off.

'Is Antonio all right?' Manuel asked.

'Yes. The friend he has studying medicine in Bologna, is Greta, his girlfriend. On our way here, we stopped to see her. He asked her to marry him, but he was so clumsy about it that they had a row. I suppose discussing medicine upset him. I think he also felt like a bit of a gooseberry.'

'Oh, I'm so sorry. I wouldn't have mentioned it if I'd known. What's a gooseberry got to do with it?'

'Sorry, it's an English expression. Our father is English. It means feeling unnecessary or unwanted. Anyway, you didn't mention it, I did.' Maria smiled, getting up and walking down to the riverbank. She half turned, back to Manuel, and tipped her head to one side, smiling. Manuel got up and approached her. They looked into each other's eyes. He put his arms around her and leant forwards to kiss her. Maria hooked her right leg behind his, took his right wrist in hers, and flicked his leg from under him. She dropped herself beside him with her left leg across his throat and applied an armlock. Manuel screamed in agony. She released the armlock.

'What did you do that for?'

'I thought you should know that I could. You can kiss me now,' she said getting up, and helping him to his feet.

'That really hurt. Are you insane? You could have broken my arm. What sort of physician would I make then? I'm going home. You should check into an asylum,' Manuel said getting up and packing his basket. He hurried back to the city gate.

'Don't go, I'm sorry. I just...' Maria called out, as Manuel strode away without turning, just raising his good arm.

Maria was sitting on the grass when Antonio returned. Her eyes were red.

'Are you alright, Maria? Where's Manuel?'

'He's gone.'

'Why? I thought you were getting along well.'

'It was me. I wanted him to kiss me, but I was scared too. So when he tried to, I threw him to the ground and snapped an armlock on.'

'Why on earth did you do that?'

'I wanted to be in control, but I—'

'In control, what do you mean?'

'Could you pour me some more wine?' Antonio refilled both their goblets, then he sat down on the grass beside her, and put his arm around her shoulders. 'Do you remember when we were thirteen? I was working in the wash house, and you were working at the forge.'

'Of course I do.'

'Do you remember the day I came home with my dress torn?'

'Yes, you were terribly upset. Mama couldn't get any sense out of you. You refused to go back there, and got a job at the mill, instead. You wouldn't talk about it to anyone.'

'The wash house owner's son, he was a bit simple, but strong. He, he forced himself on me. I struggled, but there was nothing I could do. He was too strong. I felt so helpless, so dirty.' Maria sobbed. Antonio held her tight.

'Oh, Maria, you never said anything. But we wondered what had happened. You were so withdrawn and angry.'

'I tried to forget it, to lock the memory away, pretend it never happened. But it did.' Her whole body shook, and tears ran down Antonio's cheeks too. 'When Papa and I were in Paris, there was an explorer who had sailed around the world. Pierre Malherbe, his name is. He had learnt, in India, how to put people into a trance. He taught Papa and I how to do it. When he put me in a trance, he unlocked that memory. I think Papa knows. I catch him looking at me sometimes. He seems concerned. Mama doesn't badger me so much about getting married as she did. What should I do, Antonio? I think I love Manuel, but I have to be in control. I don't know what to do.'

'I think you should let him cool down, then go and see him. Explain everything, as you did to me.'

'What if he doesn't want me, a soiled woman?'

'There's nothing soiled about you, Maria.'

'I'm not sure. I felt dirty. I can still smell his sweat sometimes. I feel dirty. I couldn't tell Manuel. I'd lose him. I love him.'

'If you want my opinion, tell him the truth. If he lets you go, it's his loss, and he wasn't worth your love.' Maria smiled.

'You're a fine one to be lecturing me about love.'

'Yes, I know. Sometimes it's easier to see things straight when you're looking at it from the side. If that makes any sense. Anyway, think about it.'

'I don't think I can tell him, I don't think I'd be able to tell him. You and Mama are the closest people in the world to me. If I can only tell you, after a few wines, and several years, how can I tell him? I may have feelings for him, but I've known him for such a short time. I have no idea how he would react, and I can't bear to relive it again. Even if it means I lose him, I can't tell him.'

# CHAPTER SIX

Maria was busy serving customers at their stall, whilst Antonio was filling flagons from the casks in the stables.

'I hope you don't run out of wine before Thomas Berry arrives,' Franz called out as he approached Maria. 'He's the English wine merchant I told you about. He'll need to take half a dozen casks back to London as samples.'

'Do you know when we might expect him?' Maria asked.

'Soon, I should think. He's a creature of habit. What's the matter with you? You look rather sullen.'

'Nothing. I have a slight headache, that's all.'

'I think I can guess. Manuel seemed rather reserved when I saw him this morning. Have you fallen out?'

'Yes, they have,' Antonio said as he joined them, and placed a crate of full flagons on the stall. 'How are you, Franz?'

'I'm very well. I was just saying that you should make sure you have at least half a dozen casks in reserve for when Thomas Berry, the English wine merchant, arrives. He should be here soon, God willing.'

'Oh, we'd better rein in a bit then. It seems to be very popular.'

'Have you told your customers where it's from?'

'No. I thought it best not to let their prejudice affect their palate.'

'Hmm, I wonder if I could sell it as a German wine, or perhaps a Swiss wine. No, I couldn't take the risk of being found out. I have a reputation to keep.'

'Look, if we need to rein in, you can spare me for an hour,' Maria interjected. 'Can you tell me where Manuel's clinic is, Franz? I need to speak to him.'

As Maria crossed the market square, a man wearing a cape with a hood held a sheet of paper out to her. She took it, and watched him passing through the crowds, handing out more sheets of paper as he went. She looked at the paper in her hands. It was printed. She read it.

Citizens should know their rights, but the corrupt city council is concealing them. We demand an elected council to replace the corrupt patricians. We demand the expulsion of the Jews, vile moneylenders. Action is coming. Be ready to join us!

Maria crumpled the paper and put it in her pocket. She found the clinic at the far end of the street on which Franz had his shop. It was a four-storey building. The timbers were painted white, and the brickwork was red. Maria pulled the rope attached to the clapper of a bell, which was suspended on a bracket next to the door. She rang it twice. There were footsteps, then the door opened.

'Do you have an appointment?' asked an attractive woman of about her own age, dressed in a neatly-pressed, plain brown dress, topped with a broad white collar, covering her neck and shoulders.

'No, I just wanted to speak with Manuel. It's a personal matter.'

'Doctor Nuñez is busy in the clinic at the moment. I'll

let him know you're here. Please come through and take a seat in the waiting room.' Maria followed the woman, who opened a door on the right of the hallway. The woman pointed to an empty chair to their right. Maria sat down. The woman went to a door at the far end of the room. She opened it, went in for a few moments, then came out and closed the door behind her. 'He'll see you, after he's attended to these patients. We aren't expecting any more today.' Then she left the waiting room.

Maria looked around. There was one old man with a walking stick, who kept coughing. There was a plump mother of around thirty, with two young boys, playing on the floor with carved wooden horses. The room was clean, but you couldn't say spotless. It looked as if it had been repainted within a year, but not within the week. Had Manuel been lying? She'd thought so at the time. But why would he lie? The floor was tiled, and the walls were painted white. After a few minutes, the door at the far end opened, and a young man of about her own age emerged, and left by the door Maria had entered. Then Manuel appeared in the doorway of his consulting room. He glanced at her, but quickly broke eye contact.

'Herr Schmidt,' he said. The old man, with the stick and cough, got up and went into the consulting room. Manuel closed the door behind him. It seemed like ages before Herr Schmidt emerged, carrying a small brown bottle. The mother and children were invited in. They seemed to take twice as long as the old man had, but eventually they emerged and left. Manuel stood in the doorway. 'Maria, what can I do for you?'

'Can we talk?'

'Yes, come into my consulting room. Ingrid won't disturb us.' She followed him in. He sat down behind a large oak desk. She sat in the chair in front of the desk.

'Is Ingrid your wife?'

'No, she's my receptionist and nurse. What did you want to speak about?'

'I wanted to apologise. I'm sorry I hurt you.'

'Hurt me? You nearly tore my bloody arm out of its socket.'

'Yes, and I'm sorry. I can't explain what happened. Can you forgive me, Manuel? Can we start again?'

'I don't know. Let's be friends. We should give ourselves time. After all, we don't really know each other.'

The sun was setting, and stall holders were packing away their merchandise. The last customers were buying flagons at Antonio and Maria's stall when Franz arrived. With him was a short, stocky, balding man in his early fifties. He had a ruddy complexion and a thick beard.

'Antonio, Maria, here he is. May I introduce Thomas Berry, from London,' Franz exclaimed. They all shook hands. 'Put those wooden goblets away. I've brought some glasses with me. Wine tastes better out of a glass.' Antonio took one flagon and filled the glasses, while everyone else sat down. All eyes were on Thomas Berry as he lifted his glass and looked at the wine. He swirled the wine around his glass and raised the rim to his nose, breathing in the aroma. Then he put the glass to his lips and took a mouthful. His cheeks joggled from side to side as he swirled the wine around his mouth. Then he swallowed. 'Well, Thomas, what do you think?'

'You did not exaggerate, Franz. It's first class,' he said, smiling. He took another mouthful. 'Yes, absolutely, first class. It takes me back years to when I first visited Rome. I love the Sangiovese. It rather fills me with regret at what I've missed these last few decades.'

'Try the brandy, Thomas,' Franz suggested. Antonio poured some brandy into a clean glass and handed it to Thomas. Thomas went through the same process of examining the colour, then the aroma, and finally, the taste.

'Are you really prepared to sell your wine for twenty-five ducats a barrel?' Thomas asked.

'Yes, but that wouldn't include shipping,' Antonio replied.

'I can arrange the shipping. But wine travels better in bottles. You must have a glassmaker in Rome. Venice is world renowned for its glassmaking. Have you been there? Bottling is the next big thing. Believe me, you should look into it. If there isn't somebody you can use in Rome, think about buying bottles from Venice,' Thomas said. Antonio thought for a while.

'We have been to Venice, but we were otherwise occupied. We didn't have time to look at their glass,' Antonio replied. 'Is the bottling essential? I can't know whether we can arrange it, nor at what price.'

'We can make a contract with options. If necessary, I can ship bottles out and fill them in Ostia. But it will be better if the wine is bottled at your vineyard. You look worried, Antonio.'

'It's just that I hadn't considered bottling. It's an unknown. I had hoped that we would find a buyer and expand our production, and we'd have to consult our father.'

'You will expand, don't worry. I'll take half a dozen barrels back to London with me. My partners will love it, and so will my discerning clients, including King James. By the time I get back to London, you can have done your research into bottling. Send me a letter via the Thurn and Taxis postal system, letting me know whether you can bottle, or whether I need to ship bottles on the outbound leg. We can have a contract written that will cover all eventualities.'

'You will pay for the six barrels, I assume?' Antonio asked.

'Of course, but it would be unwise to travel with a hundred and fifty ducats in your purse. We will have a bill of exchange drafted together with the contract. Franz knows a fellow.'

'I'm sorry, what's a bill of exchange?' Antonio asked.

'It's a promissory note. The fellow that Franz knows will draft it. He will give you a contact in Rome, where you will be able to exchange the note for a hundred and fifty ducats. It's how the financial system operates.'

'He's right, it's perfectly normal,' Franz added. 'Ask anyone in international business.'

'What do you think, Maria?' Antonio asked.

'Well, we can make some enquiries to reassure ourselves. When shall we have the contract and letter of exchange written?'

'I'll meet you here at ten o'clock by the cathedral clock, with Franz. He knows the way to the lawyer. There's no point dallying. I'm sure about your wine. We can agree a price on the brandy too. I'm assuming ten times the price of the equivalent volume of wine. That's the norm.'

'Yes, with the distilling costs, that's what we work on.'

'Very good. I'll see you in the morning then,' Thomas said. They shook hands, and Franz and Thomas left.

'What do you think, Maria? I'm worried about this bill of exchange thing. Who do you think we can ask?'

'What about the Marktmeister? I imagine he will have heard of them. We can ask him in the morning. We should also think about renaming the vineyard.'

'Rename the vineyard. Whatever for?'

'Have you forgotten that King James had father imprisoned for treason? If he's Thomas's biggest client, it's best he doesn't know it comes from the Standen vineyard.'

Antonio and Maria were up at sunrise the following morning. After breakfast, they set off to visit the Marktmeister. He reassured them that bills of exchange were perfectly normal for long-distance transactions, particularly if sizeable sums were involved. Banks used them, and moneylenders used them too. The Jews were particularly well connected. They would always know somebody who would honour your letter, whatever corner of the empire, or beyond. So Antonio and Maria went back to Wienerstraße and awaited Thomas and Franz. The cathedral clock had just finished ringing ten when they saw them crossing the square. Antonio locked the house.

Franz led them through the city to the city wall. They were admitted through a gate, onto a curved street around three hundred yards long. The houses on either side were three stories high. Some of them had cantilevered extensions jutting out over the road. They worked their way through the crowded street, bumping into people, the vast majority of whom bore the yellow armband. Then Maria saw a familiar face. She dropped back and intercepted him.

'Manuel. It's good to see you again,' she whispered.

'Maria, what are you doing here?'

'Perhaps you can give us added reassurance,' she said, lowering her voice. 'Have you heard of bills of exchange?'

'Oh yes. They're normal. My, er, a patient of mine deals in them. He lives just three doors down.'

'Thank you, I'd better catch up with the others. Good to see you.' Maria then looked for Antonio through the crowds, and saw him standing by a door, looking around for her. She re-joined him. The door opened, and they saw another familiar face. It was Edith Bamberger.

'How nice to see you kind people again,' Edith smiled. 'It looks as though you have found a buyer for your wine. Come through to the back room. It will please Daniel to help you.' Edith led them through the kitchen, where a large samovar sat on the stove. Then they passed through the dining room, then a storeroom that was full of racks of clothing; boxes of boots and shoes; shelves of cooking utensils; jewellery; pottery and paintings. She opened a door. 'Daniel, you have visitors. Look who it is.' Daniel looked up from his desk and stood up.

'Herr and Fräulein Standen, how lovely to see again, so soon, and Franz,' he said, shaking hands.

'It's good to see you, Daniel,' Franz said. 'May I introduce Thomas Berry, a wine merchant from London?'

Daniel and Thomas shook hands. 'I assume you have contacts in London who can honour a bill of exchange?'

'Of course, of course. So you have found a buyer, Antonio. I knew you would. Edith, get these nice people some tea, could you? Sit down, please.' They all sat down. Thomas explained the requirements of the contract, including the options regarding bottling. He set out the prices and volumes. Daniel made notes in a large, leather-bound book. Edith returned with a tray, which she set down on the desk. Then she gave them each a cup of green tea. She placed a bowl of sugar and a spoon on the desk.

'I'll leave you to your business. Let me know if you need more tea or sugar,' she said, picking up the tray and closing the study door behind her. Daniel waited until the others had taken their sugar, before taking two spoonfuls himself. They all drank in silence for a few minutes.

'It's a delicious tea. Do you have all the details you need, Daniel?' Thomas asked.

'Yes, I have everything I need. If you come back tomorrow, late in the afternoon, I'll have everything ready for you to sign.'

◇ ◇ ◇

Thomas Berry arrived at Antonio and Maria's stall mid-afternoon, the following day. Antonio and Maria were serving two Swiss couples some wine.

'Isn't Franz with you?' Antonio asked.

'No, he couldn't come. I think I can remember the way, though, can you?'

'Yes, I think so.'

'I hope you still have enough wine left for my samples.'

'Yes, don't worry, Thomas. We won't sell anymore after today. Once you're on your way back to London with our wine, we'll head back home, via Bologna, or Turin, if we miss the end of term. I have some making up to do with my girlfriend.'

Around half an hour later, the Swiss couples departed and Antonio and Maria shut up the stall, and locked the house. They took one wrong turning, but soon backtracked and found the curved street and the Bamberger house. Antonio rang the bell and waited. There was the sound of a door slamming from within the house. He rang the bell again, but nobody came. He tried the door handle. The door was unlocked, so he went in, followed by Maria and Thomas. Antonio called out, but there wasn't a sound from within. They made their way towards the study. Nothing seemed to be disturbed within the kitchen or the dining room. In the storeroom, there were boxes scattered across the floor. There was some jewellery on the floor, but much of what they had seen the day before seemed to be missing. The study door was closed, but there was a door open at the end of the storeroom. Maria walked over to it and stepped through the door.

'There's a passageway at the back. I can't see anyone,' she reported. Antonio called out again before opening the study door.

'My god!' Thomas exclaimed from behind him. Daniel and Edith were lying lifeless on the study floor. Antonio bent down, and felt each in turn for a pulse.

'They're dead.'

There were footsteps in the kitchen. Both Antonio and Maria were ready to fight. Then they saw it was Manuel. He just stood staring at the bodies on the floor.

'Manuel, I think they're dead, but I'm not a doctor. Do something,' Antonio said. Manuel knelt down beside Edith first. He put his ear to her mouth, then felt for a pulse in her neck. Then he did the same with Daniel.

'There is nothing I can do for them. They haven't been dead long. Did you do this?'

'No, of course not. How could you think such a thing?' Maria asked. 'We were here yesterday to get a contract and a bill of exchange. You remember, I asked you about it when we bumped into you yesterday. Thomas, here, is a London wine merchant who wants to buy our wine. Daniel said to come back today, and he'd have the documents ready for us to sign.'

'Yes, I remember,' Manuel whispered. 'We should inform the mayor.'

'I'll go, if you like,' Thomas said. 'Antonio, you'd better have a look around and see if you can find the papers. I'll be back as soon as I can,' Thomas said and left via the front door.

Antonio examined the papers on the desk. He opened the large leather-bound book Daniel had written in yesterday. It was a ledger with columns of dates, names, items, and amounts. The last page had yesterday's date against the last entry. There was a ragged paper edge in the margin where the next page had been torn out. He leafed back through the book and found that five other pages had also been torn out. Meanwhile, Maria was looking through the desk drawers. She took out a sheaf of papers that were tied together with a ribbon.

'These have got your name on, and Thomas's. Yes, this one's the letter of exchange, and this is the contract. At least we have these. Wait a minute, there's another bill of exchange,' she said, reading. 'One is for Thomas to take to London, and the other is for you to take to an address in Rome. There's another copy of the contract, too.'

'Yes, that's how bills of exchange work,' Manuel said. 'Poor Edith and Daniel lie dead, but your wine sale will be fine.'

'I'm sorry, Manuel, that was insensitive of me,' she said. 'You seem very upset. Were they your patients?'

'Yes they were.'

'That's odd. The floor's quite dusty over there, but this area seems to have been wiped. Has the murderer tried to mop up some blood?' Maria asked.

'There isn't any blood. They've both been strangled. You can tell by the marks on their necks,' Manuel whispered.

'You look as white as a sheet, Manuel,' Maria said. 'I'll see if there's any tea in that samovar. I'll put some brandy in it for you, if I can find any.'

'There's a bottle of brandy in the cupboard on the right-hand side of the dresser in the kitchen,' Manuel replied.

◇ ◇ ◇

About an hour later, Thomas returned with the mayor and the sergeant of the guard. The sergeant examined the bodies, and Antonio told him about the pages torn from the ledger.

'It looks like a robbery gone wrong, to me, sir,' the sergeant said to the mayor. 'It looks like some jewellery has been taken.'

'I agree. There isn't much we can do. I'll have a word with Rabbi Levi and get him to arrange the funeral.'

'Aren't you going to even try to find the killer?' Maria asked.

'It could be anyone. He lent a lot of money. There will be a long list of people that would have been better off for not having to repay their debt. They were Jews, and I have a lot of work to do. Nobody will be interested in the death of a couple of Jews.'

'Well, we will investigate, won't we, Antonio?'

'Yes, Maria, we will. Would you at least allow the sergeant to work with us for a few days, sir? I'd like to see if I can find any clues in the ledger. A few pages have been torn out.'

'Precisely. They've been torn out, so the evidence has gone. It's a waste of time,' Mayor Friedrich replied.

'Please, sir.' Maria said, trying to give the mayor her warmest smile.

'Oh, very well. If it's alright with you, Sergeant Voigt? But I want it wrapped up quickly.'

'I'll do my best, sir,' the sergeant said. Mayor Friedrich nodded, grimaced and left, limping. 'So, how can I help? Antonio is it? How did you discover the deaths?'

'Yes, sergeant. I'm Antonio Standen from Frascati, where we have a family vineyard. This is my twin sister,

Maria. This is Thomas Berry, a wine merchant from London. He is buying our wine, and Daniel Bamberger was writing the contract and bill of exchange. He asked us to come back this afternoon to sign and collect them.'

'I see. And who are you, sir? Your face is familiar,' the sergeant asked, turning to Manuel.

'I'm Manuel Nuñez, a physician. Daniel and Edith were patients of mine.'

'Yes, I have heard the name. We can't afford your fees, of course. It's a foreign-sounding name, sir. You're not from here, are you, sir?'

'I moved here from the Netherlands because of the war.'

'I hate to bring business into this, with these poor people on the floor,' Thomas said, 'but is there any reason why Antonio and I can't sign these documents? Then I can load their wine onto the ship I have chartered and make my way to London.'

The sergeant stroked his beard for a moment. 'I don't see why not. I can't see any motive you might have had. Do you, Herr Standen?'

'None at all. Please call me Antonio, if we're going to be working together on this.'

'Yes, that's right, business must go on,' Manuel said bitterly. Maria looked at him and tried to put her arm around him, but he moved away.

'You really cared about Daniel and Edith, didn't you? Were they more than patients?' Maria asked.

'No, just patients. I care for all my patients, of course I do.'

'But you were here yesterday, and again today. They visited our stall, and seemed quite healthy, so surely they could have gone to your clinic?' Maria asked.

'Stop asking me questions. Can I go now?' Manuel asked. The sergeant looked at Antonio. Antonio turned to Maria, who nodded.

'Yes, sergeant. I think Manuel can go,' Antonio replied.

Manuel left. An undertaker arrived and Daniel's and Edith's bodies were taken away. Antonio and Thomas read through the contract and bills of exchange. It was quite clear where they should sign. There was a witness required, and the sergeant agreed to sign as a witness.

'So, Sergeant Voigt. My plan, if you agree, is to take the ledger away and examine it. I can help Thomas load our wine then examine it,' Antonio suggested.

'But what can you hope to find, unless the murderer was interrupted and failed to tear out a relevant page?' the sergeant asked.

'I don't know, but I'll look for patterns. From what I've seen already, as the mayor said, many people came to pawn items and recover them. If I find people who may have also visited on the days that have been torn out, then they may have seen the murderer,' Antonio explained.

'I'd forgotten, but I think we interrupted the murderer, Antonio, Thomas,' Maria exclaimed. 'Don't you remember, we heard the back door slam, when we were at the front door? I think they were already dead by then, and he, I'm assuming it was a man, was wiping the floor for some reason. Heaven knows why, as there wasn't any blood. And why would he want to mop the blood up, anyway?'

'I see,' Sergeant Voigt said. 'How exactly can I help?'

'If I can find a pattern, and draw up a list of people who may have visited on the same day as the killer, then we will need your help, and authority, to interview them,' Antonio explained.

'Very good, Herr Standen. You can find me in the town hall most days, when I'm not checking the gate sentries. If I am out, I'll tell the hall porter what time I'll be back. I'll lock up here and post a notice on the door. You can all go now.'

'If it's all right with you, Antonio, I'll fetch my wagon, and drive it round to Wienerstraße. If you could help me load it, the ship's crew can help me load it onto the ship? That is, if I can pry them out of whatever tavern they're in,'

Thomas said.

'Of course, let's get that the business side of things out of the way. Then we can get on with our investigations.'

'Just out of curiosity, why do you feel obliged to investigate?' Thomas asked.

'I wondered the same thing, Herr Standen,' Sergeant Voigt added.

'I don't know. Perhaps it is curiosity.'

'Nonsense!' Maria exclaimed. 'We seem to have inherited a strong sense of justice, no matter who the victim or murderer is. I think we got it from our father.'

Antonio, Maria, and Thomas finished loading Thomas's wagon.

'How long will it take you to reach London, Thomas?' Antonio asked.

'It's around two hundred and seventy miles from here to Rotterdam. We follow the River Main to Mainz, where it flows into the Rhine, and that takes us to Rotterdam. From there it's around a hundred and eighty miles to London. It depends on the winds, of course. At least the return trip is with the flow of the river. I expect to be in London in around a fortnight, but I will have to negotiate tolls along the way. Every town and city wants more than its fair due.'

'Well, I wish you fair winds,' Antonio said.

'Don't take too long with this investigation that you seem to want to involve yourselves in. You should look into bottling. Don't forget to let me know whether or not I need to arrange the bottles.'

'We won't.' Antonio and Maria waved as Thomas flicked the reins, and the wagon rolled off. 'He's right, Maria, we mustn't spend too much time here.'

'Then you had better get stuck into examining that ledger.'

'I've been doing some thinking. I know you won't like it, but could the murderer be Manuel?'

'What?'

'Wait! Let me explain. You bumped into him near the Bamberger house on our first visit. We heard the back door slam just as we arrived on our second visit. Almost immediately after we discovered the bodies, Manuel turned up. He could have killed them, slipped out the back door, followed the passage to where it joins the street and then come back in through the front door.'

'I don't believe he's capable of murder. He cures people. You saw how upset he was.'

'Yes, but he couldn't answer your point about why he was visiting their house. Could he, Maria? And they seemed fit for their age. Why was he making house calls at all?'

'I don't know, but I don't think it's him.'

'Love is dulling your brain. It does that. I should know. Look at the complete mess I made of asking Greta to marry me.'

'It's not dulling mine. Are you going to look through that ledger, or shall I do it?'

Antonio closed the ledger and put down his quill. He examined the list of dates and names he had made. The last entry was on Monday the 15th of August 1614, the day they had found the bodies. The ledger stretched back five years. The most recent page to have been torn out was Thursday 11th August. The next page to have been torn out was Thursday 14th July, and the first one was Thursday 12th May. So Antonio assumed the killer had visited on those three Thursdays, before making an unexpected and murderous visit on a Monday. He had made a list of everyone who had visited on Thursdays. The appointments seemed to be all after lunch, at half-hour intervals. It was a long list, there were fifty-two names. Then he looked at names which appeared more than twice. He found that most people only made two visits, presumably to pawn something, then to recover it. Perhaps they'd had an unexpected expense, which required a short-term loan, which was a one-off. There were sixteen names that appeared more than twice. He looked at their positions on the daily appointment list. He wanted to find names that would give him as much coverage across the day as possible. There were six names that gave him that. They were: Heinrich Weber, Franz Müller, Karl Schmidt, Andreas Bauer, Friedrich Schröder, and Günther Zimmermann.

'Maria, look at this. The three pages which have been torn out are all Thursdays. There are fifty-two people who have visited on Thursdays, and sixteen who appeared more than twice. I've identified these six names that visited at different times of the day. I suggest we start by interviewing them.'

'Why only them?'

'We have to start somewhere, and I want it to be as efficient as possible. We need to get home, and I want to put things right with Greta on the way. We'll ask each of these six, who was leaving when they arrived, and who was arriving as they left. Then we'll see if those names are on the list. When we find one that isn't, he'll be our man.'

'That's good work, Antonio. But what if they didn't know the people who were visiting either side of them?'

'That's possible, of course. But what else have we got to go on?'

'I'm still bothered by the killer cleaning up after himself. There wasn't any blood, so what was that about? Even if there had been blood, why clean it up?'

'I don't know, but shall we give this a try? Unless you just want to set off now?'

'No, you're right we should try it. I assume Manuel isn't on any of the lists.'

'No, he isn't.'

'I need to find out what he has to do with this. It's worrying me. Let's take your lists and go and find Sergeant Voigt.'

◇ ◇ ◇

Sergeant Voigt was in the guardroom at the city hall

when Antonio and Maria arrived. Antonio explained his reasoning, and the need to question the six people on the list.

'That sounds like a good plan, let's have a look at the list,' Sergeant Voigt asked. Antonio handed him the list. The sergeant read it. 'I know some of them, but let's go to the record office, and check on the others.' He got up from his chair and led them down a corridor. He knocked on a door at the end of the corridor and opened it. They went in. A grey-haired man, with thick reading glasses, was writing at a desk. In front of the desk, there were seven rows of bookshelves, filled with identical-looking, thick, leather-bound books. 'Good morning, Wilhelm. We need to check some names and addresses,' the sergeant said, handing the record keeper Antonio's list. The record keeper examined the list. Then he got up and went along the bookshelves. He took two books down and returned, placing them on his desk.

'Do sit down, there are some chairs, over there. Bring them across,' he said, as he went back to the shelves and took down two more books. Then he sat down again and opened the first book. He leafed through the pages. 'You must know Andreas Bauer, Barnard. He has a farm outside the east gate.' He closed that book and opened the next one. 'There are several Müllers, but only one Franz Müller. He works the watermill.' He closed that book and opened another. 'There are two Karl Schmidts. You must know old Karl, who has the forge on Königstraße. But there is a tailor by that name who has a shop on Mainzerstraße. Now then, Schröder, Friedrich, yes, here he is. He has a small business running carts to move goods around the market, and also at the quayside. He also lives on Königstraße.' He closed the book and reached across for the last book and opened it. 'We only have one Heinrich Weber, the basket weaver on Rheinstraße. Zimmermann, Günther. You're in luck, just the one again. The carpenter with a workshop on Friesengasse. Shall I write those all down for you, Barnard?'

'Yes, if it's no trouble, Wilhelm.' Wilhelm, the record keeper, took a sheet of paper from his desk, dipped his quill in the ink pot and wrote out the list of names and addresses. He blew on the paper and pressed it against the blotting pad on his desk. Then he handed it to Sergeant Barnard Voigt.

'Thank you, Wilhelm, we'll leave you in peace now.'

'Where do you think we should start, Sergeant Voigt?' Antonio asked as the sergeant closed the door of the records office.

'The tailor is nearest. Why not start with him.'

It didn't take them long to reach the tailor's shop. Sergeant Voigt opened the door, and they went in. The room had several mannequins adorned with breeches, shirts, waistcoats and coats. A middle-aged man emerged through a door behind a counter.

'How can I help you? New coats perhaps, I expect we will have a hard winter again.'

'I am Sergeant Voigt of the city guard. We are here to ask you some questions concerning a murder.'

'A murder? But I know nothing of any murder. You have the wrong man, I swear it.'

'If I may, Sergeant Voigt,' Antonio said. 'We are reasonably certain that you are not the murderer. But I believe you have had occasion to pawn items to Daniel Bamberger. Is that correct?'

'Yes. I didn't want to deal with Jews, but I needed some cash, just until business picked up. I was able to pay off the loan last Thursday and recover my wife's jewellery. Why, what has happened?'

'Daniel and his wife, Edith, were murdered.' Antonio paused while the tailor held the counter for support. 'Did you visit Daniel on either 11th August, 14th July, or 12th May?'

'As I said, I visited to pay off the loan on Thursday the eleventh. I'll have to look at my appointments book to check when I took out the loan.' He felt under the counter and then placed his appointments book on the counter. He opened it. 'I took out the loan on the 12th of May, there see for yourself,' he said turning the book to face Antonio. Antonio saw that there was a gap between appointments at 2 p.m and 4:30 p.m, with Judengasse written between those times. He ran his index finger over the word. 'Judengasse is Bamberger's street in the ghetto,' the tailor explained. Antonio turned the pages until he came to the 11th August. He saw Judengasse written in at 3 p.m.

'When you repaid the loan, on the eleventh, did you see anyone leaving as you arrived?' Antonio asked.

'Yes, the miller, Franz Müller was leaving as I arrived.'

'And did you see anyone arrive as you left?'

'Let me think. Yes I did. Gerhardt Schneider arrived as I left. I'm making a coat for him. We joked about it because I wanted to know that he had the money to pay for his coat.' Antonio took his long list from his pocket and examined it.

'I see, Gerhardt Schneider only appears twice in the ledger. He will be someone we should speak with, Sergeant Voigt.'

'You don't think he's the murderer?' the tailor exclaimed. 'Please don't speak with him until I've finished his coat and got my money. I could have it finished tonight, at a push.'

'No, I simply want to find out who he may have seen arriving as he left. That's all. Where does he live, this Gerhardt Schneider?'

'He has a butcher's shop in Wienerstraße, and lives above the shop.'

'And what about when you took out the loan, on the 12th of May? Who did you see leaving and arriving then?'

'It was the butcher who arrived, just as I was finishing my tea. But it was my namesake, Karl Schmidt the blacksmith, who was leaving as I arrived.'

'Are you sure?' Antonio asked.

'Yes, I'm certain of it. I didn't see anyone else there,

apart from the Bambergers.'

'Thank you. We can go now, Sergeant.'

'Who do you think we should interview next, Herr Standen?' Sergeant Voigt asked, once they were outside the tailor's shop.

'Who's furthest away? I like the idea of working back in towards the centre. Please stop calling me Herr Standen. My name's Antonio. We may be working together for a while.'

'Well the farmer, Andreas Bauer, is furthest, Antonio. My name's Barnard.'

'Good, let's go then. Lead on!'

'Antonio, wait a minute. Can we have a private word?' Maria whispered, holding his arm.

'Yes. Just give us a minute, please, Barnard,' Antonio agreed, and they took a few paces away. 'What is it, Maria?'

'I can't help thinking about Manuel. You're right, it is strange that he was there. I don't think he's a murderer, but I want to know what he was doing there. You've got this investigation going well, the ledger book thing is brilliant. I don't see what I can add. I'm going to speak with Manuel.'

'Be careful, Maria. I don't think he's a killer either, but we wouldn't have thought the pope was, would we?'

'I can look after myself.'

'If he tries to strangle you, you can. But he's a physician. What if he offers you some mint tea with poison in it? If he thinks you suspect him, I mean.'

'I'll be careful. See you back at Wienerstraße.'

# CHAPTER SEVEN

Maria knocked on the door of Manuel's clinic. She heard footsteps approaching, then Manuel opened the door.

'I didn't expect you still to be here. Has there been a problem with your wine sale?'

'No. Thomas Berry has sailed for London with our wine samples. Can I come in?'

'Yes, of course.' He opened the door wide, and Maria brushed past him. He closed the door. 'Come into my study.' He opened a door opposite the door to the waiting room and led her inside. There was a large window behind a desk. There were two upholstered chairs facing the desk. On the desk was a strange contraption. It was a tube fixed in a stand, with a wheel on one side. At the base of the tube was a glass ledge, and below that a mirror. 'Excuse the mess,' Manuel said, taking some wooden trays from one of the chairs. 'Please sit down. Can I get you some tea, or wine perhaps?'

'No, I just want to talk,' Maria said, sitting down. Manuel walked around and sat behind the desk, facing her. He slid the contraption to one side so that they could see each other's faces.

'So if your wine has gone to London, why are you still here?'

'We're trying to find out who killed Daniel and Edith. We liked them. Antonio has examined Daniel's ledger and found pages have been torn out, we assume because they had the killer's name on them. We have persuaded the mayor to let us work with Sergeant Voigt to interview people who visited Daniel on the same day of the week as the pages that have been torn out. If there's a pattern, by asking who they saw leaving as they arrived, and arriving as they left, we may find the killer.'

'That's brilliant. But why would you do that, for a Jew, I mean?'

'What do you mean, for a Jew? Frankly, Manuel, I expected better of you. Jews are flesh and blood, and bone, just like us. As a physician, you should know that. What were you doing there? I'm sorry, I don't believe your story about visiting them as patients. They visited our stall and seemed quite healthy. They could easily have visited your clinic. Or don't you like to have Jews dirtying your waiting room, and disturbing your good Christian patients? Talking of dirtying your waiting room, it doesn't look recently decorated. Why did you lie to me when you gave us the tour? Are you lying about why you were you there, at the Bambergers too?' Maria said, thumping her fist on the desk. Manuel pulled a handkerchief from his waistcoat pocket and wiped tears from his eyes.

'Edith is my aunt.'

'You have a Jewish aunt?'

'Yes, my mother is Jewish. I am Jewish.'

'You don't wear the armband.'

'I've been living a lie. You've seen how they treat us. When I left Amsterdam, I thought life would be a lot easier if I pretended to be a Christian. It has on the outside. But inside I loathe myself.'

'So you were visiting your aunt and uncle, pretending

they were patients?'

'Yes. They were shocked at my deception, my betrayal, at first. But they came to understand. I made them swear not to write to my mother and father, or at least not to tell them about it. It would break my mother's heart, after everything she endured, as a proud and faithful Jew.'

'So it wasn't you. You didn't kill them.'

'No, of course not.'

'I think I will have a drink. Have you got any wine?'

'Yes, but not as good as yours.' Manuel got up and left the room. Maria thought about what he had said about living a lie. She was doing exactly the same. He returned with a bottle and two glasses. He poured the wine and handed a glass to Maria. Then he sat back down. 'I can't believe that you're trying to track down their killer. Why?'

'I think it's in our blood. Our father taught us some useful skills, including wrestling, but he also instilled in us a sense of justice. He hates religious sectarianism and intolerance. In England and the Netherlands, he saw a lot of it. He adored William of Orange, who wanted religious freedom for everyone. Of course, that was about Protestants and Catholics, but I'm sure it would be true of Judaism too. I'm sorry, how is your arm?'

'It's healing. You're good people.'

'Thank you. What is this tube thing?' Maria asked, pointing at the contraption on the desk.

'I call it a Janssenscope. I knew a fellow in the Netherlands called Zacharias Janssen. He was a spectacle maker and came up with the idea of mounting two lenses in a tube. Zacharias was a bit of a rogue. It was used to perfect his counterfeiting techniques. I've made a few improvements and use it for my hobby. Here, come round and have a look.' Maria got up and walked around to stand beside Manuel. Manuel looked through the tube and turned the wheel on the side. 'There, have a look.' He stepped aside. Maria bent to look through the tube, her hip brushing Manuel's.

'My god! What is that thing?'

'It's a flea.'

'But it's the size of a horse.'

'No, it's just magnified. I use it to study nature. I have a collection of seeds, grains, insects, many things. It's amazing what you can discover with it.'

'Can it discover secrets?'

'What do you mean, secrets, Maria?'

'What is going on inside someone's head?'

'No, it only magnifies what is outside.'

'Pity, it might have explained the turmoil in my head.'

'What sort of turmoil, Maria?'

'You've told me your secret, but I have one, too. I told you I couldn't explain why I hurt you. It's because I can't allow a man to have power over me.' She breathed deeply. 'When I was thirteen, I was raped. You do not know how hard it is to say those words, especially to someone I have feelings for.'

'Oh Maria, what are we going to do? I'm in turmoil, too. I am a Jew who has feelings for a Gentile, which cannot work. But when I'm near you, I want nothing more than to touch you, to feel your warmth. Can I kiss you, Maria?' She looked into his eyes.

'Yes, Manuel. I won't throw you this time. I promise.'

Maria wandered around the garden, picking flowers and singing a love song her mother had taught her. She took the flowers inside and laid them on the kitchen table, while she got three empty flagons from a cupboard. Then she took the flagons back out into the garden and set them down on the ground next to the well. Next, she poured some water from the jug kept next to the well into the hole at the top of the cast-iron hand pump to prime it. Then she pumped the handle until it drew water. She kept pumping with her right hand as she filled each flagon and finally topped up the jug of priming water. Maria went back into the kitchen with the flagons and arranged flowers in each. She was placing the last one in the sitting room and still singing when she heard the door open, and Antonio's familiar footsteps.

'So he didn't poison you then?'

'No, he didn't. How did you get on? I've got a stew on the range. It'll be ready in about an hour.'

'We only had time for two interviews before Sergeant Voigt had to report to the mayor. We spoke to the tailor, the younger of the two Karl Schmidts. Then we interviewed Andreas Bauer, the farmer. He was some way outside the city, and we had to find him working in the fields. That's why it took so long.'

'What did you find out?'

'The tailor saw the same two people, leaving and arriving on either side of his visits. They were Franz Müller, the watermill owner, and Gerhardt Schneider, the butcher. Andreas Bauer visited Daniel on the 14th of July and the 11th of August. He also saw the same two people leaving and arriving. He was after Gerhardt Schneider, the butcher, and before Heinrich Weber, the basket weaver. We hope to interview everyone else tomorrow. How were things with Manuel?'

'We've made up.'

'Did you find out what he was doing at the Bamberger house?'

'Edith was his aunt. That's why he was so upset.'

'Strewth! He could have told us. There we were trying to find the contract and letter, and he'd lost his aunt and uncle. Why didn't he say anything?'

'For all your intelligent sleuthing, you can still be a clot sometimes. Edith was his aunt. He's Jewish. The law requires him to wear a yellow armband, which he doesn't. He was hardly going to say that in front of the sergeant, was he? He's seen too much persecution of his race, and he thought when he left the Netherlands, that he'd pretend to be Christian. Wouldn't you?'

'I suppose I would. But then I'm not, am I? Nor are you, a Jew I mean. Are you seeing him again tomorrow?'

'No, he's got another operation to help with tomorrow, after his clinic. I'll come along and help you with the other interviews. Wait a minute, you don't want me to see him again, do you?'

'He's Jewish. It wouldn't be right. How could it work?'

'It could work in several ways. He can carry on being a Christian, on the surface anyway. I could convert to Judaism, but why put our children at risk, no, not an option. Or we could both just continue to be human beings. What's your problem? Are you prejudiced? No, I know you better than that. You and I share the same blood. It's that Joseph friend of Greta isn't it? The green-eyed monster lives. Even after what we've been doing to avenge the Bamberger murders, you haven't got over it.'

'Think of Mother and Father. How do you think they'd feel if you married a Jew.'

'Mama is the most loving person I know. Papa has seen enough religious bigotry, I hardly think he'd harbour any himself. You liked the Bambergers.'

'Yes, I did. But, no, you're right. It's Joseph. I'm jealous. Mea culpa. I'm still worried for you though. Promise me you won't put yourself and any nieces or nephews I may have at risk.'

'As I said, conversion is not an option.'

Sergeant Voigt, Antonio, and Maria arrived at the butcher's shop early in the morning. Antonio was carrying their shopping basket. Two women were buying meat. When the customers had left, Gerhardt Schneider turned to Sergeant Voigt.

'Good morning, Barnard, what can I do for you today? I have those sausages you like, and some tender steak.'

'I'm on business, I'm afraid, Gerhardt. You visited Daniel Bamberger, a Jewish money lender.'

'Yes, only for small loans, just to tide me over some bad debts. Why?'

'Bamberger and his wife have been murdered. Can we talk somewhere more private?'

'Heavens, yes. I'll get Gertrude to serve. Come through to the parlour.' The butcher asked his wife to mind the shop, and he led Barnard, Antonio and Maria through to a room with a table and six chairs. There was a dresser against the far wall, with crockery on the shelves. The other walls were decorated with some framed embroideries. 'Please, sit down. Murdered, you say. You can't think I've got anything to do with it.' They all sat down. Antonio took some paper, a quill, and an inkpot from the basket, and put them on the table in front of him.

'We're making enquiries of several people who visited the Bambergers. This young man will explain,' Sergeant Voigt said, turning to Antonio.

'Yes, Herr Schneider. We don't suspect you, because you appear in some pages of Daniel's ledger. The murderer appears to have torn out all pages that had his name on them. We understand from Karl Schmidt, the tailor, and Andreas Bauer, the farmer, that you visited on the Thursdays of 12th May, 14th July, and 11th August, is that right?'

'Probably, they were Thursdays. I remember talking to Karl. I don't think I've met the farmer. But on the second and third visits, the same fellow was arriving as I left.'

'Can you describe him?' Antonio asked, quill poised in his hand.

'He was younger than me, but just as well fed,' the butcher replied, smiling and rubbing his plump stomach. 'He was tall and well tanned. I suppose you would be working in the fields.'

'Yes, that sounds like him. What about the second visit, on the 14th of July? Who was leaving as you arrived?'

'Ah, I remember that. There had been a mix up. It wasn't Karl Schmidt the tailor, it was Karl Schmidt the blacksmith.'

'And who was arriving as you left on the first visit?'

'I remember him. It was Heinrich Weber, the basket weaver. His baskets are very popular with our customers. Is there anything else?'

'Why did you visit three times? Wouldn't you just pawn something, then redeem it, when you had the money?' Antonio asked.

'Daniel charged a lower fee for stage payments. That's why I used him, instead of the others.'

'Well, that all seems in order, Gerhardt. Thank you for your time,' Sergeant Voigt said. They all got up. The butcher grabbed a handful of sausages, wrapped them in paper, and handed them to Sergeant Voigt, just as they left.

It was a short walk from the butcher to the basket weaver's workshop on Rhinestraße. Sergeant Voigt opened the door, and they went in. There was a thin blond-haired man of around thirty sitting on a chair in the middle of the room. The wall to their left was lined with shelves. There were baskets of varying sizes on the shelves. To their right there were bundles of willow reeds stacked against the wall. The seated man was working on a basket. He continued weaving until he had finished the reed he was working with, then he looked up.

'Good morning. How can I help you?'

'I'm Sergeant Voigt, of the city guard. We are on official business. We understand you visited Daniel Bamberger on the Thursdays of May 12th, July 14th, and August 18th. Is that correct?'

'Probably, I can get my diary if you like.'

'Yes, please do,' Sergeant Voigt replied. The basket weaver put down the basket he was working on and got up. He went to a chest of drawers and took a book from one of the drawers. He came back to his chair, sat down, and leafed through the pages.

'I'm sorry, I don't have any chairs for guests. There isn't much room, as you can see. Yes, that's right. I had appointments at half past four on each of those Thursdays. Why do you ask?'

'I'm afraid it's a murder inquiry. Both Daniel and Edith Bamberger have been murdered.'

'My god. I'm sorry to hear that. I didn't enjoy needing to borrow money, but times have been hard. He may have been a Jew, but he always struck me as being a considerate man. There was always a cup of tea for you, and biscuits. He wanted to know how business was, how my wife was, and my children. There was never any rush to finish the business and send you on your way. You can't think I had anything to do with his murder?'

'No,' Antonio answered, as he walked over to the chest of drawers. He put his basket down and took out his paper, quill and inkpot. 'Can you tell us who was leaving when you arrived?'

'The first time that I visited, the butcher, Gerhardt Schneider, was just finishing his tea. On the second and third visits, there was a different man, about my age. He was well built and tanned, if I remember correctly.'

'Yes, that sounds like Andreas Bauer, the farmer. Who arrived as you left, on each of the Thursdays?' Antonio asked.

'It was the same man on each day. Günther Zimmermann, the carpenter. He made that chest of drawers for me. Is there anything else?'

'No, I don't think so,' Antonio replied, finishing his notes and corking the inkpot.

'I see you have one of my baskets. They're good, aren't they?'

'Yes, very good.'

The interview with Günther Zimmermann was straightforward. He was the last appointment on each of the Thursdays, and confirmed that Heinrich Weber, the basket weaver, was there when he arrived on each occasion. They left the Zimmermann carpentry workshop and crossed the street to a tavern for lunch. They were soon seated at a table and enjoying sausages with sauerkraut, washed down with beer.

'How do you think the investigations are going, Antonio?' Sergeant Voigt asked.

'Well, it's all tying together so far. We just have the blacksmith and the miller to go, I think.'

'The carpenter seems to have been the last appointment on each day. He could have strangled them both, with nobody due to arrive and catch him at it. Did you see the size of his hands?' Maria suggested.

'Yes, except for two things. They weren't murdered on a Thursday. The last entry in the ledger was Monday 15th August, the day we found the bodies. And his name was on pages that the murderer didn't tear out,' Antonio replied. 'It's not like you to miss obvious clues like that.',

'You're right,' Maria replied. 'These sausages are delicious.'

'They're a speciality of the city,' Sergeant Voigt said, smiling.

◇ ◇ ◇

They could hear the hammering from the blacksmith's forge before they turned the corner onto Königstraße. The barn-type doors were wide open, and the heat hit them as they entered. Sergeant Voigt caught Karl Schmidt's eye, and the latter stopped hammering. He was around sixty years of age and bald. He had powerful-looking arms and large, scarred hands. Sergeant Voigt explained the circumstances and purpose of their visit.

'I'm sorry to hear that. Bamberger seemed like a decent enough man for a Jew. How can I help?' the blacksmith asked.

'You visited him on the Thursdays of May 12th and July 14th, is that correct?' Antonio asked.

'Yes, that's right. I only needed a small loan, just for

that month.'

'Did you see who was leaving before your appointment and arriving afterwards, on each day?'

'Let me see. Yes, Franz Müller, the miller was before me on both days. The day I took out the loan, my namesake, the tailor, arrived as I was finishing my tea. When I paid it back, it was the butcher, Gerhardt Schneider, who arrived as I left. Is there anything else?'

'No, that all seems to tie up with what we know,' Antonio said, examining his notes.

The watermill was near to where Maria and Manuel had picnicked. As they approached it they saw the water wheel turning. The mill was set back around fifty yards from the riverbank. There was a stone channel that diverted water from the river to the wheel, then returned it to the river. They could see an iron axle penetrating the wall of the mill house. Sergeant Voigt knocked on the door, but there was no reply. He turned the handle, and they entered. They could see the axle turning above them, and a system of gears translating the motion into a vertical axis which was rotating an enormous circular millstone. That millstone was turning on a stationary stone. There was a channel cut in the stationary stone, and a stream of flour was pouring from it, down a wooden chute into a sack on the floor. A larger chute was directing the grain to the hub of the upper stone. The air was thick with fine flour dust, and flour covered the floor and coated the walls. In the corner, there was a ladder to the floor above. Sergeant Voigt walked over to the ladder just as a pair of sturdy legs appeared from above. Franz Müller was a tall man, with the physique of someone who handled sacks of flour every day. He started as he reached the ground and turned to be confronted by Sergeant Voigt, Antonio, and Maria.

'Can we have a word with you outside?' Sergeant Voigt shouted above the noise of the mill. The miller nodded, and they all went outside. Sergeant Voigt introduced Antonio and Maria before beginning his questioning. 'We understand you visited Daniel Bamberger on three Thursdays: the twelfth of May, the fourteenth of July, and the fifteenth of August. Is that correct?'

'Yes, I think so. They were all Thursdays. I'd have to check my diary for the dates. Why do you ask?'

'Because Daniel Bamberger and his wife have been murdered,' Sergeant Voigt replied. The flour dust on the miller's face couldn't quite disguise the blood draining from his face. He reached out a hand to the wall to steady himself. 'Can you remember who was leaving as you arrived on each day?'

'Nobody. I suppose I was the first.' He turned to face the wall, with both hands steadying himself. A floorboard creaked, and a door opened at the far end of the mill. A large woman of around the same age as the miller, around forty, appeared with a broom. 'Not now, Frieda. We have guests.' The woman looked at each of them in turn.

'What's the pretty young woman doing here? Who is she?'

'She and her brother are helping the sergeant with an investigation, my love.'

'What investigation? What have you been up to?'

'Nothing, I swear it. Leave the sweeping until later.' The woman turned and went back out the door, slamming it behind her. 'Excuse my wife. What were you saying?'

'What about who arrived as you left?' Sergeant Voigt continued. Maria reached out to the basket Antonio was holding and took a sheet of paper. Antonio looked at her quizzically. She put a finger to her lips and quietly slipped back into the mill.

'Karl Schmidt, the blacksmith on the first two days, and the tailor of the same name on the last.'

'Are you absolutely sure there was nobody before you?'

'Not sure, no. But I didn't see anyone,' the miller said, as Maria slipped back behind Antonio. 'Is there anything else?'

'No,' Sergeant Voigt replied, after exchanging eye contact with Antonio. 'You seem rather shaken by the death of a Jew.'

'Well, a death is shocking, isn't it? Even the death of a Jewish money lender.' The miller turned to face them. Sergeant Voigt nodded and turned to leave. Antonio and Maria followed him. Nobody spoke until they were well away from the mill.

'Well, everyone seems to have liked the Bambergers. He seemed genuinely shocked by it,' Sergeant Voigt said.

'Can we stop a moment?' Antonio asked. They stopped, and Antonio took his notes from the basket. 'On every other day, Daniel had seven appointments in the afternoon. Why would he have only six on these three days?'

'I don't know,' Voigt replied. 'Perhaps if there was an earlier appointment, it ended early. The miller may have been late for his appointment.'

'What did you slip back inside for, Maria?' Antonio asked.

'For this,' she said, unfolding the sheet of paper. 'I collected some flour dust.'

'Why?' Antonio asked.

'It's been bothering me why the floor had been cleaned when they were bloodless murders. What if the killer had left something else? What if it was flour dust he had left? You saw him, he's covered in it. He may have seen the dust on the floor and cleaned up after himself.'

'Yes,' Antonio said, stroking his beard. 'But why not tear out all the pages with his name on?'

'Maybe the cleaning up distracted him. Then we arrived, and he had to flee.'

'That's possible. But he tore out other pages.'

'He may have been tearing out the pages, then noticed the flour dust and concentrated on that instead. Then we arrived, and he had to leave.'

'You may have something there, Maria. Why did you take the flour sample?'

'He seemed to have done a good job of cleaning the floor, but I can imagine him strangling Daniel and Edith. Perhaps he left some dust on their clothing. I thought I'd get Manuel to compare it with anything we might find on their clothing. He has a Janssenscope.'

'What on earth is a Janssenscope?' Antonio asked.

'It's a tube with lenses in it. It made a flea appear to be the size of a horse.'

Maria knocked on Manuel's clinic door. Ingrid opened the door.

'I need to see Manuel,' Maria said.

'Come in. He has his last patient of the day with him. He won't be long.' Maria followed Ingrid to the waiting room. Ingrid left and closed the door behind her. Maria sat for a few moments, then got up and paced the room. Manuel's door opened, and an old man shuffled out. Manuel smiled at her as he opened the waiting room door for the old man and followed him to the front door. When he returned, he opened his mouth to greet her, but Maria beat him to it.

'Have your aunt and uncle been buried yet?'

'Yes, of course they have. It's a Jewish tradition to bury the body as soon as it has been prepared.'

'Can they be exhumed?'

'No, they certainly can't be. It would be abhorrent to disturb the deceased like that. Why would you even ask?'

'I was just trying to help. I'm sorry, I see I've upset you. It's just that I think we've found out who the murderer is. We don't have any witnesses, but I wondered why the killer cleaned the floor. I thought perhaps he had left something which would incriminate him, like flour dust. I took a sample and thought that if we found any dust on Daniel and Edith's clothes, you could compare them with your Janssenscope.' Maria saw tears well in Manuel's eyes. He took out his handkerchief and wiped them.

'I can't believe you're doing this to bring justice for my family.'

'Of course I am. I'd do it for anyone.'

'I'm not sure I believe that, but thank you. There is a chance if we hurry. Follow me, I'll explain on the way.' Manuel put on his coat and called out to Ingrid to lock up when she left. He hurried towards the Judengasse. 'The Taharah precedes a Jewish burial. That is a ritual washing of the deceased. Then the body is dressed in the Tachrichim, special white clothes representing purity and holiness. The undertaker may not have disposed of their clothes yet, if we're lucky.'

They passed the synagogue, and Manuel led the way to a small building nearby. He knocked on the door, and a man in a black robe and cap led them in.

'Is this the undertaker?' Maria whispered to Manuel.

'It is the Jewish version of one. This is where the Chevra Kadish cleans the bodies of the dead, and remains with the deceased until burial, which is normally within twenty-four hours.'

'Doctor Nuñez, what can I do to help you now?'

'Thank you, Isaac. Do you have Daniel and Edith's clothes?'

'They will be in the storeroom, I expect. Why?'

'The clothes may help us find whoever killed them.'

'It has only been a few days. If the family doesn't want them, and we know of no family here, we wait until we have enough to do a big wash, then distribute them to the poor.' He opened a door, and they went in. It was a small room with shelves on three sides. There were piles of white linen on one shelf, black ribbons on another. There was a woman folding and stacking clothes. 'Sarah, do you know where the Bambergers' clothes are?' Isaac asked.

'They will be in these piles,' the woman replied, patting two piles of clothes on the shelf to her right.

'Will you recognise them?' the undertaker asked.

'Yes, I think so.' Manuel examined the piles of folded clothing. 'Here they are,' he said, pulling out a long blue dress, a pair of brown breeches, and a white linen shirt.' He handed the dress to Maria and unfolded the shirt himself. 'There is some dust on the shirt, and a sort of stain here.'

'Yes, the dress is dusty as well. Something's stuck to it. Have you got a few sheets of clean paper and a knife please, sir?' Maria asked the undertaker.

'Yes, of course, I won't be a minute.' He left the room. The woman looked them up and down, then returned to folding garments. When the undertaker returned, he handed Maria half a dozen sheets of paper and a knife. Maria laid the paper flat on the floor, then scraped the dust onto the paper from the dress. She folded the sheet of paper. Then she laid out another sheet of paper and worked at the dried stain.

'I think this is dried dough,' she said, as she handed the knife to Manuel, while she folded the sheets of paper containing the samples. Manuel scraped the dust from the shirt onto another sheet of paper. Then he did the same with the breeches onto another sheet. 'Could we trouble you for a quill and some ink please, sir?' Maria asked the undertaker. He went away again. When he returned, Maria wrote on the folded sheets of paper. 'There, now we know which sample has come from which garment. We'd better take the clothes with us, Manuel. They're evidence.'

Maria and Manuel returned to the clinic. They went to Manuel's study, and he took a small box from a cupboard. He took six squares of clear glass from the box. Then he took a sheet of paper and a quill. He dipped his quill in the ink pot and wrote a series of headings down the page.

'Let's start with the dust from Daniel's shirt,' he said, as he unfolded the appropriate sheet of paper. He took a small paintbrush from a drawer of his desk and brushed some of the dust onto one of the squares of glass. Then he put the glass square under his Janssenscope, and peered through it, adjusting the wheels at the side. 'Do you have the sample of the miller's flour?' Maria handed him the paper with the sample of flour she had taken at the mill. Manuel brushed some onto another glass square. Then he swapped it with the glass square he had just examined. 'Yes, I'd say they are identical. Here, look for yourself.' Manuel got up from his chair, and let Maria sit at the Janssenscope. When she had examined the flour sample, he swapped the squares for her.

'I see what you mean. I can't tell the difference. So it is the miller, he's the murderer.'

'Shall we have a look at the scrapings from the stain, as well as the dust?' Manuel suggested. Maria nodded, standing up and letting Manuel take over again. Manuel placed the scrapings onto a clean square and put it under the Janssenscope. 'Well, it definitely has the flour grains in it, but there are other substances too.'

'What other substances?'

'I think there is butter or milk there. It's dough, but there's something else in the dough. I'll have to look through my collection and see if I have something similar.'

'I wonder how the milk or butter got there? Perhaps the miller was drinking some milk and spilt some down his dusty coat before he went to murder Daniel and Edith. As he was strangling them, some transferred to their clothing. Oh, I'm sorry, Manuel, I'm being insensitive again. How long will it take you to look through your samples?'

'Hours. I have over five hundred samples in my collection. Don't be sorry, I am amazed that you'd go to all this trouble for them. I feel so stupid making such a fuss about you hurting my arm. Can you forgive me?' he said, getting up from his chair. Maria looked up into his eyes and smiled. She moved closer to him and put her arms around his neck. He put his arms around her waist and leaned forwards. Their lips touched. He felt her heart pounding against his ribs. Their tongues touched and Maria was surprised that she didn't recoil.

'Tell me about your mother. You said you get your looks from her.' Maria smiled.

'I don't know where to start. She had to leave Portugal with her uncle and brother to escape the Spanish Inquisition. They boarded a ship bound for the Netherlands, but an English ship captured their ship. The English captain was so captivated by my mother that he proposed marriage to her. She refused, but he took them to London. News of her beauty spread, and Queen Elizabeth had her taken to her court. The queen gave her a tour of London in her carriage.'

'Really? Our father is English. He wasn't very impressed with Queen Elizabeth. She was very slow to reward him for his services.'

'After a few weeks, the queen granted my mother and her family safe passage to the Netherlands, where she met and married my father. Maria, if I were to propose to you, would you convert to Judaism?'

'What do you mean, if I were to propose? Are you proposing or not?'

'I've never met anyone like you, nor anyone who matched my mother's beauty. There is this massive problem though. It would break my mother's heart if we didn't have a Jewish wedding. Would you convert to Judaism?'

'What do you mean, I'd have to convert to Judaism? You've been pretending to be a Christian. Why would I have to convert to Judaism? That's crazy! You've seen how the Jews are persecuted. Would you want that for our children?'

'I've hidden my heritage, but I've never stopped revering it. We could continue to pretend to be Christian, but you would have to convert.'

'Why?'

'Because Judaism follows the mother's line. If your mother is Jewish, you are Jewish, even if the mother has converted. It really would break my mother's heart if her grandchildren weren't Jewish. Her family went through so much at the hands of the inquisition. Will you do that for me?'

'This is too much for me to take in. I love you, of course I do. But for you to have hidden your own faith, pretending to be a Christian, and now wanting me to do the opposite, I don't think I can. Why should my children carry that burden? No, I'm sorry, Manuel, I don't think I can do that. I'll help to bring your aunt and uncle's murderer to justice, but I can't let my children run the risk of someone discovering they're Jewish. I'm going to leave now. Let me know when you discover what the other substance is.'

When Maria got back to the house on Wienerstraße, Antonio was already there.

'You're late, Maria. What did you discover?'

'Less than I'd hoped, and more than I'd feared.'

'That's rather cryptic. What do you mean?'

'Pour me a goblet of wine and I'll tell you.' Antonio felt the deep sadness in his twin. He went to fetch two goblets of wine. He handed one to Maria, then sat down and took a swig himself. Maria took several gulps of wine. 'I'd better start with the hopes. I had hoped that we could find Daniel and Edith's clothes, even if we had to exhume them. I wondered if we would find that they had flour dust on their clothes. I thought Manuel could prove that the flour matched the miller's flour. We would have found the murderer, and perhaps that would make everything right between Manuel and I. I've never felt that way about anyone, you know.'

'So what happened?'

'We didn't have to exhume them. The undertaker still had their clothes. We took samples and went back to Manuel's clinic. He examined the samples taken from the clothes and compared them with the sample I took from the mill. They were a perfect match. There was something else there too. Manuel found either milk or butter, or both. He found something else too. He's going to compare it with other specimens he has.'

'Butter or milk, doesn't that point to dough, as well as flour?'

'I thought the miller might have been drinking some milk and spilt some down him.'

'Maria, you're not thinking straight. If Franz Müller were the murderer, he would have torn out the pages with his name on them. He didn't. Anyone who had been making bread or pastry might have flour and dough on their clothing. I'm sure there was somebody else who had the first appointment on those days. Either Müller didn't see them, or he's lying. But I can't see why he's lying. We need to question him more, and find out why he's lying. Who is he protecting, and why? Wait, you said you'd discovered more than you feared. What do you mean?' Antonio looked in her eyes. Maria took another long draught of wine.

'We love each other. He almost proposed to me, but on one condition.'

'What do you mean, almost proposed to you?'

'He's as inept as you are in that department. He said, if I were to propose to you, not will you marry me? He wants me to convert to Judaism, to please his mother. Don't laugh, I can see the irony. You bungled your proposal to Greta, because you made it sound as though our mother was making the proposal. Now it's his mother who has screwed up Manuel's proposal to me. It's damned crazy. He's living like a Christian to enjoy a good, and let's face it, safer life. Then he wants me to become a Jew and have Jewish children. Why would anyone want to have children and put them in danger? And heaven knows how Mama would take it.'

'I don't know, Maria. It doesn't seem to make any sense to me. Do you want to go home? I'd like to put things right with Greta on the way, then tell father about the wine deal. We need to look into bottling as well. What do you think?'

'Maybe that's best. Pour me another wine. I think I'll need it to help me sleep.'

# CHAPTER EIGHT

Maria awoke with a hangover. She went downstairs and poured herself a glass of water from the jug on the dresser. She drank it and emptied the jug into her glass. She drank that, then went into the backyard and refilled the jug from the pump. She tipped the water out and refilled the jug so that the water was fresh, not mingled with the priming water. When she got back to the kitchen, Antonio was there.

'Here, have some water. You look like you need it as much as I did.' Maria filled a glass and passed it to Antonio.

'Thanks.' He drained the glass. 'Have you thought about it? Going home I mean.'

'Yes. You go home. You need to patch things up with Greta, then go home. Hopefully she'll see sense and start a clinic in Rome. You'll work something out. The vineyard is your thing. I need to find my life.'

'How? Doing what? You can't just leave mother and father, not without explaining why.'

'You explain. Tell them I love them, but I have to find my life. I don't know how. Maybe I'll go to Paris and see how Louis is getting along. It's been two years. I wonder how Marie's regency is working out. He'll be king in his own right, eventually. I'm sure he'll find my talents useful. Just leave me half the money, my pistol and rifle. I can look after myself.'

'Don't you think there's unfinished business here?'

'I can't see a future with Manuel, if that's what you mean. He seemed sincere that he needed me to become a Jew.'

'There's also the investigation.'

'Do you have any ideas? We hit a dead end, as far as I can see.'

'Yes, I do. Let's speak with Sergeant Voigt. You can tell him about the Janssenscope, and the sample. We need him to help us put pressure on Müller. We need to know who he's protecting and why.'

'You're right. It wouldn't feel right to leave this thing half finished. Let's see him now.'

Antonio and Maria went to the city hall and found Sergeant Voigt in the guardroom, polishing his boots.

'Good morning, Barnard,' Antonio said. 'We think we're getting closer to finding the killer. I don't think it's the miller, but I am certain he knows who the killer is. Can you help us put some pressure on him?'

'I'm afraid not.'

'Why not?' Maria exclaimed.

'The mayor's orders. He thinks we're wasting our time.'

'We are getting closer. Manuel, Doctor Nuñez, that is, has a Janssenscope which magnifies objects. We were able to get Daniel and Edith's clothes from the undertaker and examine them. They had flour, dust, and dough on them. That must be what the killer was at pains to wipe from the floor. But he left traces on their clothes. Antonio is right about the ledger pages, so if it's not the miller, it might be a baker he supplies. Don't you see?'

'Yes, I see, but it doesn't change the mayor's orders.'

'But if he knows we're not wasting our time, surely he'll change his mind. Can we speak to him?' Maria asked.

'His office is at the end of the corridor, but I think you're wasting your time. His mind seemed set.'

Antonio and Maria left and went to the mayor's office. They knocked on the door and a short, plump, grey-haired man opened the door.

'We'd like to see the mayor. We've been working with Sergeant Voigt to solve the murder of the Bambergers,' Antonio explained.

'He told Barnard to drop the case.'

'Can we please just speak to the mayor?' Maria pleaded.

'I don't think he's likely to change his mind,' the grey-haired man replied, as a door opened behind him. Mayor Friedrich appeared.

'What's all the fuss about? Oh, it's you. I'm afraid I've told Voigt to drop it. You're wasting your time,' Mayor Friedrich said.

'But we're not. We are making progress. Please let us explain.' Maria asked.

'When is my next appointment, Karl?' the mayor asked.

'Not for half an hour, sir.'

'Oh, very well. Come through into my office.' Mayor Friedrich sighed, limping back into his office. Antonio and Maria followed him past the clerk's desk and through a door into a much larger room. It was well lit by windows overlooking the city square. There was a large desk and a table with twelve chairs around it. Portraits hung on the walls. The one at the end was of Mayor Friedrich. The mayor pulled out a chair at the end of the large table and indicated for Antonio and Maria to sit in the adjacent chairs. They all sat. 'So what progress do you think you're making?' He listened as Maria explained the Janssenscope and the flour, dust, and dough. Antonio explained why he didn't think the miller was the killer, but that he was covering for whoever was. Mayor Friedrich sighed. 'You may well be right, but it doesn't change my mind. I see you are disappointed. I'm sorry, but I have much greater worries than the murder of two Jews. Not a council meeting or trial takes place, without the citizens demanding to know their rights. They also demand the expulsion of the Jews. So if you were to find the citizen who murdered the Jews, it would only make things even worse for me. I'm sorry, but you must stop. Go home! Where are you from? You're wine producers, aren't you?'

'Yes, that's right, sir. We have a vineyard near Rome,' Antonio said.

'What are the rights that the citizens are demanding to know?' Maria asked. 'And why won't you tell them?'

'Well, I suppose as you'll be going back to Italy, it won't do any harm.' Mayor Friedrich smiled. 'I won't tell them their rights because it doesn't do to give in to demands. Especially when if they knew what their rights were, it would inflame matters even further.'

'I don't understand,' Maria murmured.

'It's so very ironic, I can't help telling you. It's all about the policy of tolerance. After so many decades of religious conflict, the Holy Roman Emperor decreed that each prince may decide what the official religion shall be in his lands. Other religions are to be tolerated. The citizens' rights are freedom of religion, and if they don't like the official religion, then they are free to move to the land of another prince. So how can I tell these intolerant citizens that their precious right, which they crave to know, is that they are free to leave the city? There would be a riot. If only Matthias, the Holy Roman Emperor, hadn't threatened us with removal of our rights, if we didn't swear an oath of allegiance, then there wouldn't be this demand to know what the rights are.'

'I see. But why are they so intolerant of the Jews?' Maria asked.

'That's a complex question. To start with, they're different. Not very different, but they don't eat pork, for example. We're very proud of our pork sausages here. Of course, the church doesn't help. I didn't say that, by the way. The Jews are banned from most regular trades, but they make excellent physicians, organisers and financiers. Times have been hard recently, and many citizens have had to turn to Jewish money lenders, like Bamberger. They blame me for protecting the Jews, claiming that I'm taking bribes from the Jews, which, of course, I'm not. You must see that I can't allow the trial of a citizen for the murder of the Bambergers. I fear a riot would be inevitable. I walk a narrow line. Go home! Make your wine. I trust the fair was useful to you?'

'Yes, sir,' Antonio replied. 'We found a wine merchant from London who wants our wine. We need to investigate bottling. Apparently, wine travels better in glass bottles.'

'Yes, I've heard that. So there you are then. Go back home and look into bottling.' Mayor Friedrich said, standing up, wincing. 'Damn this bloody gout! Now, if you don't mind, I need to prepare for my next meeting.' Antonio stood up, and Maria followed his lead. They shook hands and left the mayor's office.

◇ ◇ ◇

'So, I suppose that's it then.' Antonio sighed once they were outside. 'We can't put any pressure on the miller without Sergeant Voigt. He'll just refuse. If we use force against him, he'll complain to the mayor. Having told us to go, the mayor would have us arrested. So perhaps it's time I headed off to see Greta. Do you still intend to go to Paris?'

'Yes, but I still don't enjoy giving up so easily. I agree we can't put any pressure on him, but there are other ways.'

'What other ways?'

'You weren't with Papa and I in Paris. He taught me surveillance. I disguised myself as a tramp and followed the suspects after Papa had interrogated them. I got quite good at it. We should find somewhere that we can observe the watermill without being seen. Then if we see people come to collect flour, and if it's several sackfuls, then we'll follow them. If, on the other hand, he drives off with a cartload of sacks, then we follow him and see who he delivers to.'

'So if it's just a purchase of flour for domestic use, we ignore it. Yes, I see. Why would he protect somebody who wasn't an important client?' Antonio said, stroking his beard. 'That could take a while. We don't know how long it takes a baker to get through a cartload of flour. Why don't we use another skill Father taught us? We could pick the lock on his mill while he's out, and examine his ledger. We may find out who his customers are much more quickly that way.'

'I wonder what the chances of a miller being literate are. Not great, in my opinion. But if he is, then it would speed matters up, as you say. I don't know how many bakers there are in the city. Let's say there are six. What do we do once we know who they are? If we put pressure on them, how is that any different to putting pressure on the miller? They can still complain to the mayor.'

'I think he is literate, Maria. He said he'd have to consult his diary to confirm the dates. So he's bound to have a ledger as well. If that throws nothing up, could we try some kind of bluff? The bakers wouldn't know that we don't have the mayor's support. We could tell them that the miller had confessed to covering up for them. Then persuade them it would be better for them if they confessed. Would that work?'

'Unlikely, Antonio.' Maria paused, her eyes lowered to her chest. 'Manuel should still have Daniel and Edith's clothes. If the killer could transfer flour and dough to their clothes, what are the chances that the dough took a fragment of thread from the killer's apron with it? Manuel said there was something else in the dough. If he could compare a thread that is in the dough on the Bamberger clothes, with the fabric of the aprons, using the Janssenscope, he may find a match.' Maria smiled. 'If we identify all the bakers, just by walking the streets of the city, then we could have a night of lock picking and apron theft. How exciting!'

'That's brilliant, Maria. We'll have to label the aprons as we steal them. But what if all the bakers get their aprons from the same supplier, like the wicker baskets?'

'Perhaps something else got transferred with the dough? What if a hair was? Perhaps we could identify whose hair it was.'

'Why would the baker go to murder Daniel and Edith wearing his apron?'

'I don't know. Perhaps dressing for the occasion isn't at the front of your mind when you set off to kill.'

'Yes, I suppose anger drives intelligent thought aside. Although he thought to rip the pages out and wipe the floor. If we do get some evidence from the Janssenscope to identify the killer, we still have to persuade the mayor to do something about it. Do you think he will? I don't.'

'You may be right, but we will have done everything we can. We will have solved the case, even if we haven't secured justice. Perhaps that's what is drawing me back to Paris,' Maria said. Antonio looked puzzled for a second.

'Ah, yes, Épernon.'

'Yes. I think I should speak with Manuel. We need to know what he can accomplish with the Janssenscope.'

'What shall I do, Maria?'

'Take your pick. Either find somewhere that you can watch the mill without being seen, or walk the streets identifying bakeries. I may be a while, depending on how many patients Manuel has to see. I'll see you back at the house.'

Maria had a long wait in the waiting room. There was a young mother with a baby and a young son of around three. The mother was sitting on a chair in the corner of the room, furthest from Manuel's consulting room. She was cradling the baby in her arms. The boy was on the floor at her feet, playing with a carved wooden horse. There were six other patients, two middle-aged women, a young man with an arm in a sling, and two elderly men. They were all sitting next to each other in the corner diagonally opposite the young mother. Maria wondered whether the mother or her children had plague. She looked for any sign of pustules or blackness on their skin, but could see none. Nor did they appear to have a fever. Then, as the mother turned, moving the baby from one arm to the other, she saw the yellow armband on her sleeve. She wanted to shout at the others, to call out their prejudice. Instead, she breathed deeply and slowly, trying to push the anger that was squeezing her heart back down again. It wouldn't help the mother, and it certainly wouldn't help Manuel. She decided to leave and return later. She spoke to Ingrid, telling her she would be back in a couple of hours, and that she needed to speak with Manuel. Then she left.

Maria walked back to Wienerstraße. From there she walked the streets looking for bakeries. The first one she found was the grocery and bakery on the market square, where she had bought bread on the day they set up their stall. She peered in through the window. There was a queue of six women waiting to be served. The same plump young woman was serving. Maria remembered the man who had brought the bread out to her, flour dust in his hair. Vincenz, that was what the woman had called him. He'd gone back and brought gingerbread men for the little boy. He had seemed so jovial. He said he didn't know how he would pay for his daughter's wedding. So he needed money. It might be him. How could you tell? Maria didn't go in, but she lingered by the door, checking the lock. She continued walking along the street, counting her paces, until she reached a junction. Then she turned left and then left again, into a narrow alley. She counted her paces back until she felt she was at the back of the grocery and bakery. There was a wooden gate in a fence. She looked around to see if there was anyone about. She opened the gate and slipped into the yard. It wasn't huge, about eight paces by three. There was a shed. She opened the shed door and looked in. There were dozens of sacks, some open at the top. She could see onions, turnips, carrots and cabbages. On the other side of the shed there were sacks with flour dust on the surrounding floor. She closed the shed door as quietly as she could. She pressed herself against the back wall of the shop. There was a window. She stooped, so that she was just looking through a bottom corner of the window. She could see the flames of the oven and Vincenz taking some loaves out, using a long-handled sort of flat shovel. He was wearing an apron, and she could see a row of pegs on the wall. There was a coat on one peg, and another apron too. She moved away from the window and examined the lock on the back door before slipping out into the alleyway again.

Maria made for the cathedral. From there she walked the streets, keeping the cathedral to her right, but working her way further from it. The first bakery she found bore a sign "Hartmann Brot". She went inside. There were only two middle-aged women in the queue. While waiting for them to be served, Maria glanced behind her at the door. The lock wouldn't be a problem, but there were bolts at the top and bottom of the door. The women waiting were talking about their grandchildren. The woman serving went to fetch a rye loaf from the oven, and Maria tried the top bolt. It slid easily, so was clearly well used. The first woman paid for her loaf, thanked Frau Hartmann, and left. The second woman wanted a spelt loaf.

'Ernst, ein dinkelbrot, bitte,' Frau Hartmann called out. After a few seconds, Ernst Hartmann appeared from the back room with the loaf. He handed it to his wife after exchanging a few words with the customer. Ersnt Hartmann was short, plump and bald. Maria couldn't imagine him overcoming Daniel and Edith without a struggle, but his apron was covered in flour, dust, and dough. When the customer left, Maria also asked for a spelt loaf. As Frau Hartmann turned to call her husband back with another loaf, Maria edged sideways to get a view into the back room. In the oven's light, she could see the back door, which did not appear to have any bolts. Ernst Hartmann was frowning when he reappeared with the loaf. He handed it to his wife, muttered something which Maria couldn't make out, and went back to the bakery. Maria paid for the loaf and left the shop.

She continued her search for bakeries. The next one she found was called Krause Bäckerei. It was a four-storey building. The brickwork between the timbers was painted yellow. A young boy was walking towards her, holding a stick which he tapped against the walls of the buildings he passed. Maria stopped and waited for him to reach her, then she offered him the bread, which he took and thanked her. Then he ran off in the direction from which he had come. Maria entered Krause Bäckerei. A small bell above the door rang as she opened the door. There was a shelf stacked with loaves behind the counter. There was nobody in the shop, but a man in his early thirties, Maria guessed, emerged from the door behind the counter, between the stacked shelves. He was a little taller than Maria and had red curly hair, coated in flour dust. His apron was also dusty and spotted with dough. Maria asked for a spelt loaf and he went back into the bakery. Maria couldn't see past him before he reappeared with the loaf. She thanked him, paid and left. She found an alleyway which she thought should lead to the rear of Krause Bäckerei. She followed it and paced off the distance. There wasn't a yard, but there was a door which should open onto the bakery. She turned the handle very slowly. She could hear the roar of the oven as she slowly opened the door an inch. She put her eye to the crack and could see the baker needing dough on a bench beside the oven, singing as he worked. Maria opened the door another inch and glanced up and down for bolts. There were none. She saw several sacks of flour stacked against one wall. She gently closed the door and made her way back to the main street. Maria continued her search for bakeries, but hadn't found any more by the time the cathedral bells rang four o'clock. She turned and set off for Manuel's clinic.

Manuel smiled at Maria when he opened the door. She smiled back. He stood aside to let her in, and she went straight to his study. He followed her.

'I'm afraid I haven't discovered what the other substance is yet. I have had very little free time. Do sit down. How is your investigation going, Maria?'

'Not as well as we would have liked. The mayor has forbidden Sergeant Voigt from helping us, so we're unable to interrogate the suspects. They'd just protest to the mayor, and he'd have us imprisoned or expelled.'

'Why has he done that?'

'He's afraid there will be a riot. Since Emperor Matthias threatened removal of citizens' rights, if they didn't swear an oath of allegiance, they've been demanding to know what their rights are. Since they're also demanding expulsion of the Jews, he doesn't want to tell them that their rights are freedom of religion, and the right to leave if they don't like it.'

'Yet you're still pursuing the murderer. Have you had second thoughts about marriage?'

'Not unless you have. I can't see how anyone would want to be a Jew. In your waiting room this morning, there was a young mother with a baby and a young son. I thought they must have the plague, from the way the others treated them. Then I saw the yellow armband. It's inhuman. Why do they have to wear the armbands? You don't.'

'Because they can't tell us from them without the armband. They can't see that we're Jews by the colour of our skin. I'd decided not to be identified as a Jew before I arrived here, so I can pull it off. I attend mass. It's not so bad, unless the bishop preaches against us. Easter's the worst. I enjoy the Gregorian chants. I keep my Jewish faith, but don't risk attending synagogue. I still want my children to be Jewish though, albeit secretly.'

'I just don't understand you, Manuel.'

'No, I suppose you don't. I don't understand myself, half the time. So what have you come for?'

'Antonio and I think the killer is probably a baker. We wondered if the other substance in the dough scrapings might identify which baker it was. Perhaps there's a hair of his, or a thread from his apron. We're planning to identify all the bakers in the city and steal their aprons by night. Then you could use your Janssenscope to compare the dough and fibres on each apron with the stains on your aunt and uncle's clothes. Do you think that's possible?'

'There's not much you can tell from hair, other than colour, and whether it's human or animal.'

'Well, only one baker I've visited today had red, curly hair, so that would be a start.'

'As for fibres from an apron, I could tell cotton from wool, or linen made from flax.'

'Good. There's a full moon tonight, so we'll go collecting aprons. Can you please make some time to get on with your part of this investigation? We want to get home.'

'Yes, alright. But I'll miss you. I've never met anyone like you before. It can be done, you know. Being a secret Jew. I'm the living proof.'

'Yes, but why would I?'

'For love.'

'I could say the same to you. Someone I used to know said, "Paris is well worth a mass." It seems to me that you'll go to mass to save your skin, but not for me.'

'Who was that who said Paris is well worth a mass?'

'Henry the fourth of France.'

Maria was making a stew when she heard the front door open and her twin's familiar footsteps. She sliced the remaining carrots and tossed them into the pot on the range, then gave it a good stir.

'That smells good,' Antonio said, peering over her shoulder.

'How did you get on?'

'I found a spot by the riverbank, under an oak tree, from where I watched the mill. I saw the miller loading sacks onto his wagon, then I followed him as he went into the city. He made deliveries to six bakeries. The first two were near to the cathedral, Hartmann and Krause they were called.'

'Yes, I found them too. I checked out the locks. Hartmann won't be hard to pick, but there are sturdy bolts on the Krause door. It looked like we could get in the back door, though.'

'Then there was a bakery called Meyer, about a quarter of a mile east of the cathedral. Then we started making our way back round the south side of the cathedral. There were two more, first Becker, then Koch. The last delivery was near here, Fettmilch. That was a grocery and a bakery.'

'I know it. That's where I buy our bread and vegetables. Anything else?'

'I was just getting to that. He had one smaller sack left on the cart, spelt flour. He has all his sacks printed with the type of flour, so I'm pretty sure he is literate. He stopped just a few doors away from the Fettmilch shop and knocked on a door. An attractive woman of about thirty, with long blonde hair, opened the door. They kissed, and he carried his sack inside. He was there for about half an hour and then left. I followed him back to the mill, then I came back here.'

'Well, I think we can guess what he was getting from the blonde. No wonder his wife was so suspicious,' Maria said. 'There's a full moon tonight, so I suggest we go around the bakeries collecting aprons. Manuel thinks he can tell the difference between fibres of cotton, wool and linen. So if the something else that was in the dough on Daniel and Edith's clothes turns out to be a piece of fibre, we might be able to narrow it down.'

'Hasn't he already compared this something else with samples of fibre?'

'No, he's been too busy with patients. The man's infuriating. I've urged him to get on with it. It will speed things up if we have the aprons available when he gets around to it. I found some labels in a drawer of the dresser. I suggest we write the names of the bakers on them before we set out tonight. Then we can label each apron as we take it, so we don't get them mixed up.'

'Good idea, Maria. I take it you haven't patched things up with Manuel then?'

'No. He still insists on me becoming a Jew. I just don't get it. Most of the Christians hate them so much, yet even Manuel, who masquerades as a Christian, clings to his Judaism. Why?'

'Don't you remember what Daniel said? They were expelled by the crusaders and the Muslims from their homeland. They became refugees, yet with little refuge. I can understand why they might cling to their heritage. All they seem to have is each other. Their heritage binds them together.'

'It's not my heritage, though. Why do I have to be the one to change when he already has?'

'Is it so much of a change, Maria? After the Sarpi affair, neither of us has had much regard for the Catholic Church. I can't say I like these Lutherans much either.'

'You're right, of course. I wouldn't mind taking the risk myself. But if we had children, then I'm sure I wouldn't want them exposed to such a risk.'

'Talking of risk. Is that stew ready yet? It'll be dark soon, and we've got some apron liberating to do.'

They started their pilfering at the furthest bakery and worked their way back towards Wienerstraße. When they got to the Krause bakery, Maria led Antonio to the back door. She looked all around. There were windows overlooking them, but she couldn't see any faces at the windows.

'You keep watch. I'll pick the lock,' Maria whispered.

'Wouldn't it be quicker if I picked it? I learnt faster than you.'

'But I've been practising more. Leave it to me.' Maria took her lock picks from the pocket of her coat. She crouched down and inserted the pick into the key hole, followed by the tensioner. She kept a steady pressure on the bolt of the mortice lock with the tensioner. Then she felt for the levers with the pick. She felt the first gate, the lever lift, and the bolt turn a fraction. The next gate was a false gate, so she probed further into the lock. Then she heard heavy footsteps approaching and froze. The footsteps passed the end of the alleyway and gradually receded.

'It was Sergeant Voigt and two guardsmen,' Antonio whispered. 'They're probably off to relieve the guard at the city gate.'

Maria continued picking the lock. The next lever lifted, and the bolt turned further. Within a minute, she had opened the lock. She turned the handle, and the door opened. The heat from the cooling oven hit her as she tiptoed inside. In the moonlight, she saw pegs on the wall and two aprons hanging up. She ran her fingers over each one and lifted them in turn to her nose. One smelt, and felt clean. She took the other one. As she turned, her right foot hit something and there was the sound of a pot breaking. She looked down and could just make out the shape of a ceramic pot on its side. She stood still for a few moments, listening for any sound of movement upstairs. There was none. She re-joined Antonio outside.

'Shall we lock up again?' Antonio whispered.

'Why? It'll take longer. If we leave them unlocked, they'll think that they forgot to lock up.'

'Yes, but if we lock up, it'll be a mystery. They'll assume they mislaid the apron themselves. It won't take long. I'll do it, if you like.' Maria nodded. She attached the label she had prepared, folded the apron, and put it in the sack she had brought. Antonio used his pick and tensioner to relock the door. Maria peered round the corner onto the street. It was deserted, and they set off for the Hartmann bakery, which wasn't far. They repeated the process there with no problems. As they were walking towards the Meyer bakery, Antonio looked around and grabbed Maria's sleeve.

'What is it? Have you heard something?' she whispered.

'No, look!'

'Oh my god,' she exclaimed, seeing the trail of footprints. She looked down at her boots, which were covered in paint. 'I accidentally kicked over a pot at the Krause bakery. It must have been paint.'

'We're leaving a trail. You'll have to get rid of the boots.'

'I don't want Sergeant Voigt finding them and coming looking for someone who fits them. We'll be his prime suspect in the case of the disappearing aprons.'

'Good point, Maria. Let's bury them in the garden, or throw them in the river. Stick them in the bottom of the sack for now.'

All went well at the Becker and Koch bakeries. Their ultimate target was the Fettmilch grocery and bakery. They went down the alleyway, and Maria opened the wooden gate to the backyard. Antonio kept watch, while Maria picked the lock. She felt and smelt for the dirtiest apron, and took it from the peg. In the moonlight she saw a row of little men on the work surface. She took two and slipped back outside. Antonio locked up, while Maria labelled the apron, folded it, and placed it in the sack with the others.

'I took these. I've never tried one, have you?'

'No, what are they?' Antonio whispered.

'I think he called them ginger men, or gingerbread men, something like that.' She bit off the head of one, and handed Antonio the other. 'Hungry work, pilfering isn't it? Let's get back to the house.'

The following morning, just after sunrise, Maria got up. She took her boots from the cupboard she had hidden them in. In the sunlight she saw that it was yellow paint. She went to Antonio's bedroom and shook him by the shoulder.

'Antonio, I'm going to take the aprons around to Manuel. Could you dispose of my boots in the river, then buy me a new pair. You know my size.'

'Of course. Are you going to Manuel's barefoot? Won't that attract attention?'

'I'll wear a long dress. I found one in the wardrobe that will cover my feet.'

She took the sack of aprons to Manuel's clinic. She had to knock on the door several times before Manuel opened the door in his nightshirt.

'Hello, Maria. What are you doing here at this ungodly hour?'

'Can I come in, I've brought something?'

'Of course,' Manuel replied, stepping aside to let her in. Then he shut the door. Maria was already making her way with the sack to his study. Maria took the aprons one by one out of the sack, and placed them on his desk. 'What are these?' he asked.

'What do they look like? They're the aprons from the six bakers. I've labelled each one. Now it's your turn to discover who killed Daniel and Edith. We need a match between the stains found on their clothes, and the stains on these aprons. Don't just stand there gawping! Do you want to find their killer, or not?'

'But how did you get hold of them?'

'We took them last night, from the bakeries.'

'Weren't they locked?'

'We can open locks. Another skill our father taught us.'

'Is he a thief?'

'No, he was a spy. But a thief taught him how to do it. How long is it going to take?'

'I don't know.'

'Then you'd better get started. Let us know when you've found something. I'll let myself out. You look good

in your nightshirt, by the way,' she smiled.
    'You look good in anything.'

# CHAPTER NINE

Manuel smiled as he shut the door after Maria disappeared from sight.

There is clearly still a physical attraction. Why does she have to be so unreasonable? It's not as if I want her to abandon her faith. Simply add mine. If I can do it, why can't she? We wouldn't endanger any children we might have. I could teach them how to disguise their faith, or rather faiths, and she could certainly teach them to defend themselves. The bloody woman nearly tore my rotator cuff. Still, I can't imagine what it must have been like to be raped. Fear, well, I know that old friend. To feel soiled, really soiled, not the taunts and abuse hurled at you by Christians, but physically defiled. Yes, that must scar you. She's still the most beautiful woman I've ever seen. And her courage and sense of justice, that is remarkable. I wonder if her brother feels that too, or is he just doing as she tells him? Either way, I should do my bit as well. Let's have a look at these aprons. I've got a few hours before my first patient is due.

Manuel got dressed and settled at his desk with the Janssenscope. He took some sheets of paper from a drawer and copied the names of the baker onto each of the labels.

Then he used a scalpel to remove some thread from each apron in turn, and place them on the relevant sheets. From another desk drawer, he took out the slides he had prepared after recovering Daniel and Edith's clothes. He reached into another desk drawer and took out his box of blank glass slides. He got up and went to a cupboard to get his glue bottle, and the iodine. Then he settled down again. He used his tweezers to place the sample of the Hartmann baker's thread on a slide. Then he dipped a needle into the iodine bottle, and let a drop fall on the thread in order to stain it. He took one of the thinner glass slides from his box and lowered it over the thread, still using his tweezers. He didn't want any air to get trapped between the slides. He cut the word Hartmann from the paper and glued it to the end of the slide. Then he placed the slide under the Janssenscope and examined it. He made some notes in his notebook, then removed the slide and replaced it with the slide he had made from Edith's clothes. He didn't see any similarity. The mystery substance wasn't that thread. He prepared samples from each of the other aprons and examined them all. There were minor differences between the apron fabrics, but nothing matched the mystery substance. He had previously compared the mystery substance with his samples of egg, milk, and many types of flour. There had been egg and milk in the samples taken from Daniel and Edith's clothes, also rye, wheat and spelt flour. But what this other substance was, he didn't know. He thumbed through his notebook, re-reading the descriptions he had made of plant and animal matter. His observations went back to his time at medical school.

This is bloody annoying. She's not going to be very impressed with me, is she? She walks through locked doors in moonlight to gather evidence, at risk of arrest, and heaven knows what, and what can I do with it? Nothing. I don't deserve her. That's the truth of it. Frau Schmidt will be here soon. I'd better get ready. What can this substance be? What else might you put in dough? I know what I'll do.

Aunt Edith kept a notebook of recipes. I'll go to their house after clinic and fetch it. That might give me some ideas.

After his last patient left, Manuel asked Ingrid to wait, in case Maria returned. Then he put on his coat and set off for Judengasse. His pace slowed as he turned onto Judengasse. The ghetto was even more crowded than normal. A ladder leaning against a house was impeding people and carts. A man was at the top of the ladder replacing a pane of glass in a window. Further along there were more broken windows awaiting repair. Benjamin Kosoff, one of his patients, was painting the wall of his house. Manuel could just make out the word "JUDE" in large yellow letters, before Kosoff painted over it.

'I thought you only redecorated last year, Benjamin,' Manuel said, as he stopped beside him.

'I did. A group of thugs came through last night, throwing stones through windows and daubing walls with "Jews go home!" As if we wouldn't if we could. It's getting worse, I tell you, Doctor Nuñez. I'm sorry, Doctor, I know you liked the Bambergers. At least nobody was murdered last night. That's something, at least.'

Manuel patted his shoulder and continued pushing his way through the crowded streets to his aunt and uncle's house. He took his key from his pocket and let himself in. The house was cold. Dust glittered in the rays of the setting sun. He looked around the kitchen. A layer of dust coated the surfaces that Edith had so fastidiously cleaned. He went over to the shelf and took down his aunt's recipe book. He took one more look around the room, then left and locked up.

Ingrid said that there had been no visitors or messengers. Then she went home. She had already lit a fire in his study. He took a taper from the basket next to the fireplace, lit it in the fire, and used it to light the oil lamp on his desk. Then he sat down and leafed through the recipe book. Finally, he came to a recipe for gingerbread.

Ginger, I don't think I've ever examined ginger. It seems to be a ground root that's used. Good for nausea and morning sickness. I gave some to Frau Schipmann earlier this year.

He got up and went to his consulting room. He ran his eyes along the row of jars on his shelves and took down the jar of ginger. He took out a root and sliced a piece off with a scalpel. Then he put the rest of the root back in the jar, put the stopper in, and replaced it on the shelf. He got a pestle and mortar from a cupboard. Then he put the slice of ginger in the mortar and pounded it with the pestle. He scraped some of the ground ginger onto the tip of his scalpel and took it through to his study. He prepared a slide and put it under the Janssenscope. He peered, but the sun had set and the light of the oil lamp was too dim for him to see the specimen clearly enough.

Damn, this will need to wait until the morning.

Manuel got up with the sunrise and examined the slides he had prepared the previous evening. He studied the ginger under the Janssenscope. Then he replaced the ginger slide with the dough sample taken from Daniel's clothing. He peered, adjusting the focus until the mystery substance was clear. He swapped the slides over several times.

That's it! Ginger is the mystery substance.

Manuel then made slides from the dough stains on each apron, labelling each slide with the name of the baker. He examined each making notes during and after each examination.

There are two dough samples with ginger in, Krause and Fettmilch. I can't wait to tell Maria. I think I've done my bit. Nearly time for the clinic. Ingrid will be here any minute.

The cathedral bell was chiming the hour as he heard Ingrid's key turn in the lock. A minute later, she knocked and opened the study door.

'Good morning, Ingrid.'

'Good morning, Doctor Nuñez. You seem very pleased with yourself. Has your romance blossomed?'

'Not yet, but I have high hopes. If Maria calls around this morning, will you call me?'

'Even if you're seeing the mayor about his gout?'

'Yes, even if I'm with the mayor.'

'Isn't there anything else you can do, Manuel? It's so damn painful.'

'I've told you, Hans. We know gout as the rich man's disease because it's prevalent in diets with high meat content. Cut back on your meat intake.'

'Can't you give me a potion or something? A man has to eat, especially me. There are so many lunches and dinners I have to attend as mayor.'

'I haven't heard of an effective potion yet,' Manuel said as there was a knock at the door. He opened it.

'She's here,' Ingrid whispered.

'Would you excuse me a moment, Hans?'

'Of course, Manuel,' Mayor Hans Friedrich replied. Ingrid and Manuel left the consulting room. Hans winced as he stood up and limped across the room. He put his ear to the door.

'Come to my study, Maria. We can't talk in the waiting room,' Manuel said.

'I've found out what the mystery substance is, Maria,' Manuel exclaimed as he shut the study door behind them. 'It's ground ginger root. I went and recovered Edith's cookery book to see what else might be included in the dough. She had a recipe for gingerbread. I made a slide from some ginger I use to treat nausea. When I was able to compare the sample from Daniel's clothes with the ginger, the ginger was a perfect match for the mystery substance.'

'That's great work, Manuel. Now all we have to do is identify which bakers make gingerbread. I know Fettmilch does. I tried some of his the night we took the aprons.'

'And so does Krause. I found ginger on just those two aprons.'

'Brilliant!'

'Thank you. I see you've gone back to more modest attire. That long dress suited you.'

'Do you think so? I only wore it to disguise my bare feet.'

'Why did you have bare feet?'

'It's a long story. Don't you have to get back to your patient?'

'I shouldn't keep the mayor waiting, but I'm intrigued. Go on!'

'When we were taking the aprons, I kicked over a paint pot at the Krause bakery. It was a pot of yellow paint. I got it all over my boots and was leaving a trail on the pavement. Antonio spotted it, so I had to take off my boots. I wanted to get the aprons over to you as quickly as I could. So in the morning, I sent Antonio off to dispose of my boots in the river, and buy me some new ones. I put a long dress on and brought the aprons over to you. You seem distant.'

'Sorry, I was just thinking about yellow paint. When I went to recover Edith's recipe book, they were clearing up in the ghetto. A bunch of thugs had been smashing windows and daubing slogans on the walls. One read "Jews go home" in yellow paint.'

'So Krause and Fettmilch are a match for the dough transferred to Daniel and Edith's clothes. Neither of them appear in Daniel's ledger, but may have been on the pages torn out. Krause keeps a pot of yellow paint, so he may have been daubing vile slogans on the walls in the ghetto. Both Fettmilch and Krause are customers of the miller, who claims not to have seen whoever had the appointments before him. It looks as if the balance of the evidence points to Krause.'

'Fettmilch might have a pot of yellow paint, too. Maria, I mustn't keep the mayor waiting.'

'No, of course not. I'd better go and talk this through with Antonio. Don't tell the mayor about this just yet.'

Maria rushed back to Wienerstraße and told Antonio about the ginger and the yellow paint. Antonio paced the kitchen.

'So what do we do next?' he asked.

'We could search the Fettmilch place again by night, taking an oil lamp with us. I knew where the aprons would be, but we'd have to make a more thorough search looking for paint.'

'Anyone might have a pot of yellow paint. The buildings are all quite colourful, many of them yellow. I think the Krause building was painted yellow. I can't remember what colour the Fettmilch one was, can you?'

'No, that's something we should check before risking a night-time search. I don't see why anyone would keep a pot of paint, especially for daubing slogans. They'd use whatever was handy, don't you think?'

'That makes sense, Maria. But how can we really know how a murderer's mind works? I'd have taken my apron off, but I'm thinking clearly and coolly. The armbands the Jews have to wear are yellow. Perhaps that's why the thugs are using yellow paint. It may have some significance that we're unaware of. The other thing that worries me is why the miller appears to be covering up for the murderer. He has other customers, and if one of his bakers goes out of business, people will still need bread. They'll either bake it themselves, or one of the other bakers will expand production. They'll still need his flour.'

'As you said, he might not be thinking that clearly.'

'Why not? We don't think he's the murderer. I've had

another thought. I saw the miller visiting that woman a few doors down from the Fettmilch shop. If it's a regular thing, either Fettmilch or his wife are bound to have seen him entering or leaving. If Fettmilch threatened to tell the miller's wife about the affair, I can imagine that would be a much better motive to lie than losing a customer.'

'That's possible, Antonio. But how do we prove any of this? The mayor doesn't seem inclined to take any action. Should we visit the miller again, and threaten to tell his wife about his affair, unless he admits he was covering for Fettmilch?'

'I don't like it, it feels dirty. It's blackmail in the name of justice. If it came to trial, the miller's wife would be certain to find out.'

'Why shouldn't she know about her husband's infidelity?'

'I don't know. I just don't like it. I'd rather hand it over to the mayor and Sergeant Voigt.'

'Alright, what if we keep Fettmilch and Krause under observation?' Maria suggested.

'Why? What do you think we might discover?'

'Well, someone seems to want the Jews to leave. The mob of thugs will surely strike again. We can at least find out whether Fettmilch or Krause are involved. You keep Fettmilch under observation. I'll take Krause.'

# CHAPTER TEN

The mayor's clerk opened the door for Sergeant Voigt and closed it behind him.

'You asked to see me, sir,' Sergeant Voigt said.

'Yes, sit down, Barnard. I've had some complaints from bakers about aprons going missing. They all seem to have gone missing on the same night, the night before last. They can't understand it because there was no sign of forced entry. Each baker says they locked up at night, and their doors were still securely locked in the morning. No windows were broken, so they can't understand it.'

'Neither can I, sir. We have had nothing like that in my experience. Fuchs, the locksmith, is the only man I can think of who could have done that, but why would he? I'll talk to him if you like.'

'Yes, please do that. Ask him if those Italian winemakers have employed him.'

'They've gone though, haven't they?'

'No. I was seeing Doctor Nuñez about my gout yesterday. The girl came to see him. I recognised her voice. I couldn't hear anything because they went off to his study. He didn't come back for about a quarter of an hour. They were so keen to prove who killed the Bambergers, and they had this idea that it was a baker. I think they must have taken the aprons to try to prove it. They must have bribed Fuchs to help them with the locks. Start by putting pressure on Fuchs. Tell him he won't be punished if he admits who bribed him to do it. Then lean on Doctor Nuñez. See if he knows anything. Find out why she came to see him. Report back to me as soon as you have something. I don't want them stirring up trouble.'

'Talking of trouble, sir, there have been complaints from Rabbi Levi again. More windows have been broken and slogans painted on walls in the Judengasse. If you could let me have some more men, sir, I could post some men there to monitor things.'

'I don't know. It wouldn't look good if I were seen to be protecting the Jews from our own citizens. On the other hand, we mustn't let the situation get out of control. I'll let you recruit two more men for the city guard. Put two of your experienced men to watch Judengasse.'

'Thank you, sir.'

Sergeant Voigt asked Guardsman Lehmann if his adolescent sons would like to join the guard. As they weren't showing any particular aptitude for anything else, Guardsman Lehmann jumped at the opportunity. Sergeant Voigt told him to take them under his own wing on duty at the South Gate. Then he set off for the South Gate and told Heinrich and Günther that as soon as they were relieved, they were to patrol Judengasse. Then he went to see Fuchs, the locksmith.

'Barnard, to what do I owe this pleasure? Has someone lost the key to a city gate again?'

'No, Heinrich. Have you been helping two young Italians to enter bakeries?'

'No, of course not. Why do you ask?'

'Because someone has been stealing aprons. They appear to be getting in without breaking in, and locking up behind themselves again. You are the only person I know who could do that.'

'To steal aprons? Why would I do that? I have my own apron. Do you have a fever, Barnard?'

'No, I'm perfectly serious. If you've taken money from these young Italians, I'm authorised to let you off. You won't face any punishment. It's the foreigners stirring trouble that we're after, not you. Just admit it, and you'll hear no more about it.'

'I would if I had anything to admit, but I don't. When were these aprons supposed to have been taken?'

'The night before last.'

'Well, it definitely wasn't me then. I was in the bierkeller with friends. We overdid it and I passed out. Bergmann, the landlord, had to carry me down to the cot that he keeps in the cellar for such occasions. Ask him, he'll confirm it. I don't think I'll ever hear the last of it.'

'I see. Have you taught any strangers how to pick locks?'

'Of course not. It takes months to learn how to pick a lock. I couldn't interest my own sons into becoming locksmiths. They became carpenters, as you know. There's more money in it. Who are these young Italians?'

'Winemakers.'

'Well, it certainly won't be them then. Why would you waste your time learning to pick locks when you own a vineyard?'

'I see you have a point. Well, it's a mystery then. I'll be on my way.'

Sergeant Voigt insisted on seeing Manuel straight away. Ingrid told him he would have to wait until he had finished with his current patient. She didn't want the patients in the waiting room gossiping about why Sergeant Voigt wanted to see Doctor Nuñez, so she asked him to wait in the study. When the patient emerged from the consulting room, Ingrid slipped in and told Manuel about his visitor.

'Tell them I shouldn't be long, and apologise, Ingrid.'

Manuel went to his study. 'What can I do for you, Sergeant Voigt?'

'I understand from the mayor that Maria Standen came to visit you during the mayor's appointment. Why did she come, and why was it important enough to delay the mayor?'

'It's a personal matter.'

'What sort of personal matter?'

'We're in love, or at least, I'm in love with her. I hope she feels the same, but it appears she doesn't.'

'I'm sorry to hear that. It doesn't have anything to do with aprons, does it?' Manuel hesitated before replying.

'Aprons? No, of course not. Why would it?'

'Come along, Doctor Nuñez. Don't lie to me. I know you were helping her with some sort of telescope to examine flour and dough found on the Bambergers. The mayor told me about how they had tried to coerce him into allowing the investigation to continue. He insisted they go home to Italy. So tell me again why she came to see you?' Manuel hesitated again. It looked as though Maria was in trouble.

'She told me our brief romance was over and that they were returning to Frascati.'

'So she didn't bring you six aprons she had stolen, then?'

'No, she didn't.'

'That's odd, because while I was waiting for you, I had a look around your study.'

'How dare you!'

'I dare with the mayor's authority. The six aprons in the cupboard there, labelled with the names of the bakers. Might they not be the ones she delivered to you?'

'What are you going to do with her?'

'I don't know yet, Doctor Nuñez. I'll have to ask the mayor.'

'Tell him that if he wants his gout to get any better, he mustn't harm a hair on her head.'

'I'll tell him, Doctor Nuñez.'

'They've only been helping you to find a murderer. What's the problem with that?'

'The mayor has other issues to weigh in the balance. Important issues for the peace of the city.'

'More important than finding a murderer?'

'In this instance, the mayor appears to think so, Doctor Nuñez. Good day to you.'

# CHAPTER ELEVEN

Vincenz Fettmilch walked proudly down the short aisle of a side chapel of the cathedral, his daughter Ursula by his side. Victor Krause's son, Günther, stood up, smiling at his beautiful bride to be. Günther and Ursula turned to face the priest. Vincenz took a few steps back and sat on a bench beside his wife Hilda. There were Gregorian chants being sung in the main body of the cathedral. He found them somehow calming. The priest read a few verses about the Wedding at Cana. Vincenz's calmness melted away again. The wedding had cost him dearly, and he didn't appreciate water being turned into wine at some other man's daughter's wedding. Hilda reached her hand out to his. He took it and she elbowed him.

'Don't squeeze my hand. Be gentle!' she whispered.

'Sorry!'

They sang more hymns, vows were taken, and then Vincenz and Victor signed the register, along with the newlyweds, the priest, and other witnesses. Guests were filing out as Vincenz followed Günther and Ursula out of the cathedral.

'I hope you'll all join us for a reception in the bierkeller. There will be meat, vegetables, ale and wine, and some excellent bread, of course.' He shouted over the excited babble. Then he led the way across the square towards the bierkeller.

The smell of roast pork was in the air, as the guests entered the bierkeller. A dog was trudging around inside a caged wheel, which was connected via pulleys and ropes to the spit, turning slowly above the fire. Flames shot up whenever fat dripped from the pig into the fire. The landlord's young son would prod the dog with a stick, poked through the cage, if he thought the spit wasn't turning fast enough. Tables were set out with bowls of bread, jugs of beer, and jugs of wine. Waitresses were scurrying around laying plates. More waitresses appeared from the kitchen with bowls of sauerkraut. The guests took seats and helped themselves to food and drink.

'This must have cost you a fortune,' Victor Krause said into Vincenz's ear.

'Yes, but Ursula deserves a decent wedding.'

'My brother-in-law, Franz, has been staying with us for a few days. He's from Mainz, you remember.'

'Yes, a farrier, isn't he?'

'That's right. He said that, he was told by their mayor, that their citizens' right is that their prince can choose the official religion.'

'Is that so?' Vincenz replied. 'Well, ours is Catholicism. So why do we have to put up with all these Jews?'

'It must be as you said yourself, it's corruption. All the patriarchs are taking their cut from the excessive fees the Jews charge on loans. It's nothing short of criminal, that's what it is. We've been trying to make our point known, but it's falling on deaf ears. Some of us have been taking matters into our own hands.'

'So have I,' Vincenz murmured.

'I thought you'd been too pre-occupied with the wedding. I hope I haven't stepped out of line. You've been our best spokesman at the council meetings and trials. I would have left it to you to lead us, but what with the wedding to organise, I thought you seemed too busy. It's just been a few of us, breaking windows and painting slogans in the Judengasse. We think we need to shake things up a bit more, don't you?'

'Yes, I do, Victor. They're in it together, these corrupt councillors and Jews. We should strike at both.'

'What, the council too? What about the guard?'

'They've just drafted Lehmann's worthless kids into the guard. There are far more of us than them. We'll agree a date. Spread the word. We'll talk again after the feast and the speeches.'

Karl, the mayor's clerk, came out of the mayor's office. He nodded to Sergeant Voigt and closed the door after Voigt had gone inside. The mayor looked up from the letter he was writing.

'The locksmith, Fuchs, denies picking the bakers' locks, sir.'

'Do you believe him?'

'I do, sir. He has an alibi for the night of the apron thefts. I've checked it out. He couldn't have been at any of the bakeries, and he wasn't capable of opening the locks, even if he had been.'

'How so?'

'He was blind drunk and unconscious in the bierkeller, sir.'

'I see. So who did gain entry then?'

'I went to interview Doctor Nuñez, as you instructed, sir. The aprons are all in a cupboard in his study. It must have been the Standen twins, sir. Fuchs swore he hadn't taught them to pick locks. He says it takes months to train someone, sir. But I don't see who else it could have been. They had this idea that they could find evidence to match the dough on an apron with the stains on the Bamberger clothes. Perhaps they got hold of spare keys.'

'What for every bakery? That seems implausible. No, I think they must be thieves themselves. Perhaps this whole winemaker story is a cover. I think they're here to break into the cathedral treasury and steal the jewels.'

'If so, why haven't they done it and fled? Why would they be working on finding the killer of a couple of Jews?'

'You're right, of course. It's this bloody gout. Who knows why they're trying to find the Jews' killer? But it must be them. Arrest them and put them in the dungeon. I'll get Karl to schedule a date for their trial.'

'Should I arrest Doctor Nuñez, sir?'

'What? No. He doesn't seem to have any effective remedy for my gout. He just gives me useless advice about dieting and cutting out meat. How could I? Lunches and dinners are part of the job. But he is the best physician in the city. Give him a severe warning, but leave him to do his work.'

'I'm not sure I should, sir, but he asked me to warn you too, sir. He said that if a hair on Maria's head was harmed, he wouldn't do anything to help your gout.'

'Did he? The impudent pup! He has done nothing for my gout, anyway. Arrest the Standen twins. Search them to see if they have any lock picks on them. Did you post guards on the Judengasse?'

'Of course, sir. There has been no recurrence of the trouble.'

'Good! That will be all, Sergeant Voigt.'

Maria answered the door to see Sergeant Voigt and two guards with muskets. She went to slam the door, but Sergeant Voigt had put his foot in it. The guards levelled their muskets at her. Voigt pushed past her.

'Who is it, Maria?' Antonio asked as he came into the hallway.

'Don't try anything, Antonio, or your sister will be shot. You're both under arrest.'

'What for?'

'Breaking into bakeries and stealing aprons.'

'We were trying to find a killer. We were helping you,' Antonio said.

'Yes, but Mayor Friedrich had instructed you not to, and to go home. You didn't. You'll have to come to city hall with us, and await trial.' Antonio looked at Maria, but she signalled that resistance was useless. The guards were keeping a distance. She couldn't take them both out before one of them let off a shot. They were too far to attack, but too close to miss. 'Put your arms behind your back, both of you,' Voigt ordered. He took some cord from his pocket and bound Antonios's wrists. Then he did the same to Maria. They were both marched away.

Antonio and Maria were frogmarched to city hall, and across the foyer. Friedrich, the Marktmeister, gazed at them, speechless, as they were marched past him towards a spiral stone staircase in the corner of the foyer area. When they reached the bottom, they all had to wait for their eyes to adjust. They were in a dank room, around twenty feet wide by ten feet deep. In front of them were two sets of steps down to heavily-studded wooden doors, with small grills at head height. The steps were around ten feet apart. Maria looked behind her. There was a bench against the wall. Two guards were standing at attention in front of the bench. To their right, at the far end of the room, was a desk. Behind the desk, another guard was standing at attention. The only light came from a window in the wall above the desk. There were bars set into the wall outside the window. The window was open. It was still summer, but it was cold, despite a warm breeze blowing in. Sergeant Voigt looked at the guard behind the desk. The guard saluted. Voigt returned the salute.

'Hans, we will need to search them both. Fetch Heidi, the washerwoman, she can search Maria.' Hans went back up the spiral staircase. 'Fritz, keep them both covered with your musket. I'll search Antonio.' He frisked Antonio and felt in his pockets. 'What have we here? Lock picks, I've seen Fuchs using similar. Now what's a winemaker doing with lock picks? Well? Explain! Did you come to sell wine, or was that just a cover? The mayor thinks you intend to steal the city jewels from the cathedral treasury.'

'Our father was an English spy. He taught us many things, like languages, ciphers, wrestling, and picking locks. We were just here to sell wine. Then, as you know, we've been investigating the Bamberger murders. That's all. We used our lock picks to gather evidence from the bakeries. We now know that the killer is either Fettmilch or Krause. We were going to keep them under observation, but we couldn't gate crash a wedding,' Antonio explained. Hans reappeared, followed by a middle-aged woman. They led Maria off to a small cell where the washerwoman searched her. She found her lock picks.

'How do you know it's either Fettmilch or Krause?' Voigt asked.

'Manuel used his Janssenscope to examine the dough on each apron and compare it with the stains on Daniel and Edith's clothes. There was ginger in the dough, and the only aprons with ginger in the dough were theirs,' Antonio explained, as Maria and the washerwoman returned. The washerwoman handed Maria's lock picks to Sergeant Voigt.

'Can you use these too?' Sergeant Voigt asked Maria.

'Yes, of course.'

'I see. Your brother has explained why. You should have left this to us.'

'You weren't going to get anywhere, were you?' Maria said.

'Well, look where it's got you. You'll be tried for theft. Hans put Maria in the women's cell. Fritz put Antonio in the men's. I've got them covered. You can untie their hands now.'

# CHAPTER TWELVE

Anthony rode into Rome to visit the Thurn and Taxis office. They ran a postal system covering the Holy Roman Empire, and major cities outside the empire, too. He tried to look in every few months to see if there was any post for him. His brother Edmund wrote to him occasionally. Edmund was doing very well in his legal career. He was Master of the Petty Bag, which was only one rank below Lord Chancellor. Their father would have been very proud of him. The queue wasn't long. Soon the man in front of him was handed a parcel, paid the clerk, and left.

'Good afternoon, Giuseppe,' Anthony greeted the clerk. 'Is there anything for me?'

'Not exactly, Sir Anthony. It is from London, so I assume it's from your brother. It's addressed to Antonio. A slip of the pen, perhaps?'

'My eldest son is Antonio. I'll take it for him.'

'Two lira, Sir Anthony please.' Anthony opened his purse and took out the coins and handed them to Giuseppe.

'Thank you, Giuseppe.' Anthony went to one of the small desks that were available for drafting letters. He opened the letter and read it. It was from a London wine merchant named Thomas Berry. The letter set out a schedule of wine and brandy orders, with scheduled shipping dates from the port in Ostia, at the mouth of the Tiber, where they kept Maia their own yacht. It also specified requirements for bottling in glass. Anthony read the letter again. This should be good news. Antonio and Maria had clearly reached Frankfurt safely and achieved their aim. This was an important order. It would make the existing vineyard very profitable and allow them to expand on the neighbouring land. What worried him was how Thomas Berry had managed to return to London, establish the demand for their Sangiovese wine, and send this letter before Antonio and Maria had returned. Images of them dead in a ditch flashed through his mind. Without realising it, he had screwed the letter into a ball in his sweaty palm. He flattened it on the desk and folded it carefully.

'Will there be a reply, Sir Anthony?' Giuseppe asked. Anthony was the only customer left in the office.

'No. Is there a glassworks in the city?'

'Yes, several. I've heard there's a good one near Santa Maria di Trastevere.'

'Thank you, Giuseppe.' Anthony put the letter in his pocket as he stood up and left the office. He untied his horse, Lightning, from the rail and swung himself into the saddle. He stroked Lightning's mane. The horse was twitchy, sensing Anthony's concern. 'I know. I'm worried too. But what can I do? If I rode to Frankfurt, we could pass like ships in the night. The only logical thing to do is to find out about buying some glass bottles.'

Anthony tried to hide his concerns. He didn't mention the letter to Francesca. He spent more time tending the vines than usual. When he wasn't in the fields or the winery, he devoted himself to the children's lessons. William was eight now and fluent in seven languages. Anna was six and Catherine was four. He was starting the girls on Latin. It was familiar to their everyday Italian and would help them with the other romance languages. When they needed a break from the classroom, he coached them in wrestling. He drew some comfort from knowing that Antonio and Maria could handle themselves in a fight, but worried they might not be cautious enough to stay out of one.

'There you are,' Francesca called out. 'I've hardly seen you since you got back from Rome. What's wrong?'

'Nothing's wrong, darling. I've just been busy. That's all.'

'For an ex-spy, you're a terrible liar. Is it that Cardinal Aldobrandini? Has he gone back on his deal or something?'

'No.'

'Then what is it?'

'Nothing.'

'Please don't lie to me. The children sense it too. I'm expecting Catherine to talk to me in Arabic any minute, the amount of time you're spending on their lessons. Whatever it is, keeping it to yourself won't help.' Anthony put his arms around her and pulled her tight. Francesca hugged him back and felt his tears fall on her face. She felt him shudder and held him, swaying, rocking him to the rhythm she rocked the children. When she felt him regain his composure, she kissed him. 'What is it?'

'Antonio and Maria should be back by now.'

'Frankfurt's a long way. We don't know how long it will take them to find a buyer and get back. You shouldn't worry. They're strong, and they have those rifles. They can look after themselves, you've seen to that.'

'Yes, you're right. We don't know how long it will take them.' Francesca looked up at him, studying his face.

'You're still lying. You know something. What is it? Tell me!'

'There was a letter for Antonio in Rome. It was from a London wine merchant. They must have finished their business months ago. Why aren't they back yet?'

'Perhaps they've gone to see Greta. Antonio doesn't see her as much as he should.'

'Yes, maybe that's it. How do you do it?'

'How do I do what?'

'Be so optimistic. You seem to be so hopeful.'

'I had all those years after you had to leave Florence. You didn't know it, but you'd left me with Antonio and Maria. I had to look after them. There was no time to worry about where you were or when you were coming back. All I had was them, and hope, and love. You find you don't need more. There's always hope.'

Anthony's worries increased with every passing day. When William ran into the winery to tell him that he could see a wagon coming up the lane, Anthony ran outside. William followed. William ran down the lane, stopped, and ran back again.

'It isn't them, Papa.' Anthony's face fell. The wagon drew to a halt, and the driver climbed down.

'I've got your glass bottles. Where do you want them, sir?'

'In the winery. We'll give you a hand.' Anthony and William helped the driver unload the wagon and stack the crates of bottles in the winery. The driver handed Anthony the invoice.

'You'll have to pay at the glassworks, sir. The owner won't let the drivers collect money. Either he doesn't trust us or thinks we might get robbed. Thieves and bandits at every corner, that's what he sees.'

◇ ◇ ◇

More weeks passed. Anthony rode into Rome again to pay the glassmaker. The bill came to around half of his remaining fortune. He called in at the Thurn and Taxis office, but there were no more letters. Anthony and William bottled the wine and brandy, as per Thomas Berry's instructions. It would soon be time to take the first delivery to Ostia.

'How are we going to get the wine to the port without

our cart, Papa?' William asked.

'Our cart? Oh, yes. Surely they must be home soon.'

'But what if they're not, Papa?'

'Then I don't know what we'll do. What will it all have been for?'

'I'll help you, Papa. I'm nearly grown up now. I can carry two crates at a time. We'll manage.' Anthony ran his fingers through William's hair.

'Yes, you're a good boy. Poor old Niccolo had a cart in his barn. Perhaps we could use that. We'll ride over on Lightning and bring the cart back here.'

Anthony drove into Roberto Cavalli's boatyard. Roberto was caulking a boat in his yard.

'Anthony, what a pleasure. Are you off on Maia again? We've been looking after her. We scraped her bottom last week. Hello, William, are you looking forward to another sail?'

'No, Roberto. We're delivering a cargo of wine. Has an English ship called the Spirit of Kent arrived?' Anthony replied.

'Yes, she arrived yesterday. That's her, the two-masted brigantine, over there.' Roberto replied, pointing.

'Thanks, Roberto. We'll see you later.' Anthony flicked the reins and drove the wagon round to the ship. He found the captain in the harbour master's office. They completed the customs formalities and helped the crew load their cargo aboard. The captain gave Anthony a receipt for the cargo.

'Mr Berry said that a letter of exchange will be with the Medici bank in Rome for you, within a month of the cargo reaching London,' the captain said.

'Yes, I understand. It was all in his letter.' Anthony and William rode back to the Cavalli boatyard. Anthony stabled Lightning, then he and William boarded Maia. They would ride back to Frascati tomorrow. William was soon asleep in his hammock. Anthony tossed and turned in his cot. Every creak of the hull reminded him of Maria. She had wanted him to build her a boat. She had been with him on her sailing trials, and on her maiden voyage to Tunis. They had fought off the Barbary pirates together. Where on earth was she now?

# CHAPTER THIRTEEN

A toothless woman of about Maria's age stood scratching her groin area.

'Hello luvvie, aren't you a pretty one. You're not here to muscle in on our trade are you?'

'What trade is that?' Maria asked.

'Oh, she can't guess.' The woman cackled to the other women, sitting on the straw strewn on the floor. 'Ain't she posh.'

'I see. No, I'm not in your line of business,' Maria replied. She looked around, trying to tell where the stench was coming from.

'The cesspit's over there in the corner, luvvie.' She cackled. 'It was cleaned out only a month ago, so it ain't too bad. What are you in here for then? My name's Anna, what's yours?'

'Maria.'

'So what are you in here for then?'

'We stole some aprons.'

'Aprons, they won't fetch much. I could buy twenty aprons from ten minutes' work with a sailor. What do you want to steal aprons for?'

'It's a long story.'

'Do we look like we're short of time? We likes a good story, don't we girls? Sit down and tell us all about it.' When

Maria had finished telling her story Anna thought for a moment. 'You picked a bad time to steal them aprons. Normally you'd be fined. If you didn't have the money, they'd stick you in the stocks and we'd all enjoy throwing rotten vegetables and horse shit at you. It's a shame you chose to do it now.'

'What do you mean?' Maria asked.

'There's such trouble with the merchants. The bakers are making a right fuss. I think they'll make an example of you, to please them.'

'What sort of example?'

'I've seen thieves have their hand chopped off, sometimes an ear. People know what you've done, see! Are you right or left handed?'

'Right handed.'

'My tip, Maria, is try to convince them you're left handed. Then they'll chop off the left one. It's such a shame, a beautiful girl like you. You'd make a fortune in my game.'

Antonio was pushed into the men's cell, and the door was locked behind him. He could see four men slumped against the wall to his left. One of them was taller than the others, and powerfully built. His eyes focussed on Antonio. He got to his feet.

'I don't recognise you. Where are you from?'

'Frascati.'

'Where's that?'

'Near Rome.'

'Italian eh. I don't like foreigners.'

'That's your problem.'

'Then I'll make it your problem.' The big man took two paces towards Antonio. The other prisoners sat up to watch. The big man swung a right hook at Antonio's head. Antonio dodged the punch and used a sweep of his left foot to flick his opponent's right foot as he grabbed the man's right arm. He harnessed the momentum of the punch to send him spinning to the ground, and dropped into the familiar hold, with his left leg pinning down the man's neck. He applied an arm lock. The big man screamed.

'That wasn't very friendly,' Antonio said. 'Don't struggle,' he suggested, as he increased the pressure on the armlock. The man screamed. 'Do you yield?'

'Yes,' the big man screamed. Antonio released the hold and jumped to his feet, moving an arm and a half clear, as the big man slowly got to his feet, his left hand cradling his right elbow. 'What kind of fighting is that?'

'Wrestling. Our father taught us. He also taught us some killer blows. If you're attacked by a number of men, you need to make each blow count. They mustn't be able to get up again. I thought I'd be gentle with you.'

'That was gentle, shit! Us, you said. Where's the other one?'

'They put my sister in the women's cell.'

'What are you in here for?'

'We stole some bakers' aprons. What are you in here for?'

'Drunk and disorderly. What's your name?' the big man asked as he rubbed his right elbow.

'Antonio. What's yours?'

'Klaus.'

'What do you do when you're not locked up, Klaus?'

'I'm a sailor, working the barges on the river.'

'I've done some sailing too. Our father has a boat. Are you going to introduce me to the others?'

'The blond one on the left is Jürgen, he's a farm labourer. Next to him is Nils, he's a wagoner. The other one is Ludwig. He's a cook's assistant in the bierkeller. What's a rich man's son from Rome doing stealing bakers' aprons?'

'Well it all began with a barking dog,' Antonio began. His audience listened in silence as he told his story.

'So you're here because you tried to find the killer of some Jews. You're crazy. They'll probably hack your hand off, to quieten the bakers. You poor stupid sod. Why?'

'We'd met them, the Jews that is. They were good people.'

'Jews, good people? That ain't what the bishop says. Killed Christ they did. They don't eat pork either.'

'Neither did Christ. He was a Jew.'

Antonio explored every inch of the cell. He asked Klaus if he could stand on his shoulders to examine the gratings over the light well. They were very secure. When meals were brought in, a sentry remained outside with a musket. The meals consisted of bread and boiled vegetables or sauerkraut, with beer. The bowls were wooden, as were the spoons, and the goblets. There was nothing to fashion a rudimentary lock pick from. Antonio slumped down onto the straw and leant against the wall.

Why didn't we go home when I suggested it? I'd be on my way to make up with Greta now, with two hands to hold her with, caress her with. What will she think of a one-handed husband? What a grisly prospect I'll be. It's going to be much harder picking grapes. We'll need more seasonal labour, which will drive costs up and profits down. If they take my right hand it'll make writing a challenge. I'll never pick a lock again, not that that matters much. Why didn't we go home as the mayor ordered? Maria and her sense of justice, that's why we're here awaiting our fate. No, that's not entirely fair. I felt it too. What am I going to do? Maybe, when they bring in the food next time, I could overpower the guard. If I'm quick enough, I could use him as a shield against the sentry's musket. Klaus and the others could overcome the sentry. They could only do that if the sentry had already fired his musket. What if the musket ball goes right through the guard? I'd be dead. Father said the ball went right through that fellow's head, when he was almost burnt to death. If it can go through a skull, I don't see a few ribs stopping it. I haven't tried the grating over the cesspit. If I could loosen that, just before mealtime, and lower myself in. I can't believe I'm even thinking this. If I lowered myself in, and braced myself against the sides, and if Klaus put the grating back in place, I'd be missing. Would they think of looking in the cesspit? Would Klaus and the others be able to overcome them, as they searched frantically for the missing prisoner?

Antonio stood up and took his shirt off. He ripped a sleeve off, and bit into the frayed edge, then tore it in two. He wrapped the cloth around each hand then went over to the cesspit grating. He vomited as he bent down and took hold of the shit-encrusted bars. He braced himself and pulled with every ounce of strength. It wouldn't move.

'It usually takes longer to go crazy,' Klaus exclaimed. 'What the hell are you doing?'

'I thought if I could get this loose, just before mealtime, I could hide down here. They'd be a prisoner missing and confused. In the confusion you might be able to overpower them and help me out. Then we could escape. Will you help me try and shift the grating?'

'Not a chance. In less than a week, I'll have had some rotten vegetables thrown at me, and be a free man.'

Maria had thought through all the possible methods of escape, just as Antonio had, with the exception of the cesspit. She had wondered if Anna, who was the most attractive of the prisoners, might entice one of the guards with her female charms. If she could, then she might be able to overpower him. Anna said that they'd tried that, and the guards were under strict orders not to fall for that trick.

I wonder what Manuel will think of me with a missing hand? Why do I care? I am attracted to him, in a way I have never been attracted before. He's so good looking. He's intelligent. He's a very good physician, a healer, that's a good thing to be. He makes good money, although not the sort of money I can make, with Papa's skills. After I've lost my hand though, that life will be behind me. Why does he have to be so dogmatic about me converting to Judaism?

When I do lose my hand, I'll be far less able to defend myself, let alone children. I'm not even sure if I could teach them to wrestle, with only one hand. Living as a secret Jew would be too dangerous. Why is he so stubborn about it? If it's so damn important to him, why doesn't he fight for it? Does he have a backbone? What a waste. What will Greta think of Antonio with only one hand? I hope they make up. I'd like to be an aunt, if I'm not to be a mother. Why didn't I listen to Antonio when he suggested we leave? Why couldn't I just leave Daniel and Edith's killer to the authorities? What business did I have shoving my nose in? The loss of Antonio's hand will always be my fault, on my conscience. I thought I had become invincible, not anymore. If Manuel doesn't want me after this, I wonder if I'll find anyone else? Why would I want anyone else? Why would they want me? Just the same way as that rat at the wash house did, before I'd learnt to fight. It looks like I've come full circle.

# CHAPTER FOURTEEN

Vincenz and Victor had persuaded thirty merchants to join them, in the bierkeller. Everyone had been struggling with the high food prices, and the charges the Jewish moneylenders levied. It was surely as Vincenz said, that the patriarchs were taking a cut. The city council was corrupt to its core. The gunsmith had brought six muskets, with powder and balls. Franz Müller had brought a cutlass that had been his grandfather's. The others all had clubs that they had fashioned themselves. Heinrich Weber had made a dozen torches.

'It's time,' Vincenz shouted. 'It's time for change, for freedom. Are you with me?'

'We're with you,' the mob shouted.

'Then light your torches in the fire. Victor and I will lead, with the other four musketeers. We'll need two torch carriers with us. Thank you, Franz and Karl,' he said as they stepped forwards. 'The rest follow us. We're sure to get more muskets, pikes, and swords when we take the city hall. Then we expel the Jews. For freedom!' Vincenz led the mob up the steps and out of the bierkeller. The light from the torches glimmered off the walls, as they marched towards the city square. The newly-recruited Lehmann brothers were on guard at the entrance to the city hall. As the mob approached, they looked at each other.

'Stop, or we'll fire!' shouted Nikoli Lehmann, the eldest brother.

'Get out of our way, Nikoli,' Vincenz shouted back. 'You have no quarrel with us.' Nikoli raised his musket, as he'd been taught. Johannes, did the same. They tried to aim, but their arms were shaking. Nicoli fired first, then Johannes. Both shots flew over the heads of the mob. They dropped their muskets and ran. 'To the mayor's office!' Vincenz pushed Karl, the mayor's clerk aside and opened the mayor's door. Hans Friedrich was working in the glow of an oil lamp on his desk.

'Are you out of your mind, Fettmilch? What is the meaning of this?'

'Am I incensed, do you mean? Yes, we all are. I'm going to see the charter, our citizens' rights that you've kept from us.'

'It's not here. It's in the, er, the cathedral treasury.'

'You lie. I've been told it's in a casket on the mantlepiece. That one, I'm guessing.' Vincenz said, pointing. He walked over to the fireplace and took a silver casket from the mantlepiece. It was locked. 'Give me the key.'

'It's at home. I hardly ever need to open it. I know what's in it.'

'Never mind. Heinrich, would you oblige please?' Vincenz ordered. Heinrich Fuchs, the locksmith, stepped forwards. He took the casket, and placed it on the desk, looking sheepishly at Mayor Friedrich. He took out his lock picks and soon had it open. Vincenz took the parchment from inside, unfolded, it and began reading. His breathing grew quicker, and his brow creased. 'So the Jews are to be tolerated, and we have the right to leave our homes if we don't like it. What kind of rights are those? It's unbelievable, and it's all because you're milking the Jews for the interest on the money they lend us. Well we've had enough. To the Judengasse, men. We'll settle this once and for all.'

'Vincenz, I'll catch you up,' Victor said. 'My wife's younger sister Anna is in the cells. I promised her I'd get her out. Let me have a few men, please?'

'Of course, Victor. Take Ex-Mayor Friedrich with you and lock him in the cells. We will hold his trial for corruption in due course. Follow us as soon as you can.'

Vincenz Fettmilch was infuriated by the charter of citizens' rights. It seemed even more just that they should expel the Jews. Why should he have to leave the city where he was born, if he didn't like the way they ran it? His father and his grandfather had been born here, and his grandfathers with as many greats before them as he could count, just like the patriarchs. There was something rotten about the council, enshrined in the place's architecture. Perhaps he should tear down the tiers of benches. He didn't like the patriarchs looking down on him and his fellow artisans. Vincenz Fettmilch prided himself on his sense of justice and fair play. He would hold elections. Citizens should be able to vote for the councillors who would represent them. Why should it just be handed down through the richest families? It wasn't right, and it wasn't just. He would make Frankfurt a model city. Others would follow his example. Why should he stop there? The Holy Roman Emperor, Mathias, was weak. Why else would they have been forced to swear this rotten oath of allegiance? They swore it under the threat of losing rights that weren't rights at all. It all made Vincenz's blood boil. He took some deep breaths. The attack on the city hall had gone well. They were now even better armed. But his loyal lieutenant, Victor Krause, hadn't been seen since he had gone to liberate his sister-in-law from the cells. The men were ready. He couldn't wait any longer. He would have to re-organise.

'Gather round men! Sadly, Victor seems to have been delayed. I will lead the rearguard. It is from the rear that they will come after us. Heinrich,' he called out to Heinrich

Weber, the basket weaver, 'Will you lead the advance party, instead off Victor?'

'Yes, Vincenz. What do we need to do?'

'You must advance quickly and quietly to the far end of Judengasse. If the Jews sense what is happening, they'll lock and bolt their doors and window shutters. Pick a couple of houses on either side of the street, and throw one of these jars of lamp oil through a window or door, quickly followed by a torch. Fuchs installed most of the locks and has provided some master keys. Hand them out would you, Fuchs? There, now once we see the flames, we will do the same at this end of Judengasse. The flames will spread through the shared roof space. The main body of Jews, in the middle section of the street, will not lock themselves in, so our brave men in the centre, led by Franz Müller, can recover our treasures. Those treasures that have been taken from us by the extortionate money lenders. Christ turned over the tables of the moneylenders in the temple. The Jews convicted him and handed him to the Romans for crucifixion. Are you ready to take back what is ours, and avenge our saviour?' The mob cheered. 'Then advance!'

They were almost at the start of the Judengasse. Vincenz felt the tingle of excitement around him. This would be his finest hour. He looked behind him. In the glow from their torches, he saw the glint of blades and the brave smiles of his fellow merchants and artisans. As he turned his head back, something caught his eye. He stopped, and the column of men stopped too. Up the side street to his right was a well, and a pond. In his eyes, it was bathed in sunlight. Children of his own age were splashing in the pond, and laughing. His mother was a few steps ahead of him, and he toddled off to the pond to join in the fun.

'Juden!' his mother screamed. There was a blend of fear, anger, and panic in her scream that he'd only heard once before. It was when she had crossed the road to get away from a beggar with pustules on his face. He'd gone closer to look at the beggar. He looked at the children's faces. Their smiles faded. They didn't seem to have the pustules of plague victims, but they must carry some awful disease. Why else would his mother be so scared? He took a deep breath and held it. Whatever it was, he didn't want to catch it.

'Vincenz, what's the matter?' Franz Müller asked.

'Nothing, Franz, just a memory.' Vincenz started walking forwards, towards the Judengasse. The memory was churning in his mind. He remembered that he'd held his breath when he strangled the Bambergers.

Vincenz watched the first party advance up the Judengasse. They soon disappeared from view around the curve. He could hear laughter and singing coming from the nearby houses. He could see lights from the windows, so they were not yet shuttered. When he thought that Weber must be approaching the far end, he tapped Franz Müller on the shoulder. Müller led his group off, carrying empty sacks for the loot in one hand, and their weapons in the other. They had four torch bearers in their party. They too soon disappeared around the curve in the street. It felt as if he waited for hours, but it was probably only a quarter of an hour before the glow could be seen where the end of the Judengasse would be. The glow warmed his heart.

'This is it, men, advance!' He took a jar of lamp oil from the crate that his son-in-law, Günther, was carrying. He hurled it through the window of the first Jewish house on his right. 'Throw in the torch!' he shouted at Albert Fuchs, one of the locksmith's sons. Albert seemed to hesitate, so he took the torch from him and threw it through the broken window. The living room erupted in flames. A woman opened the front door, stared at him for a second, then ran towards the road with the pond, her dress in flames. 'You two, start on the other side,' Vincenz shouted. Once it had started, it didn't take long for the fire to spread. Human torches were running around in circles, screaming. The plan was working beautifully. Vincenz led his party towards the main group, who would be collecting the spoils. He spotted Franz Müller ahead and raced forwards to join him. 'It's going well, Franz.'

'Yes, Vincenz. Look at them. They're bringing our treasure out to us. All we have to do is cut them down.' Jews, men, women, and children were indeed running out into the street, clutching whatever valuables they could carry. Fettmilch's men were chasing them, clubbing them, or slashing their blades at them, to regain their rightful belongings. 'You remember your promise, not a word to Frieda.'

'Of course, Franz, your secret is safe with me. Keep up the good work. I'm going forward to see how Heinrich Weber's men are getting on. I'll see you later.'

There was a good five- or six-hundred-yard stretch of the Judengasse that was not yet burning. Some Jews were getting past his men, but not many of them. Some were probably using the back alleyway, the one he had used to escape from the Bamberger house. He soon met Heinrich Weber, leading the forward party back to share in the spoils.

'Good work, Heinrich.'

'It was a good plan, Vincenz.'

'Yes, gather as much loot as you can, as quickly as you can, and get it back to the bierkeller. We'll divide the spoils there. Then we will organise our people's council, and plan for elections. The bishop will be behind us, now that we've dealt with the Jews.'

'Praise the Lord, Vincenz, praise the Lord.'

# CHAPTER FIFTEEN

The sound of shouting echoed down the spiral staircase. One of the guards climbed halfway up and took a boot in his chest, which sent him tumbling down. The other guard fired his musket as Victor appeared, and caught him in the leg. He collapsed on the ground at the bottom of the stairs. The guard took out his powder flask to reload, but was clubbed over the head by Franz Müller, just as he dropped his powder flask and reached for his sword instead.

'Are you alright, Victor?' Franz asked.

'I've been hit in the leg. We need to stop the bleeding.'

'Let me out. I can help. I've treated wounds like that before,' Maria shouted through the bars. 'The keys are on his belt.'

'Yes, let them out,' Victor gasped. Franz took the bunch of keys from the guard's belt and went to the women's cell door. He opened it with the second key he tried. Maria rushed out first.

'Give me a knife, and open the men's cell,' she said. Franz took a knife from the sheath on his belt, and passed it to her. 'You'd better truss up the guards. There's some rope hanging on the hook over there.' Maria examined Victor's wound. The ball had passed straight through. 'Has anyone got some brandy?'

'I have,' Heinrich, the son of the bierkeller landlord said, as he handed her a flask. Maria took it and poured some over the wound. Then she cut off one of Victor's shirt sleeves, and used it to bandage the wound.

'It's not too bad, you'll live,' she reassured him. 'What's happening?'

'We've had enough corruption. We're fighting back,' Victor winced. 'We've taken the city hall, now we're going to throw the Jews out.'

'There is no corruption. You've got it all wrong, and you're going to pay for it,' Mayor Hans Friedrich shouted as he was shoved into the men's cell. Antonio joined Maria at Victor's side.

'Good job, Maria. Now shall we get out of here?' Antonio asked.

'Yes, I thought we'd both lose our hands.'

'So did I. Did you see what they did with our lock picks?'

'Yes, they're in the desk drawer.' They recovered them. The mob were bundling the guards into the men's cell as Maria and Antonio rushed up the stairs. In the vestibule they noticed the Marktmeister, Friedrich Schulz, cowering under a table. Antonio stopped.

'Friedrich, we're leaving now. How much rent do we owe you? I don't have any money on me, but we'll leave it on the kitchen table.'

'One thaler.'

'Right, thanks,' Antonio said, Maria tugging his arm.

'Are you mad, we need to be going?'

'I don't want to be jailed again, for something we're actually guilty of.'

Antonio and Maria ran back to the house on Wienerstraße. Antonio harnessed Bellezza and Allegro to the cart, while Maria gathered all their things. They loaded the cart, then Antonio rushed back inside and left a thaler on the kitchen table. Antonio opened the stable door and Maria flicked the reins. The horses and cart trundled out.

Antonio shut the stable door and climbed up onto the seat beside Maria. Maria flicked the reins again, and they set off.

'I didn't see Sergeant Voigt anywhere, did you?' Antonio asked.

'No. If he's at the city gate, he's not going to let us pass.'

'We'd better hope he's gone to help at the city hall.'

'Yes, but load the rifles and pistols while I'm driving, just in case.' Antonio reached behind him and felt for the gun case. He dragged it up onto the seat, and began loading the weapons. He had to do it by feel, in the dim light of the half-moon and the light from torches mounted in brackets along the street walls. They were just trundling past Manuel's house when Maria reined in the horses. 'I have to say goodbye to Manuel. I won't be a minute,' she said jumping down. Antonio looked all around, nursing one of the rifles in his arms. Maria knocked on Manuel's door. Ingrid opened it. 'Is Manuel in? We're leaving.'

'No, he's been called out. There's trouble in the ghetto.'

'Shit, he's in danger. Antonio, head for Judengasse!' she said, as she climbed back onto the cart.

They made easy progress through empty streets to begin with. They could see a red and yellow glow above the rooftops ahead of them. Then the streets became busier. Two men were walking towards them carrying a chest between them. Maria recognised one of them as Karl Schmidt, the tailor. Maria reigned in Bellezza and Allegro. She peered at the chest which was full of fabrics.

'Karl, have you seen Doctor Nuñez?' she asked. He looked up surprised.

'Oh, it's you. He was in Judengasse, treating the wounded Jews. I suppose it's that oath they swear. Why else would you help Jews?' Maria flicked the reins and they trundled on. They encountered many more of the mob, few of whom they recognised. They were all carrying loot of one sort or another. One man had a string of pearls around his neck. When they turned into Judengasse, they came to an abrupt halt. Bellezza and Allegro reared in fright. The buildings either side of them were ablaze. They could see one woman screaming from an upstair's window in a burning building. Men, women and children were rushing out of buildings and fleeing from the inferno.

'We can't go any further with the horses, Maria.'

'No. We don't have room to turn around. Hop down and see if you can back them up!' Antonio jumped down. He spoke softly to Bellezza, stroking her mane. She calmed a little and Allegro followed her lead. 'Back we go, there, that's right,' he said, walking them backwards. 'There's a side street behind us with a grass square, a well, and a pond. I'll turn them in there.' It was a small haven from the hell they had seen. Maria jumped down. They unhitched the horses, who seemed happy to drink and graze. 'Do you think it's safe to leave the cart and horses here, Maria?'

'We have no choice. We'll take a rifle and pistol each, powder flasks and lead balls. Grab our money, the contract and bill of exchange. Anything else that's left when we get back is a bonus. Now let's find Manuel.'

# CHAPTER SIXTEEN

Before leaving his surgery, Manuel had packed his medical bag with a few extra things he thought might be required. These included an extra two bottles of laudanum, a clean scalpel, forceps, needles and surgical thread. Then he had told Ingrid to give his apologies and send the waiting patients home. He'd rushed out of the door and followed Sam Cohen, who was already twenty yards ahead.

'Wait, Sam. I don't want to trip in the dark. I have bottles in the bag,' Manuel called ahead.

'Sorry, Doctor. I'll guide you. I thought you knew the way.'

'I know the way well enough, in the daylight. It's the uneven cobbles that worry me.'

'I'll carry the bag, if you like, Doctor. My eyes are younger that yours.'

'No, lead on.'

After another three hundred yards, Manuel's path was well illuminated. The fire stretched along the Judengasse on both sides. As they continued, and could see more of the street around the long sweeping curve, he could see that the fire had reached about a third of the way along. He had to blink as the sweat ran into his eyes. They passed Daniel and Edith's house. The door hung open, on the bottom hinge.

The top half of the door had burnt away. Manuel paused. They had been so kind to him. They'd been the only people he could really talk to about his mother. They said it had been bad in Portugal, before they fled. But they'd never described anything that even faintly resembled this hell. It must have been an accident, surely.

'Did it start in the bakery?' Manuel asked.

'No, Doctor, a mob of merchants came through, with torches, swords and muskets. They cut down anyone who resisted, seized their valuables, and set fire to the buildings.'

'Why? What harm were the Jews causing? Isn't anyone doing anything? We need to get buckets. There's a pond and a well in the lane we just passed. We need to set up a chain of men with buckets and dowse the flames.'

'I think it's beyond that, Doctor. You're needed in the synagogue. That's where we're taking the injured.' Manuel grabbed the sleeve of a man running past.

'Get some buckets! Get some more men and form a chain from the well and the pond. We must dowse these flames.' The man shook his head and ran off. 'My god, what will be left after this, if we do nothing to save it?'

'Doctor, sir, there will be nobody to save it for, if you don't come to the synagogue.' Manuel turned to look Sam in the eye. Sam grabbed his hand and pulled. Manuel ran with him to the synagogue.

◇ ◇ ◇

Burnt and bloodied bodies lay on the floor of the synagogue. Wails and screams echoed around the walls. Manuel caught Rabbi Levi's eye, and the Rabbi threaded his way through the injured to reach him.

'Manuel, thank the Lord, you're here at last. What should we do?'

'We need to group the casualties. Are there any dead here?'

'I've had the dead carried down to the crypt.'

'You're sure they're dead?'

'Manuel, I've seen enough death to know its face,'

Rabbi Levi whispered.

'Yes. We need to sort the casualties into three groups. The beyond hope, those who can wait, and those needing urgent treatment. Lay them out with enough room between them for two people to pass.'

'I'll put those without hope against the east wall, nearest Jerusalem,' Rabbi Levi said.

'We will need sheets and blankets. Can you set up a fire, tripod and pot to boil water? I'll need lots of sterile water. Brandy, I'll need brandy to sterilise my instruments. Who are you?' Manuel asked a teenage girl, who he recognised, but couldn't quite place.

'I'm Sarah.'

'Sarah, can you write?'

'Yes, Doctor.'

'Get some paper, and something to make a mark with. Charred wood will do. There's enough of that around. I'll examine each patient and raise one, two, or three fingers. You make a corresponding mark, and place it at the patient's feet. One will be those without hope. Sam, you find helpers and get those carried over to the east wall. The twos will be the non-urgent cases, and the threes will be the urgent ones. They go nearest the west wall.'

'Where will I get some paper?' Sarah asked.

'Rabbi Levi, we need paper. Lots of it!' Manuel called out. Rabbi Levi was already trying to organise a fire where the ceiling was highest.

'I have some I use to write my derashas!' he shouted back.

'Tear pages from the Torah if you must.'

'I'll find enough.'

Manuel began examining the casualties. Sarah soon joined him, clutching a sheaf of paper and a charred piece of wood. Sam and four young men soon joined them. Manuel backtracked to the first casualty and gave the hand signals. They worked through the casualties. Manuel assessed the gravity of the injuries, and told Sarah to label them with a 1, 2, or 3. Other uninjured Jews came offering help. Manuel instructed them in elevating bleeding wounds, applying clean folded sheets against a wound, and using boiled water, once it had cooled on burns. Within half an hour, the sorting process was complete, and Manuel began work on the urgent cases. More casualties were being brought in all the time. Sarah and Sam did their best to organise them along the lines Manuel had shown them.

'Sarah, I'm sure I've seen you before. Are you the undertaker's niece?'

'That's right, Doctor. I was named after Isaac's wife.'

# CHAPTER SEVENTEEN

After checking on the prisoners, Sergeant Barnard Voigt had checked the city gates before making his way to the Judengasse. He walked along the curving street towards the city gate at the far end, where his guardroom was established in a tower. All seemed quiet. There were many windows that remained broken, and had been boarded over. There were also still anti-Semitic slogans that hadn't been whitewashed. The few Jews he met on the street scurried away from him, anxious not to be caught out in the curfew. When he reached the gatehouse, he found Corporal Heinrich Schulz inside. Schulz stood up from his chair behind a desk and saluted. Voigt returned the salute.

'Is all well, corporal?'

'Yes, sergeant. Would you like to see for yourself?'

'Of course.' Corporal Schulz led the way up the narrow, spiral staircase to the viewing platform. Guardsman Köhler was peering through the crenellations towards the river and the quayside. He turned and stood at attention as he heard the footsteps behind him.

'At ease, Köhler. Any sign of trouble tonight?'

'None, sergeant. It's been quiet. There's some unloading going on. Over there on the quayside. I was just wondering if it might be smuggling, and whether I should check.'

'Good idea. I'll come with you. I think arresting those Italians who were poking their noses in may have helped appease the vandals. Corporal, you can watch over us from up here. Cover us with your musket.'

'Very good, sergeant.'

Sergeant Voigt led the way back down the tower, followed by Guardsman Köhler. He opened the door on the river side of the tower, and they made their way towards the small gang of men unloading a barge. They kept to the right-hand side of the path as far as they could. Then Sergeant Voigt drew his sword and stepped out of the shadow.

'What's going on here?'

'Heavens, Barnard. You startled me.'

'Oscar?'

'Of course. We're working late on an urgent job. The bierkeller was almost out of beer. The barge from the brewery arrived on the tide an hour ago. The landlord is paying the overtime to get it unloaded as soon as possible. The paperwork is all in order, if you want to come to the office and check?'

'No, that won't be necessary,' Voigt replied. He knew that Oscar Baumann was honest enough. Just then, there was a shout from Corporal Schulz. Voigt and Köhler rushed back to the guardroom and up the steps of the tower. 'What is it, Heinrich?'

'Over there, fire. At the far end of the Judengasse!' Corporal Schulz said. Sergeant Voigt peered through the crenellations and along the curve of the Judengasse. The fires were most intense at the far end, nearest the city. He stared beyond the Judengasse, but he couldn't see any sign of fire within the city itself, just the very dim glow of the torches lighting the streets. His gaze shifted back along the Judengasse. He squinted and thought he could see dim lights moving towards him. He rubbed his eyes and stared again.

'Schulz, Köhler, tell me what you see.' The corporal and the guardsman stared down the Judengasse.

'Fire, sergeant,' they both replied.

'Yes, but describe it, you first, Köhler.' Barnard Voigt wanted the untainted opinion of the youngest eyes first.

'Well, sergeant, I think the buildings are on fire. It's spreading along the street towards us. There are smaller pinpricks, almost, of light moving this way. Sparks from the fire, perhaps?' Voigt licked his finger and held it up.

'They can't be sparks. The wind, what there is of it, would be blowing them away from us.' Barnard Voigt bit his lip. They had to be torches. That was the mob, and there were a lot of them. He could run and hide, or face them, with two men, two muskets, two bayonets, and his own sword. He breathed deeply, trying to calm his racing heart, that seemed to be trying to claw its way up his chest. 'We must investigate. Fix bayonets and follow me!' He saw his men exchange eye contact, then draw their bayonets and fix them in place. Köhler's hands were shaking as he did so.

Voigt paused as he left the guardroom. He could lead his men directly down Judengasse, and confront the mob head on. That was what he felt he should do. But Köhler was newly married. When they confronted the mob head on, what would happen? How might the mob be armed? They should have some respect for his authority, surely? He would order them back to their homes. But they had started something that they must know could not go unpunished. Would they listen? Somehow, he doubted it. They would get off two shots. He thought Schulz would hit his mark, but Köhler's hands were shaking. He could imagine him running. If the ringleader went down, how would the mob react? With anger or fear? We must circle around and pick them off from the rear. Their leader, probably Krause or Fettmilch, will be at the front. If we can create panic at the rear, we might survive this night. Köhler's wife might not be a widow, so soon.

'Listen to me, men! We're going back through the gate into the city and onto Praliger Gaß. Then we'll head back towards the far end of Judengasse. That way, we'll get behind them. These men might be your neighbours, your friends even, but they are rebels now, and you have sworn to defend law and order. I will call on them to surrender, but if they do not drop their weapons, you are to shoot to kill. Reload immediately and be prepared to use your bayonets if necessary. Do I make myself clear?'

'Yes, sergeant,' Corporal Schulz replied.

'Yes, sergeant,' Guardsman Köhler added, his mind reeling, images of his wife, Heidi, and perhaps his unborn child flashing past his eyes.

'Sergeant, if they don't surrender, what do we do then?' Corporal Schulz asked. It was a good question. Voigt thought for a few moments. They couldn't lock them in a burning building. How could they be sure that they wouldn't re-join the fight? They couldn't just kill them on the spot. There would have to be a trial.

'The synagogue is towards the far end. It has a crypt. We will take a coil of rope with us and bind the wrists of the prisoners. You, corporal, will march the prisoners to the synagogue. Lock them in the crypt, then re-join Köhler and I. We will advance towards the leaders of the mob. We'll pick them off, a few at a time, with you ferrying them back to the synagogue.' Voigt thought that Schulz's greater experience and authority would deter any escape attempts. He also wanted to keep Köhler under his protective wing.

'Yes, sergeant.'

'Right. let's go.' Sergeant Voigt took a coil of rope from a hook on the guardroom wall and led the way out of the tower.

Praliger Gaß was almost deserted, and Voigt, Schulz, and Köhler soon reached the far end of Judengasse. It was a scene straight out of hell. Every building was aflame, except for the stone-built synagogue. Rabbi Levi was marshalling the uninjured to carry the casualties to the synagogue. A woman was screaming from an upstairs window of a burning building. Six men were holding a stretched blanket beneath the window, shouting at her to jump. Only when they saw the flames licking around her, did she jump. The blanket softened her fall, but they heard a sickening crack as she hit the ground. Her dress was charred, her legs too.

They found that many of the rebels had been drinking, and weren't difficult to immobilise. Sergeant Voigt and Corporal Schulz tied them up, while Guardsman Köhler covered them.

'Take these to the crypt, corporal, and re-join us as soon as you can.'

'Yes, sergeant.' Schulz set off with the prisoners to the synagogue, giving them the occasional prod with his bayonet.

By the time that Schulz caught up with them, Voigt and Köhler had taken more easy prisoners.

'Here's your next batch, Schulz. We'll continue working our way up behind them. Re-join us as soon as you can.'

Corporal Heinrich Schulz ran out of the synagogue and headed back up Judengasse. He'd just made his first delivery of prisoners. It was slow going, pushing through the tide of fleeing Jews, and rebels fleeing with their loot. He heard a girl screaming. He stopped to see where the screams were coming from. There was a girl at the first-floor window, in a burning building to his right. He could see the flames in the room behind her.

'Has anyone got a ladder?' he shouted. People ignored him, barging past him to reach safety. He looked up into her terrified eyes. She was probably in her late teens. He knew he should get back to Sergeant Voigt and Köhler, but he had to do something. 'Listen to me, jump. I'll catch you.'

'I can't!' she screamed.

'What's your name?'

'Ruth. It's too high.'

'Ruth, you have to jump. Climb out onto the window cill. Let your legs dangle over. Hold on to the window frame. It's not far.'

'I'm scared. I'll break my neck.'

'No, you won't, I'll catch you, I promise.' He could see the flames getting closer. She looked behind her, then she put one leg over the window cill, followed by the other one. She sat frozen on the cill, gripping the frame, her knuckles white. She screamed as the flames licked her dress. 'Jump, for God's sake, jump!' She fell forward, and he caught her. He rolled her on the ground and beat out the flames with his hands. Her burns looked bad, particularly the facial ones. He carried her into the synagogue. Then he set off again to find the others.

# CHAPTER EIGHTEEN

Manuel's assistants were doing well. He had them well trained in bandaging wounds, applying splints to broken limbs, and cooling burns. He wondered where Maria was now. Sergeant Voigt had seemed determined to stop her investigation. Had they arrested her? Could she have got away? Might she have fought off Voigt? She was an accomplished fighter. He still had the aches to prove it. But if so, where was she now? She and her brother would have gone back to their vineyard, if they had any sense. Perhaps when it was over, he'd take a trip to Frascati, and see if he could find her. The mayor miscalculated if he thought he could keep a lid on this hatred. So who was he fooling? She wouldn't go home, leaving this hell behind her. It wasn't in her nature. She'll be out there, trying to help. She deserves someone better, someone unafraid of who they are.

'Doctor Nuñez, I think you should look at this girl,' Sarah called over to him. He rushed over to her, and knelt down beside the casualty. Her face was badly burnt. She was Maria's height and age, he thought. Oh my god, no, it can't be. 'Doctor Nuñez, what do we do?' Manuel studied her face. It was difficult to tell. It might be her, it might not. She had partial depth burns all over her face. Blisters were forming. She was grotesquely disfigured. It could be her.

She had good teeth, just like Maria. Her hands were the same. The girl squeezed his hand as he felt them. She tried to speak, but had inhaled too much smoke. Each breath was a fight for life. She was trying to tell him something. Was it that she loved him? Was this the end? He put his ear to her mouth, trying to hear what she wanted to say. He had to do something to calm her, so he kissed her. Then his inner training took charge.

'Keep cooling her face with the sterilised water.' The girl was coughing up blood. 'She's inhaled a lot of smoke. Help me roll her on her side. There will be fluid building up in her lungs.' Manuel examined her torso, checking her burns, and deciding where they could turn her without causing too much additional pain. 'It's not her, thank God! Her musculature is all wrong.'

'She's not who, Doctor Nuñez?' Sarah asked.

'Nothing, it doesn't matter. I'll lift her knee and use that as a lever to roll her towards me. You help her turn, trying to avoid touching her burns. Ready? One, two, three, roll!' They got the girl on her side, and she coughed up brown mucus, which dripped on Manuel's shoes. The girl started breathing more easily. 'Keep cooling her burns. Try to make her comfortable on her side, like that. Sam, can you bring over some blankets?' Sam did as requested, and they used the blankets to prop the girl into a more comfortable position on her side. She kept coughing up mucus, but was breathing more easily. Manuel left her in Sarah's care and went with Sam to check on some new arrivals.

'Rabbi Levi, I thought we were moving the dead to the crypt. What are these bodies doing here? They'll upset the living.'

'I'm sorry, but Corporal Schulz is bringing prisoners and locking them in the crypt. We can't risk unlocking it unless he's here to prevent an escape.'

'Where is he then? Why don't they take them to city hall?'

'There's only him, Sergeant Voigt, and young Köhler.

They're taking on the mob alone. They need somewhere secure, and nearby, as a temporary jail.'

'I see.' Voigt might know where Maria is, Manuel thought. 'Let me know when Schulz next appears. I want a quick word with him.'

'Manuel, he's here, Corporal Schulz!' Rabbi Levi shouted. Manuel left Sam bandaging a wound and rushed across to the door to the crypt. Corporal Schulz pushed a prisoner down the stairs and locked the door.

'Corporal, can you ask Sergeant Voigt something for me, please?'

'We have little time for talking, Doctor Nuñez.'

'Just ask him if he knows where Maria Standen is, please.'

'Maria, who?'

'Maria Standen. She and her brother were helping him on a murder case.'

'Well, if I get the chance, Doctor Nuñez, I will. I've got to go now.' Corporal Schulz turned and ran out of the synagogue.

'Who is this girl, Manuel?' Rabbi Levi asked.

'The girl I love.'

'Tell me about her. Don't worry, Sam and Sarah seem to be managing. We all need a rest from this unfathomable violence. I'd like to hear about love on a day like today. Tell me, what is she like?'

'To look at she's the most beautiful woman in the world. She's Venus, Aphrodite, and Eve rolled into one. No, they pale in comparison. She has their voluptuousness, but in a more masculine way.'

'Masculine way? What do you mean?'

'Masculine is the wrong word. It's just that her curves are sculpted, somehow. It's that Greek image of feminine beauty, sculpted by Olympian athleticism. Yes that's it, she's athletically voluptuous.'

'She sounds like a rare beauty.'

'Yes, but that's just on the outside. She's even more beautiful on the inside.'

'How do you mean?'

'As I said, she and her brother were helping Sergeant Voigt to investigate Daniel and Edith's murders, Daniel and Edith Bamberger.'

'I know who they are, Manuel. Why were Maria and her brother helping the investigation?'

'Actually, they were more than helping him. There wouldn't have been an investigation at all, if it hadn't been for her. The mayor would have brushed it under the rug as soon as he could. He wouldn't waste time on Jews. He seemed to have more on his mind.'

'Is she Jewish, this Maria?'

'No, she isn't. That's what makes her so special. She seems to be driven to seek justice. Her brother is too, just not so much. He's clever though, he came up with the main line of inquiry.'

'What was that?'

'There were pages torn from Daniel's ledger. He guessed that the murderer must have been ripping out the pages that had his name on. He thought that if he could find a pattern of appointments on particular dates, then he might be able to work out who the killer was.'

'Yes, Daniel was a man of habit. Won't it be a problem for you, though, that Maria is a Gentile, I mean?' Rabbi Levi nodded. 'You might find it difficult to marry a Gentile.'

'Oh, so you know then,' Manuel whispered.

'That you're Jewish?'

'Yes.'

'I had my suspicions. I'd seen you visiting Daniel and Edith. They said that you were just a friend of theirs, but I saw a familial likeness. It was only a suspicion, but you just confirmed it. But she isn't Jewish.'

'No, but I love her. I'm hoping she'll convert.'

'Why should she, when you hide your own faith? I don't blame you, of course. In this city, you couldn't be the physician you are, if you were open about your faith. You wouldn't be here saving lives now. God works in mysterious ways. He will guide you and her. Sam is beckoning for you.'

# CHAPTER NINETEEN

When Schulz re-joined them after his second delivery of prisoners, the pickings were looking much less easy. The smoke was thickening.

'Advance!' Voigt ordered, and they made their way through the smoke, along the curve of Judengasse. The next members of the mob that they encountered were three men. One of them was the miller, Franz Müller. His silhouette was unmistakable. He had a sword in his right hand and a flaming torch in his left. The other two had muskets. Voigt didn't recognise them from the back. 'Drop your weapons, in the name of the law!' He shouted. They turned. Voigt recognised one of them as Karl Weber, the basket weaver's eldest son. The other was Rolf Zimmermann, the carpenter's son.

'Shoot!' Müller shouted. Karl Weber levelled his musket, and there was a crack. Weber slumped to the ground, clutching his chest. Young Zimmermann dropped his musket and ran away, up the Judengasse. Müller chased after him. Voigt looked around. Corporal Schultz was busy reloading his musket. Guardsman Köhler was staring, open mouthed, at the body on the ground. Voigt knelt next to young Weber. There was no point feeling for a pulse, Schultz had hit him in the heart.

'Good shot, Heinrich!' Voigt said. 'That's their

rearguard dealt with. Müller will race ahead to inform the leader, Fettmilch or Krause. I don't expect as much resistance from the next rebels we meet, not until they take action to shore up their rear. Let's move on.' Voigt was right. As they worked their way forward, they met little resistance. The street was littered with dead and dying Jews. Rebels were returning from the front with their loot. Men wore strings of pearls around their necks. Some were wearing furs, too tight for a man to fasten. All pockets were bulging. Two men staggered past, carrying a wooden chest. They turned their faces away as they rushed past the guard, but Barnard Voigt would remember their names. Karl Schmidt, the tailor, dodged past them, with a bundle of cloth under each arm. After sixty or seventy yards, they met two armed men. 'Drop your weapons!' Voigt commanded. Schulz and Köhler aimed their muskets. From the corner of his eye, Voigt was pleased to see that Köhler's aim was steady. The muzzle was not waving about as it had been. He'd had his baptism of fire. Günther Zimmermann and Heinrich Weber dropped their cutlasses. Voigt bound their wrists behind their backs, whilst Schulz and Köhler kept watch. 'Take them to the crypt, corporal, and get back as soon as you can. Köhler and I will press on ahead.'

It seemed to become easier the further they went. From the smell of their breath, the rebels had been helping themselves to kosher wine. Corporal Schulz had made four deliveries of prisoners to the synagogue crypt by the time Sergeant Voigt and Guardsman Köhler ran into Vincenz Fettmilch, Günther Krause, his new son-in-law, and Franz Müller.

The smell of burning human flesh turned Barnard Voigt's stomach. Smoke filled the street. Torches had been abandoned; they were no longer required. Almost every building was burning, and the glow of the flames lit the streets with flickering, dancing light. Through the flickering light, Voigt saw the silhouettes of Vincenz Fettmilch and

Franz Müller ahead. Between them was Günther Krause, Vincenz's son-in-law. There were others, but they were swaying, guzzling from flagons. Fettmilch and Müller were armed with swords, Günther had a musket. They were sifting through some wooden chests, looking for valuables.

'The odds are good, only three of them to two of us, Köhler,' Voigt whispered. 'I shall command them to surrender. If they don't, young Günther, with the musket, is your target. Aim for the chest. I'll take on the others. A baker and a miller will be no match for an old soldier.' He hoped he'd steadied Köhler with the bravado he was far from feeling himself. 'Surrender! Drop your weapons, in the name of the law!' Voigt commanded.

# CHAPTER TWENTY

Vincenz Fettmilch grinned. His plan was working better than he could have hoped. The city guards were nowhere to be seen. They had probably locked themselves into their guardrooms. Thanks to Heinrich Fuchs and his master keys, they would soon deal with them. Only one thing was troubling him. The men were drinking too much. They obviously felt they had earned it, and that was true. Perhaps the danger was past. It was too late anyway. The men running around him, and sitting in the street counting their jewels in the light of the burning houses, would not be sober for hours. At least Günther, his son-in-law, and son of his friend Victor Krause, was sober. Ursula had chosen well. Vincenz put his arms around Günther and hugged him.

'This is all for you and Ursula, Günther. You deserve a better life than I've had. No worries about money for you and your children. No begging for loans from Jews for you. You will vote in free elections for who runs this great city. Why, you will stand with me and become a councillor too. Your father will be my deputy mayor, of course. Where is he? He should have freed your aunt by now.' A familiar figure pushed his way through the crowd of wine-guzzling rebels. It was Franz Müller. Close behind him was Rolf Zimmermann, the carpenter's son.

'Vincenz, the guards are coming. We tried to hold them. They shot Karl Weber. I think he's dead.'

'Who? Who shot him?'

'Corporal Schulz, I think. It might have been Frederick Köhler. They both had muskets, Voigt had a sword.'

'Damn them! Damn them to hell!' Vincenz looked around him. Who could he rely on? 'Did you wound any of them? Did you see any more guards?'

'No, just them. Karl got off a shot. He might have hit one of them.'

'What do you mean, he might have hit one of them? Did he, or didn't he?'

'I couldn't tell. Karl fell like a stone, then Rolf ran, and —'

'And so did you.'

'I'm sorry, Vincenz. I didn't know what else to do. I'm only a miller. Voigt and Schulz are trained killers. Vincenz, was it you who killed the Bambergers? I did as you asked. I didn't tell them I saw you there.'

'What does it matter? They were Jews.'

'I owed them money too, but I never considered killing them.'

'I had a wedding to pay for, my beautiful daughter's wedding. The wife was making me tea. He was counting out my money, and writing in that damned book of his. That box of his was open. There were enough thalers in there to pay for a dozen weddings. It seemed like the best solution. If you're having second thoughts, I will tell Frieda about your young blond friend, Lena.'

'No, Vincenz, please don't. She'd kill me.'

'Don't worry, Franz, it doesn't matter now, does it? Who will worry about two filthy Jews after our glorious victory against our oppressors? The patriarchs are finished, and so are the Jews.'

'There's still Voigt and Schulz, Vincenz. They're fierce fighters.'

'They're paid killers, but we humble artisans are

stronger. You're stronger through the sacks of flour you carry. They fight for money, while we fight for our families and our friends. God is on our side, and we will never be defeated.'

'You're right, Vincenz. I'm sorry we ran.'

'Don't worry, Franz, you'll get your chance to redeem yourself. Here they come.'

Fettmilch, Müller, and young Günther Krause looked up. Fettmilch smiled. He sensed the fear behind Voigt's call to surrender. 'Surrender? To you and whose army? You and young Frederick Köhler? Where's Schulz? Has he run away?' Fettmilch jeered.

'Surrender, and you'll get a fair trial. Resist and we'll cut you down.' Voigt commanded. Fettmilch felt that his cutting riposte had struck home; he was sure of it. How could they dare to put him and his freedom fighters on trial? It was they who would be on trial. He glanced to his right and left. He could see the new determination and courage that he had instilled in Franz Müller.

Günther had his musket aimed. Good lad! He nodded to him and the musket cracked. The muzzle leapt up, as flame and smoke flew from it.

'We're in charge now. It'll be you going on trial, along with the corrupt patriarchs.' Fettmilch glanced at Günther. He and Ursula deserved a better future, free of the famine, worries, and debts he had endured. Günther had his musket aimed at Köhler. Fettmilch nodded. The musket cracked, flame and smoke shot from the muzzle. Köhler fired, but he had already been hit in his side. He rolled onto his back, staring up at the grey face of Barnard Voigt.

Günther vomited, dropped his musket, then turned and ran. Fettmilch and Müller advanced towards Voigt, their blades glinting in the firelight. Fury surged though Voigt.

He tried desperately to harness it, and use it. Fettmilch lunged first, Voigt parried it, and turned to slash at Müller. He caught him on his left arm. Müller stepped back, and Fettmilch launched a furious attack, slashing wildly. Voigt countered each slash with a bind, deflecting Fettmilch's blade to the diagonally opposite line, high left to low right, then low right to high left. Fettmilch's frustration drove him to an ever more furious assault. He glanced at Müller, whose sword arm was bleeding. He changed hands and tried to re-enter the fight. He circled around behind Voigt. Fettmilch smiled and launched another slashing assault. Voigt again countered with a series of binds, curving as he retreated, to keep Müller from getting behind him. As Voigt sensed Fettmilch was tiring, he switched to a ceding parry, circling his blade around Fettmilch's as Fettmilch lunged, deflecting it, and at the same time launching a kick into Fettmilch's groin. Müller caught Voigt with a slashing blow to his side while he was off balance. Voigt engaged Müller with a series of lunges, at which point Müller turned and ran. Voigt looked around for Fettmilch, but he was limping away ahead of Müller. Voigt rushed over to Köhler, who was lying on the ground, clutching his side. His hand was bloody.

'Let me take a look.' He didn't like the look of it. 'Do you think you can walk?'

'I'll try.' Köhler staggered to his feet, but then Voigt could see the strength draining from him. He wasted no time, grabbing Köhler's right wrist with his left hand, and raising it. He ducked down, thrusting his right arm between Köhler's legs. As Köhler's torso dropped over Voigt's shoulders, Voigt stood up, Köhler perfectly balanced over Voigt's right shoulder. He set off towards the sanctuary of the synagogue, feeling the warmth of Köhler's blood running down his back.

# CHAPTER TWENTY-ONE

Schulz made his way along the Judengasse towards the guard tower. His eyes scanned the crowds for danger and for his comrades. The muzzle of his musket followed his eyes, firelight glinting off the polished bayonet. The crowd was becoming less of a threat. They were thinning out, having made their way home with their spoils. Those who remained were drunk. He struggled to comprehend the violence. Smoke swirled around him. He squinted, peering through the smoke. Its acrid bite seemed to eat into his lungs. He began to cough uncontrollably, and then he stumbled. He rolled himself up onto his knees, scanning around, searching for the fatal blow that would emerge from the fog. He clutched his musket in his right hand, and put his left hand down to help himself up again. He recoiled. His hand was bloody. Beside him lay a woman's body. Her face was badly burnt. Her arm was broken, perhaps she had jumped. She didn't look old, not much more than twenty, if that. Why would they do this? Corporal Heinrich Schulz was no stranger to violence. His labourer father had beaten his mother whenever she dared criticise him for his drinking, or for the lack of money. He had beaten him as a child, his brothers and his sisters too. Heinrich couldn't get away from him fast enough. He'd enlisted in the Spanish army when they marched through the city, with Italian recruits, on their way to Flanders. He'd seen plenty of violence there. When he got home, and found his mother covered in bruises, he'd told his father, at the point of his musket, that if he ever hit her again, he'd kill him. He'd meant it, and his father never did hit her again. His father had died before he'd thought to ask him why he'd hurt her. He must have loved her, so why beat her? She'd always said he didn't mean to do it, that it was the drink. Years later he'd asked his uncle Tomas about it. He'd said that she knew how to wind him up. She would turn the screw, turn and turn, until he broke. Why was a mystery. Perhaps she felt some perverse sense of control over him. He would never know, but order, his order, had prevailed. What was this all around him? Why this violence and criminality? Why here? Why now? He didn't understand it. From what he'd been told, the ringleaders were from the merchant class. They didn't struggle to put bread on the table. Many of them baked it. Well, without crime, there would be no need for the guard. Then he'd be looking for another job. Perhaps Klara would moan at him about money to feed their children. The boys, Heinrich junior and Ralph, would soon be old enough to work themselves. Heinrich wanted to be a blacksmith. Ralph wanted to join the guard, like his father. Katherina wanted to be a princess. Where were Barnard and Frederick?

# CHAPTER TWENTY-TWO

Vincenz was panting for breath. The fight had taken everything from him. He tried to remember what had happened. Young Köhler had crumpled and fallen. Vincenz was so proud of his new son-in-law. He'd patted Günther on the shoulder, but he'd throw up. Then Günther had turned and ran. Vincenz had wanted to shout after him, to call him back, so that he could bask in their victory, to celebrate his kill, but there wasn't time. It was then two against one. Vincenz had launched his attack, burning with fury, Franz at his side. Then, through some devilish trickery, Voigt had managed to wound Franz's left arm. Vincenz had pressed on with his attack, giving Franz time to recover. To his delight, he had seen Franz trying to circle around Voigt. Then the breath left him, as Voigt kicked him in the groin. He'd watched Franz launch an attack as he fought for breath. He got him. Voigt had been wounded. No, he was fighting back. Vincenz had wanted to shout encouragement, but only the most feeble croak emerged. Then Franz turned and ran. Vincenz had no choice. He would have to regroup, rally his troops. He turned and limped away after Franz, as best he could.

He caught up with Franz first. 'You did well, Franz, you wounded him.'

'I'm sorry, Vincenz, I ran again. I thought the wound

would stop him, but he fought like a devil.'

'You were wounded yourself. I don't blame you. We must find shelter and get a dressing on your arm. The guard tower is ahead, and Fuchs gave me a key. Come, it's not far.'

Günther was already at the base of the tower when they arrived. He was looking a little green. Vincenz took out his key and unlocked the door. He helped Franz inside, and Günther followed them.

Vincenz looked around. The guardroom was lit by candles. He climbed the spiral stairs to see what was up there. At the top of the stairs, a door opened out onto a viewing platform, protected by stone walls with crenellations from which you could fire muskets. He gazed down at the scene below. They had done well. The homes of the Jews were charred wrecks. Bodies littered the streets. He could see his men carrying off the spoils of victory. There was no sign of Sergeant Voigt or his pathetic guards. He went back down the stairs.

'We have secured a glorious victory, Franz, Günther. Now let's have a proper look at your arm, Franz.' The miller's right arm was still bleeding from a wound above the elbow. Vincenz looked around. There was a cloak hanging from a peg on the wall. He used his sword to cut a strip of cloth from the cape. He wrapped it around Franz's wound and tied it. 'There, how's that?'

'Better, Vincenz, thank you. Are we truly victorious?'

'We are, Franz. Come up to the viewing platform and see for yourself. You too, Günther.' Günther had been looking at a rack of cutlasses in the guardroom. He took one, swished it around, then followed his father-in-law and Franz up the staircase.

They followed him up the spiral staircase and gazed down at the scene below.

'I'm thirsty, Vincenz,' Franz croaked.

'It's the loss of blood, I expect. Look, there's a water barrel over there.' Vincenz crossed the viewing platform to where a barrel rested on a wooden stand. There were four wooden goblets on the floor. He filled three of them from the tap in the barrel. He handed one to Franz, and the other to Günther. Then he raised the third to his own lips. 'It should be wine, but let's make a toast. To victory, freedom and justice.'

'Victory, freedom and justice.' Franz and Günther repeated and drank. Franz sat down, resting his back against the parapet wall. Günther did the same against the opposite wall. Vincenz sat where he had a view down the Judengasse. He surveyed the scene and smiled.

Vincenz was drifting off to sleep when he heard a voice. Someone was in the guardroom below, calling out. He listened. The voice was calling for Sergeant Voigt. It had to be Corporal Schulz, damn him. Vincenz shook Franz and Günther, whispering a warning to them. They both scrambled to their feet. Franz wasn't sure he would be effective with a sword, so he took a cudgel from his pocket. Günther picked up Franz's sword. Vincenz could hear footsteps coming up the stairs. He put his finger to his lips, then he lay his sword down. He picked up the water barrel and hurled it down the steps. Then he snatched up his sword and ran down the stairs. Günther followed him, then Franz. As he ran round the final spiral, he saw Corporal Schulz sprawling on the floor. He raised his sword and ran at him, desperate to kill him before he could aim his musket. Flame and smoke shot from the muzzle before he heard the crack. He expected to fall, but didn't. There was a scream in his ear, and Günther fell against him. He turned. Blood was spurting from Günther's leg. Schulz had done this. Schulz who was scrambling to his feet. Vincenz rushed at him, slashing at him with the sword. Schulz was parrying his blows with the musket. Schultz's musket was longer than his sword. He kept thrusting in at him, but Vincenz could parry the blows. They circled. Then he smiled, as he looked into Franz's eyes, over Schulz's shoulder. Franz's cudgel came crashing down on Schulz's head, and he fell to the floor. Vincenz stepped forward to finish him.

'Father, help me!' Günther screamed. He turned. Günther was on the floor, clutching his thigh. Blood was pumping out.

'He needs a doctor, Vincenz.' Franz Müller said, putting down his cudgel. He tried to take his coat off, but it was difficult with the injury to his left arm. 'Vincenz, take your shirt off. Cut off the sleeve and wrap it around Günther's wound.' Vincenz did as he was instructed. 'Tie it tight.' The blood soon started showing through again. 'Cut off the other sleeve, and bind that around over the top.' Vincenz cut off the other sleeve from his shirt and bound it over the first one. The blood soon showed through again. 'We've got to get him to a doctor, Vincenz, or your daughter will be a widow.'

'Not till I've killed the bastard who did it.'

'No, Vincenz, carry the boy, every second counts.' Vincenz hesitated, then scooped Günther up in his arms. He left the tower, Franz following him. Vincenz felt the warm blood of his potential grandchildren running out down his bare back. They made their way back down the Judengasse towards the city. As they drew level with the synagogue, a Jew was carrying a burnt child towards it.

'Where are you going with the child?' Franz asked.

'Doctor Nuñez is treating the wounded in the synagogue,' the man replied, without glancing at them.

'Vincenz, take him into the synagogue,' Franz said.

'I'm not taking my son-in-law into a synagogue with all those dirty Jews.'

'Vincenz, it's his only hope. Nuñez is the best doctor in the city, by a long way. I heard Mayor Friedrich won't see anyone else.'

'No, not in there, not on your life.'

'Vincenz, it's not my life, it's Günther's.'

Vincenz hesitated, then barged past the Jew with the

child and ran towards the synagogue.

# CHAPTER TWENTY-THREE

Two men were standing at the door of the synagogue as Barnard Voigt staggered in, Köhler over his shoulder. 'Is there a doctor here?' Voigt shouted.

'Yes, Doctor Nuñez is here. Come this way,' the elder of the two men said. Men and women were lying in rows on the floor. In one row, the bodies had blankets covering them completely. Many people knelt beside their loved ones, comforting them as best they could. Two boys sat in front of the eastern wall with scissors and a knife, cutting sheets into bandages. Behind them was a wooden structure supporting a large chest, almost completely obscured by curtains. Above that was gold lettering on a black background, strange lettering, Hebrew he assumed. Ahead of him, Barnard could see Doctor Nuñez, bent over a patient.

'Doctor Nuñez, treat this man!' Barnard Voigt commanded. Manuel looked up, as Barnard lay Frederick Köhler gently down beside him. Manuel examined Köhler's wound. He turned and took a bandage from a bag.

'Here, hold this against the wound. Keep pressure on it. I'll have to get the ball out, but not now,' Manuel said, turning back to the man he had been treating.

'Do it now, Doctor Nuñez. Frederick is newly married. That's an old Jew.'

'So he may be, but his blood is no different to your friend's, except that he's lost much more of it. Your friend will live, but this man will die if I don't finish cleaning and stitching his wound.'

'What about that woman? The one with Rabbi Levi. She looks even worse.'

'She is. There's nothing more I can do for her.' Manuel soaked a bandage in brandy from a cask beside him, and continued cleaning the wound of his patient. Then he threaded a needle, dowsed the needle and thread in brandy, and began stitching. Barnard bit his lip and pressed on the bandage over Frederick's wound.

'You'll be alright, Frederick. Doctor Nuñez will see to you in a minute. He's a good doctor, the mayor tells me. The best there is. Does it hurt?'

'It hurts like hell, sergeant.' Köhler winced. 'Sergeant, if I don't make it, will you do something for me?'

'Of course. What is it?'

'Tell my wife Heidi, that I love her.' Barnard squeezed Köhler's hand. 'We only have a rented room. I don't know what she'll do without my wage. We may have a child that I'll never see. Could you keep an eye on them for me, sergeant?'

'Of course, Frederick. Doctor Nuñez, will you hurry up for God's sake?'

'I'm thirsty. Is there any water?' Köhler groaned.

'Sarah, water!' Manuel shouted. A young woman looked up. She was tending a pot that had been set up on a tripod over a fire. She took a jug from beside the pot and a beaker. She filled the beaker and brought it over. She knelt beside Frederick, put her hand under his head, and lifted it.

'Here, just sip it. It's been boiled, but it's cool enough now,' she said soothingly. Frederick took a sip, then a larger sip.

'Thank you,' he said. Sarah grabbed a blanket from a pile beside her, folded it and placed it under his head, before she lowered it down.

'Right, let's have another look at you,' Manuel said, turning to Frederick. 'Take the bandage away now, sergeant. I'm going to cut the shirt away, so I can get a good look.' He turned back towards the patient he had been tending and grabbed a large leather bag. He put it down beside him and rummaged in it. He took out a scalpel and dowsed it in brandy. Then he cut the bloodied shirt away from the wound. He turned again to his bag and took out a small pair of forceps. He dowsed those in brandy too. He bent over Frederick and inserted the forceps into the wound. He opened the jaws slightly. Frederick screamed. 'You're going to be fine. I can see the musket ball. It hasn't hit anything vital. We can't have you screaming like that, and upsetting the other patients. I'll give you some laudanum, a tincture of opium. That will stop the pain.' Manuel reached again into his bag, and brought out a brown, glass bottle. He poured some into the goblet of water and handed it to Frederick. 'Drink this, and I'll operate in about a quarter of an hour.'

Manuel sterilised the forceps in brandy and removed the dressing from Köhler's wound. The musket ball was easy enough to remove, but it had hit a rib. Having removed the musket ball, he removed the pieces of splintered rib. He examined what was left, and he didn't like it. It wasn't helping that Sergeant Voigt was peering over his shoulder. The remaining section of the rib was jagged. If left in, it could puncture a lung or blood vessel.

'Is he going to be alright, doctor? You've got the musket ball out.' Voigt asked, his voice wavering.

'If I leave this jagged piece of rib in, it could pierce a lung. I'm will have to take the rib out too.'

'Will he live, Doctor Nuñez?'

'I hope so. You aren't helping, staring over my shoulder. For heaven's sake, go and see the rabbi. Ask him to pray. Pray yourself! Anything, just leave me to get on with this.' Voigt hesitated for a moment, then walked away. Manuel selected a fine saw from his bag and sterilised it. He cleaned the wound again, with brandy, then he placed the saw edge against the rib, and began sawing, with gentle, short strokes. He found the repetitive motion soothing, in a way. His mind drifted to Maria, as it did more and more often every day, despite his best efforts. Why should she convert to Judaism? There is nothing about Judaism to be ashamed of, far from it. But it had become a stigma, and he was hiding his true identity himself. He should be proud to be Jewish, yet Rabbi Levi was right. He wouldn't be in the position he was, if he had been true to himself, not here anyway. Frankfurt was fundamentally anti-Semitic. But if he sold up and left, maybe he could live his true life. Where? He'd fled Flanders in the war. Rome perhaps? If the Italians were all like Maria, maybe they were happy with the Jews in their midst. No, there's nobody like Maria, or her brother, come to that. The saw was passing the halfway point. Not far to go now. I've got to stop sitting on the fence, one way or another. Yes, it'll hurt my mother, but I'll be baptised. I can't lose Maria. When this is over, I'll sell up, and ride to Frascati. She'll have to teach me Italian, of course. I'm a good learner. By the time I've found a suitable practice, I'll be fluent enough. We'll have Christian children, free of prejudice. Mother will love them anyway, I'm sure she will. Something inside her will bleed, but something in all of us bleeds. There, that's it. Manuel put down the saw and sterilised the forceps again. He removed the piece of rib, then took a brandy-soaked cloth and cleaned away the sawdust from the wound. Then he threaded his needle, sterilised it, and started to sew.

# CHAPTER TWENTY-FOUR

Franz scurried ahead of Vincenz and opened the synagogue door for him. The synagogue was bathed in candlelight. The floor was covered in regimented rows of the injured. Their loved ones were at their sides, murmuring reassurance, and praying.

'This way, Vincenz, I see Doctor Nuñez, over there.' Franz led the way through the injured, Vincenz followed him, with Günther over his shoulder. Manuel had his back to them as they approached. He was bent over a man, working on the injured man's side, sewing.

Manuel was sewing Köhler's wound as a shadow approached. He sensed a body being lowered to the ground beside him. Then he was told to stop what he was doing and attend to the new arrival. It was somebody's son-in-law. Manuel focussed on the wound in hand. It wouldn't take a minute, then he'd be able to attend to it. He was rather pleased with his handiwork. "Leave the Jew" got his attention.

'Doctor Nuñez, this man needs your help!' Fettmilch shouted. Manuel didn't reply. He was concentrating on sewing Köhler's abdomen. Vincenz lay Günther on the floor next to Köhler, without looking at Köhler's face.

'Leave him, doctor, this is my son-in-law. You must save him.' Manuel glanced at Günther.

'Yes, I will, as soon as I've stitched this wound. I won't be a minute.'

'Now, doctor, leave the Jew. They're worthless.'

'As it happens, he isn't a Jew,' Manuel murmured, as he neatly stitched Köhler's wound. 'But if a Jew were in greater need, I'd treat the Jew.'

'Jewish scum, what would a doctor help Jews for?' Vincenz spat the words.

'Possibly, because I'm a Jew myself.'

Before he knew what he'd said, Manuel recognised the Jew hater as a grocer and baker, Fettmilch. That was the name. Gingerbread, the speciality. Fettmilch wanted to take his son-in-law to a "decent doctor" but his companion, correctly, argued that he didn't have time. Then Sergeant Voigt returned, wanting to know how Köhler was. In what could only have been two seconds, at most, Manuel finished stitching Köhler's wound. In the same two seconds, he felt the most immense sense of relief. He had become Jewish again, no longer hiding or acting a role. Manuel was his mother's son. Where did that leave Maria? Did it matter? It mattered more than anything. He needed her. He ached for her, only her. Where was she? She's a meddler. She proved that when Edith and Daniel were murdered. She has justice stamped in the centre of every exquisite bone in her body. If it had been her rib he had sawn through, a golden glow would have been shining out. Maria would have been drawn to this slaughter, like a needle to a lodestone. She'd have interfered and is probably dead. Yahweh, please forgive me. Please spare Maria, let her live. I vow not to forsake you again, if only you spare her. Please spare her.

Vincenz was speechless. He turned to pick Günther up again. He'd carry him into the city, find some decent doctor.

'No, Vincenz, we don't have time. It has to be Doctor Nuñez. Look, he's nearly finished with that fellow, haven't you, doctor?' Then Franz recognised the patient, Guardsman Köhler, Günther's only victim.

'How is he, doctor?' Sergeant Voigt asked, returning with two goblets of water. Voigt dropped the goblets when he recognised Fettmilch and Müller. He drew his sword. Vincenz drew his sword, and Franz fumbled in his pocket with his left hand for his cudgel. 'Drop your weapons!'

'Not a chance, Voigt. Drop yours! There's going to be a new council, and I will be mayor. You'll answer to me, or you'll swing at the gallows. Which is it to be?' Vincenz snarled.

Manuel was dragged back to the present as Fettmilch and Voigt fought, their swords clashing over him. His first instinct was to shield his patient, but there had to be something else he could do. The son-in-law had been lain the other side of Köhler. He had a gunshot wound in the thigh. It was serious. It had hit an artery. The leg would have to come off, and a tourniquet applied to stop the bleeding. Then he'd sew a flap of skin over the wound. He couldn't do that with swords clashing overhead. When Mayor Friedrich had visited him about his gout, he had told him that Fettmilch had been demanding expulsion of the Jews, and wanting to know his rights. It must have been he who had caused all this death and destruction. Maria had thought Fettmilch might have been the murderer. The monster who had strangled his aunt and uncle might be there, above him. As sword pounded sword, he looked around at the dying and the maimed. He wondered how he would continue operating with his trembling hands. His tongue ran over his lips and tasted the salt of the sweat which was running from his brow. His superficial temporal artery was pounding, and his chest was tightening. He felt a little dizzy. He wondered if he was having a heart attack. If he was going to die, he might as well do something for his people, something for Daniel and Edith. He reached into his surgeon's bag and pulled out his longest scalpel. His body unwound, turning and rising. His legs shook as he focussed on Fettmilch's femoral artery. Manuel's right hand gripped the scalpel as it traversed towards Fettmilch's thigh. From the corner of his left eye, something black was descending.

# CHAPTER TWENTY-FIVE

Maria clutched her rifle as she and Antonio ran back into Judengasse. They dodged around the bodies in the street. A man bumped into her and dropped a sack. 'Sorry!' he said as he bent down and pushed two silver candle sticks back into the sack, then ran off, back towards the city. They stooped as they ran, in a vain attempt to avoid the heat of the burning buildings. Maria recognised the Jewish undertaker, Isaac. He was staring at his burning building. She ran over to him.

'Have you seen Doctor Nuñez?' she yelled at him. He didn't seem to hear her, he just stared into the flames.

'She's dead. She couldn't get out. It should be me in there.'

'Who's dead?' Maria asked.

'Sarah, my wife. She couldn't get out. It was so quick. One second we were eating, the next we were burning. Why? Who did this?'

'Have you seen Doctor Nuñez?' Maria asked again.

'They're taking bodies to the synagogue. I should go in and get Sarah. She needs to be taken there. I shouldn't have left her.'

Maria ran towards the synagogue; Antonio ran after her. He glanced over his shoulder and saw the undertaker walk into the flames. Antonio stumbled, then caught up with Maria. The synagogue seemed bigger than it had been the last time they had passed it. Maria was a pace ahead of Antonio as she raced through the open doorway. The air inside the high-walled stone structure was cool. They stopped, their eyes scanning the scene, wails and screams flooding their ears. Maria saw him. He was bent over a body and reaching into his bag. Fettmilch parried a lunge by Voigt and was about to lunge himself. Müller had a club raised and was about to strike Manuel. She caught Antonio's glance from the corner of her eye. Nothing needed to be said. She knew her twin, and his mind was her mind. Her thumb pulled back the hammer of her rifle as the butt thumped into her shoulder. The muzzle rose, and she squeezed the trigger. The recoil twisted her to her right, and she saw the smoke spilling from Antonio's rifle. As her gaze flashed back to Manuel, she saw Müller's club falling from his hand. Her shot had hit his shoulder. Antonio had hit Fettmilch, also in the shoulder. They both slumped to the floor. Maria ran towards Manuel. She was screaming his name, but couldn't hear her own words. There was only silence. Her eyes met his. A scalpel fell from his hand. It hit the stone floor, but she didn't hear the tinkle of impact. His arms enveloped her. His arms squeezed her and her fingers danced across his back. She couldn't breathe, but she didn't need to. A great white light was flooding through her, washing away her pain and her shame. She writhed as it cleansed her, letting it soak every part of her, from the tips of her hair to her toenails. Gradually, the ringing in her ears became voices. Müller and Fettmilch were screaming. Sergeant Voigt had his arm around Antonio.

'I suppose you'd better tell me about Judaism,' she smiled.

Antonio smiled as he watched his twin sister's passionate embrace. He was happy for her. She hadn't been really happy since that day at the washhouse. Then his thoughts turned to Greta. He tried to picture her, her smile, her hair, the shape of her. Something, someone, was intruding on his image of her. It was that Jew, Joseph, her medical student friend. His smile dissolved. If he had to, he would fight him. He'd fight to keep the girl he loved. His blood pounded in his head.

'What are you doing here? You were in jail,' Sergeant Barnard Voigt asked as he stood over Fettmilch and Müller, who had their hands pressed against their shoulder wounds. Antonio looked up.

'Aren't you happy we are? I just saved your life.'

'Yes, of course I'm grateful, but I don't understand. We took your lock picks.'

'Before they vented their anger here, Fettmilch and his mob attacked the city hall. They released us, along with the other prisoners. Your boss, the mayor, is in the jail now.'

'I should go there and release him. Will you help me get these two into the crypt?' Voigt asked, pointing his sword tip at Fettmilch and Müller.

'I'd better look at their wounds first,' Manuel suggested, smiling at Maria, and releasing his embrace.

'Let them bleed to death, doctor. It's no loss, and they'll die anyway, after this.' Sergeant Voigt replied.

'Perhaps, but I've sworn an oath. I have to, however much I hate them.' Manuel examined the prisoners. Then he reached into his medical bag and started work on them.

'Sergeant, thank God you're all right.' They all looked around as Corporal Schulz walked towards them, rubbing the back of his head.

'I'm all right. What happened to you?' Voigt asked.

'They were in the guard tower. I got a shot off at him,' Schulz said, pointing at Günther. 'I was fighting with Fettmilch and the next thing I knew, I woke up with a pounding head, on the floor.'

'Thank God you're here. I must go to city hall and release the mayor. Can you guard these prisoners until I get back? I'm sure Herr Standen here will help, won't you?' Sergeant Voigt asked, turning to Antonio.

'Yes, of course, but where do we stand?'

'Erm, here with Schulz. They don't look like they'll cause too much trouble. Tie them up as soon as the doctor has finished with them, and get them secured in the crypt with the other prisoners. I'll be back as soon as I can.'

'No, Barnard, I mean where do Maria and I stand regarding being escaped prisoners? The mayor had us locked up.'

'Oh, I see what you mean. I don't know. I'll tell him you saved my life. That should count in your favour. But if he thinks he could have kept a lid on this, if you hadn't started interfering and investigating the Bamberger murders, well, I don't know. Perhaps you should leave the city. You too, Doctor Nuñez. You were involved in the apron thefts.'

'Nothing would give me greater pleasure,' Manuel murmured, without looking up from Fettmilch's shoulder. 'But I will need a few weeks to sell the surgery and pack my things.'

'Yes, of course.' Sergeant Voigt stroked his beard. Then he put his arm around Antonio's shoulder and guided him a few steps away from the others. 'The three of you can stay at my house until you are ready to leave. That is, if the mayor still considers you criminals rather than heroes. He'll never think I might be harbouring you myself. I'm going to be busy, but my house is painted red and green. It's on Wilhelm Straße, just off the market square. Tell my wife Gertrude, I sent you.'

'She must be a trusting soul to take three strangers in, after all this rioting.'

'She isn't that trusting. Tell her, let me think. Tell her große würst sent you.'

'Is that her pet name for you?' Antonio asked, smiling, as Voigt turned red.

It took another hour before Manuel was satisfied that he had done as much as he could. Sam had been sent to rouse other local doctors, and Ingrid had come to help with nursing. Antonio, Maria and Manuel arrived on the Standen cart at Sergeant Voigt's house. Gertrude hadn't gone to bed. She'd heard the rioting and had been sitting in her rocking chair in the kitchen worrying about Barnard. When she heard the knocking on the door, she expected the worst. She got up, took a poker from the fire, and went to the door. Her face was white in the light of the candles in the wall brackets. She unlocked and opened the door, clutching the poker behind her back.

'Gertrude, Barnard said to tell you that große würst sent us,' Antonio said. Colour returned to Gertrude's face. In fact, she turned quite red.

'Is he alright? I've heard there's been trouble.'

'Yes, he's alright. Can you let us in, please? We'll tell you all about it.' Antonio replied. 'Is there somewhere we can put our cart and horses?'

'Yes, I'll show you. Why, it's Doctor Nuñez. Please go through to the kitchen. You too, miss.' Gertrude went outside with Antonio and opened the stable door. She waited while he unharnessed Allegro and Bellezza. There was plenty of straw for them, and Antonio took some carrots from a sack on the cart. Antonio comforted them and fed them the carrots. He took a flagon of wine from the cart, then followed Gertrude back inside. Gertrude gave them some bread and cheese, which they ate voraciously, accompanied by the wine. Antonio explained the events of the evening, while Maria and Manuel held hands and gazed into each other's eyes. Antonio was just about to recount how he had shot Fettmilch in the shoulder when they heard Barnard's key in the door. Gertrude leapt to her feet. When he came through the kitchen door, she threw her arms around his neck. 'I was so worried. It must have been terrible. I could see the flames from here.'

'Yes, darling, it was. I owe my life to Antonio here, and his sister Maria. Thanks to them, we have the ringleaders in custody. We hope the rest will disperse. I explained everything to the mayor. You have nothing to fear,' he said, turning to Antonio and Maria. 'You're welcome to stay here or return to the rented house. It's up to you.'

'Come and stay with me,' Manuel said. 'We have a lot of talking to do.'

Despite the exhaustion of recent events, Maria found it hard to sleep. She wondered what life might have been like without her right hand. Would Manuel still have loved her? What will life be like now? She still held reservations about converting to Judaism. She couldn't understand why the Jews were hated so much, but they were. The evidence of that would be scarred on her memory for all her days. She feared for their children. Can a child understand how to conceal what they have been taught to believe? She would teach them to wrestle and fight, but could she teach them to control their emotions? She imagined situations in which they might angrily reveal their Jewishness. Then the white light that had flooded through her, engulfed her again, and carried her to the land of dreams, dreams of Manuel, his arms, his lips, his…

Manuel had the table laid for breakfast when Maria came down. Antonio was already eating some bread and honey, washed down with beer. Manuel embraced her and they kissed again. Antonio looked away, put his bread down, and drained his goblet of beer. Then he refilled it.

'I could do this for ever, but I think you should eat, my darling,' Manuel whispered, releasing her and pulling out a chair for her. Maria sat down, and Manuel sat opposite her. 'So have you decided that you want to convert to Judaism? Secretly, I mean, of course.'

'Yes, for you, if it's so important to you. I can't say it doesn't worry me, not for myself, but if we have children.'

'I understand. It's funny, back in the synagogue, I'd decided to marry you, if you'd have me, whether or not you'd convert. Then I realised how your sense of right and wrong would draw you in. I imagined you in that hell. Fear for your safety overcame me. I prayed to Yahweh to save you. I vowed not to forsake him, if he protected you.'

'Who is Yahweh?' Maria asked.

'Yahweh is what we call God.'

'What would constitute forsaking? Are you suggesting we have to be openly Jewish? That our children have to wear yellow armbands?'

'I haven't thought it through. No, I don't think so. I don't think I could inflict that on you, let alone our children. I think our faith would have to remain concealed, and yet, I made a vow.' Manuel stared at his plate.

'Talking of concealment, why did you lie about your surgery being decorated? It clearly hadn't been. I wondered if you were having an affair with Ingrid.'

'No, but it does concern Ingrid. From the moment I set eyes on you, I couldn't stop thinking about you. I wanted to see you again as soon as I could. I told Ingrid that I'd been called away to an emergency, and left her looking after the patients. I could hardly stroll into the surgery and say the emergency had been a false alarm and I'm taking Maria and Antonio on a city tour instead. I don't like lying, and as you can tell, I'm not very good at it.'

'I don't want to interfere,' Antonio interjected, 'but it seems to me that the persecution isn't your fault. Why should you accept it? I don't think you'd be able to do all the good you do as a doctor if they condemned you to the fringe of society.'

'That's unusually eloquent for you, brother.'

'I'm not the dumb brother I pretend to be.'

'It's not pretence, but thank you. Although I suppose you must share my intelligence, you just like to save it, for special occasions.'

'It seems like a special occasion. Anyway, I don't see what's wrong with being both Jewish and Christian. Jesus was a Jew. So was Saint Paul. Who says you can't be both?

Be Christian when you're with Christians, and Jewish when you're with Jews. What is the difference, anyway?'

'Yes, Manuel. You'd better tell me about Judaism, as it appears I'm going to convert, or at least add it to my repertoire,' Maria said.

'The festivals are different. There are some foods we don't eat, and we prepare food in a particular way. It's to do with eating healthily in a hot country. Actually, not just hot countries. You'd be appalled to know how many Germans have tapeworms from eating pork. We believe in one God who has always existed and will always exist. God rewards those who follow his laws, and punishes those who do not, but God is not vengeful. God loves all creation, all people, all animals, all plants, and so must we. God is neither man nor woman. We believe God made a covenant with us, and that we are chosen to be an example to the world. There is much more, but that is the essence.'

'Well, it doesn't sound that bad to me, sister. What do you think?'

'It sounds quite laudable to me too, brother. You say there is much more. How much more, Manuel?'

'The Torah is our bible, which starts with the five Books of Moses together with the prophets. There are 613 commandments, 248 do's and 365 do not's.'

'I thought there were only ten commandments,' Maria exclaimed.

'They're the big ones, but the Old Testament has all 613 in there. I'm particularly looking forward to number fourteen. That's from Deuteronomy, chapter ten, verse nineteen.'

'What is it?' Maria asked.

'Well, there is a slight difference between what it says, and what it means. It says, "You shall love the stranger, for you were strangers in the land of Egypt." What it means is love converts.'

'Then I shall look forward to being converted. What do we do next?' Maria asked. 'Do you want to stay here, now that the mayor seems to have forgiven us?'

'No, I don't think I want to live in the city where Edith and Daniel were murdered. The ringleaders may have been caught, but I will always look in a patient's eyes, wondering if they were at the burning of the Judengasse. I'll find a buyer for the practice and go wherever will suit us best.'

'How about Rome?' Antonio suggested. 'That's what our mother will want. Perhaps you could set up a medical practice with my girlfriend, Greta, if she'll forgive me.'

'My mother lives in Amsterdam. It's not a bad place to live and work, and raise children,' Manuel replied.

'I have another idea,' Maria said. 'How about Paris?'

'Why Paris?' Manuel asked. 'I speak a little French, but my Italian will quickly improve with your help.'

'Prince Louis is a friend of mine. His mother is ruling as regent, but he'll be king in his own right before long. Royal patronage is not to be sniffed at. Besides, I want to keep an eye on him. I became rather fond of him. We can work on your French.'

'I don't have a rival, do I?'

'Of course not, he's only twelve.'

They had just cleared away the breakfast things when Ingrid arrived. They heard her footsteps leading to the consulting room.

'We're in the kitchen, Ingrid!' Manuel called out. The kitchen door opened.

'Oh, you have company. What shall I do? Should I prepare for the patients? With everything going on, I don't know.'

'You mean last night's riots?' Manuel asked.

'Last night was awful, but it isn't over. There's a mob throwing rocks at city hall. They say that the Jews have all fled the city and have set up an encampment outside.'

'We caught the ringleaders. I thought it was all over,' Maria said.

'Ingrid, do you know what's happening at the synagogue?' Manuel asked.

'I heard some rioters are still there, but I don't know.'

'I must go,' Manuel said, grabbing his medical bag.

'We're coming with you,' Maria said. Antonio was already loading the rifles.

◇ ◇ ◇

They could hear the shouting from the market square as soon as they left Manuel's house. There was a large crowd throwing stones at the city hall. There were occasional shots fired from the broken windows of the city hall. They could hear Sergeant Voigt's voice, calling on the rioters to disperse. They didn't seem in the mood to comply.

'Should we try to help?' Antonio asked.

'I don't see what we could do,' Manuel replied. 'It's the wounded in the synagogue I want to see. If there are rioters there, I'll need your help.'

'We'll help you, darling. Is there a route off the major streets?'

'Yes, follow me.'

Manuel led them away from the market square. It was a long detour, but they arrived at the Judengasse. Jagged brick walls stood between charred wooden columns. Beams had burnt away. Broken pottery, bent and twisted ironwork, and burnt fabrics littered the street. Stray dogs approached them and sniffed at them. A cat ran past with a rat between its teeth. As they approached the synagogue, they saw a small group pelting the walls and windows with bricks they were collecting from burnt houses. There were two men directing them, but most of the group were boys, no older than ten. They were shouting "Jews go home!". Maria held her rifle in her left hand, and pulled her flintlock pistol from her belt with her right hand. She cocked the hammer with her thumb and fired into the air. The shouting stopped. Antonio had his rifle aimed at the tallest of the two men.

'No, you go home!' Maria shouted, as she tucked her

pistol into her belt and aimed her rifle. The men looked at them. One child started to cry. Then the men led the children away, past Maria, Antonio and Manuel. The men glowered at them, and some boys poked their tongues out. Maria waved the muzzle of her rifle, directing them away from the synagogue. Manuel ran to the door of the synagogue, and knocked. He shouted something that neither Maria nor Antonio understood, but they heard the door being unlocked. 'Antonio, can you keep guard? I want to be with Manuel.'

'Of course.'

When Maria entered the synagogue, there seemed to be more order than the night before. Sam and Sarah were still there. Sarah was making hot drinks, and Sam was taking the drinks around to the wounded and their families. Manuel was talking with Rabbi Levi and two men. She went over to them.

'Heinrich, Edwin, it's been so good of you to help,' Manuel said.

'Not at all, Manuel. When we heard that a good Christian doctor like yourself was ministering to the Jewish wounded, we thought we should help too, whatever the bishop might say. Anyway, I haven't treated as many wounds since I served in the war in the Low Countries,' Heinrich replied. Maria saw Manuel swallow, then smile.

'Isn't there a hospital that the wounded could be moved to?' Maria asked.

'Gentlemen, can I introduce my fiancée, Maria? Maria, these are fellow surgeons, Heinrich and Edwin.' The surgeons bowed their heads. 'The church runs the hospitals, Maria, darling. They don't admit Jewish patients.'

'You seem remarkably well armed, for such a beautiful young lady, Maria,' Heinrich commented.

'The rifle has been useful, hasn't it, Manuel?'

'Yes, she saved my life last night when the mob broke in. She's a formidable woman. So, Heinrich, Edwin, shall we get back to work?'

The doctors walked together up and down the rows of wounded, pausing at some, before continuing.

'Manuel, I've given your proposal a lot of thought, and I accept,' Heinrich said. Maria saw Manuel and Heinrich shake hands.

'Manuel is a lucky man, Maria,' Rabbi Levi said.

'I think I'm a lucky woman. I've never felt quite as I do now. I feel, I don't know, clean.'

'Cleaner than your clothes, I'm sure. Clean in spirit?'

'Yes, I suppose you could put it like that. I'm going to learn about Judaism, wish me luck. There are hundreds of things to learn, Manuel says.'

'Yes, but loving is the greatest thing. You're off to a good start.'

'Is the crypt still full of prisoners?'

'No, the guards took them all back to the jail in city hall last night, after things quietened down a bit. I understand you'll be leaving with Manuel. He's asked Heinrich to take over his practice. I don't know if he will, but if he does, where will you go?'

'I think they have agreed to that already. They just shook hands. We're not sure where we'll go yet. My parents live near Rome. His mother is in Amsterdam. I have a friend in Paris who could be very helpful. We shall have to think about it. Are you going to stay, after this I mean?'

'Of course. There is much rebuilding to do. My kehillot kodesh, or congregation, as you would say, need me. They are camping outside the city for now. We must rebuild their homes and the synagogue. It will take time.'

'How can you bear the hatred? I don't understand it.'

'We have become used to it. Together, we are strong. We trust in Yahweh.' Maria heard footsteps and felt Manuel's arms reach around her.

'Darling, I'm needed here for a few days. Heinrich is going to take over my practice and run it alongside his own. His son has just graduated from medical school, so it's perfect. I think we should be able to leave by the end of the week. But in the meantime, the wounded need my attention.'

'Is it safe here? The mob may return.'

'Don't worry, Maria,' Rabbi Levi said. 'Once our people are safely established outside the city, a party of men are coming back to defend the synagogue. I think the mob has achieved their aims here, for the present.'

'Maria, it's silent outside now,' Antonio called across from the doorway. 'I think I'll see what I can do for Sergeant Voigt.' Maria looked from Manuel to Antonio and back again.

'Go with Antonio, dearest. I'll be fine here. After all, Heinrich and Edwin will vouch for me.'

# CHAPTER TWENTY-SIX

Maria and Antonio made their way back to the market square. Antonio peered around the corner of the street across from it. There were some bodies on the ground. The rioters appeared to be sheltering behind the fountain, from where they were firing the occasional shot at city hall, and the guards then returned fire.

'There's no chance of getting in the front door. Let's see if we can get around the back,' Antonio whispered. They went back the way they had come, then turned left into a side street. Ahead of them they saw some sacks piled against the wall on the left. They approached it. Behind the sacks was a door. 'I wonder why these sacks are here?'

'Look at the hinges. The door opens outwards. They've tried to prevent escape this way. Let's shift these sacks.' They soon had the sacks clear and tried the door. It was locked. Maria took out her lock picks and soon had the door open.

'What if the rebels come back to check, and pile the sacks back? They could trap us.'

'Look up, there are windows. We could climb down a rope if necessary. Do you want to find out how Sergeant Voigt is or not? I'm happy to leave them to it and get back to Manuel.'

'Yes.' Antonio opened the door, and they went inside.

Maria locked the door behind them. They were in a corridor with a high ceiling. Windows set high in the wall provided light. To their left there appeared to be a dead end, so they crept off to their right, staying close to the wall. At the end, there was another corridor to their left. Antonio peered around the corner. 'All clear.' They made their way along that corridor. When they were about halfway along, they could see the entrance hall ahead of them. Desks had been piled against the huge oak doors. They edged into the hall and looked around. The shutters had been closed on the lower windows. Light filtered in from the fanlights above. Papers were scattered across the tiled floor. Portraits of the city's mayors had been torn from the wall, and lay ripped in their smashed frames on the floor. They saw the office of the Marktmeister, abandoned. They climbed the stairs and headed for where the sporadic shots seemed to be coming from. Antonio peered around the door. He could see Sergeant Voigt, Corporal Schulz, and several other guards crouched by the windows of what had been a banqueting hall. Mayor Friedrich was sitting on the floor behind an overturned dining table. 'Barnard, it's Antonio and Maria,' Antonio called out. Barnard whipped around, levelling his musket. 'Don't shoot! It's us.'

'What are you doing here? How did you get in?' Sergeant Voigt asked, the pitch of his voice higher than normal.

'We moved some sacks that were piled against the back door and picked the lock. Don't worry, we locked it again. We wondered if you needed any help?'

'Good God, I thought you'd be halfway back to Rome by now,' Sergeant Voigt replied, as Antonio and Maria crawled across the floor towards him.

'Maria's going to marry Manuel, Doctor Nuñez. We have to wait until he's finished treating the wounded, then we'll be on our way.'

'But why did you come here?'

'To see how you were. We worked together. I wanted to

know.'

'You must be insane, but I'm touched. Well, as you can tell, although we have Fettmilch, Müller, Fuchs, and a few of the other ringleaders in the cells, many of the rebels are continuing to fight. We've sent a messenger to the emperor seeking help. We're hoping the army will arrive soon. Until then, we can hold out here. We have plenty of food, water, and ammunition.'

'Why are they still fighting?' Maria asked.

'Ask the mayor.' Mayor Hans Friedrich crawled to the edge of the table and peered around it.

'I hadn't appreciated how widespread the anger was. I thought it was just Fettmilch, Krause, and Müller, they did all the talking. There was nothing I could do about it. I'd appealed to the emperor to fund the construction of grain silos, but heard nothing back. The Jews had the emperor's protection, so I couldn't do anything about them either. I certainly wasn't going to give them elections to the town council. We city fathers have run the city for generations. They have their representatives. That should be sufficient.'

'It would appear not,' Maria murmured.

'Well, they'll pay with their lives for this.' Spittle flew from the mayor's lips as he spoke.

'How is the guardsman that you carried to the synagogue?' Antonio asked, wiping the mayor's spittle from his face.

'Köhler, yes, he's recovering, thanks to Doctor Nuñez. He's at home with his wife,' Barnard replied. 'You were right, you know, about the Bambergers. It was Vincenz Fettmilch who killed them. We got a confession from Franz Müller. He'd lied for him. Fettmilch was going to tell his wife about a woman he was seeing if he didn't. That was before the mob sobered up and started again. Could you get a message to Gertrude? Tell her we're well, and holding out. Ask her to check on Klara Schulz and Bridgette Köhler. Will you do that?'

'Yes, of course,' Antonio replied. 'Could you spare a

guard to cover us from a rear window as we make our escape?'

'Lehmann. Go to the rear. Shoot anyone who tries to intercept them,' Sergeant Voigt ordered, and one guardsman crawled back from the window. 'Antonio, would you pile the sacks back the way they were? It would be better if they didn't know we'd had visitors.'

Maria worked at the lock with her lock picks. She kept a gentle pressure on the tensioner as she tried to remember which order the true and false gates came in. It was taking her longer than she hoped.

'I'm feeling bad about running from this fight,' Antonio whispered.

'Why?'

'I don't know, just that I like Barnard. He seems like a decent man.'

'Barnard locked us in the cells. He'd have watched as they chopped our hands off. Barnard might even have held your hand on the block, as the axeman did his work. It's not our fight. It seems to me that the rebels had some legitimate gripes. Don't you want to get to Turin and make up with Greta?'

'Yes, of course. But I fear it too. What if she doesn't forgive me?'

'That's her problem. Will you shut up, I'm trying to get this door open.'

'Do you want me to have a go?'

'No! Just shut up. There, that's got it. I remembered the false gates in the order that I opened the door, but that was the other side. Is it all clear?'

'Wait!' Guardsman Lehmann called down from the window above. Someone's coming. Two of them, armed with clubs. 'They've seen the sacks. They're running to the door.' Lehmann fired his musket. 'Damn, missed. They're at the door.' Maria glanced at her twin and knew that his doubt had dissolved. She flung open the door, feeling it hit someone as it opened. Antonio was right behind her. One rioter had been thrown to his knees as the door flew open. The other had raised a club and was poised to strike Maria. Antonio flew at him, head butting him in the solar plexus. The other rioter sprang to his feet, but Maria snatched his wrist, judged her moment, sank into a crouch, twisting and thrusting her leg to become the pivot, then threw him over her. He landed with a thump on his back, the wind knocked out of him.

'Reinforce the door!' Antonio shouted up to Guardsman Lehmann as they ran down the street. When they got to the corner, Antonio peered around. There was a party of three running from the fountain towards them. Musket balls bounced off the cobbles at their feet as the defenders fired from the front windows. 'This way, Maria, run!' Antonio shouted as he ran off, away from their pursuers. They ran as fast as they could, darting down side streets, left then right. Only after half a mile did they stop and look back. There was no sign of the rioters.

'We seem to be clear,' Maria panted.

'What about the defenders? We had to leave the door unlocked. Do you think they might have stormed the building?'

'Perhaps, but what can we do about it? You shouted for the defenders to reinforce the door. What else could we have done?'

'Stayed and fought?'

'This isn't our fight, Antonio. I'd fight anyone or anything to save Manuel. But we need to get away from this place.'

'I suppose, but what about Gertrude? We must warn her.'

'You're right about that. It's this way, isn't it?'

Antonio knocked, and Gertrude opened the door.

'It's you. Barnard isn't here.'

'We know. We've just come from him.'

'Come in then,' Gertrude said, standing aside as they entered, then closing, locking, and bolting the door behind them. 'Where is he? Is he safe?'

'He's defending the city hall and the mayor,' Antonio replied. 'He has good men with him. A messenger has gone to the emperor, and they hope an army will arrive in a few days. They have enough food, water, and ammunition to hold out until then. He's worried about you and the other wives. He asks if you'll check on Klara Schulz and Bridgette Köhler. I think he's worried that they might try to take you hostage.'

'Oh Lord! Yes, of course. He'd be forced to give up then. I couldn't put him through that.'

'Is there somewhere you could go with the other wives? Somewhere the rioters wouldn't think of?' Maria asked. Gertrude paced the hallway, clenching and unclenching her fists. She turned to face them, tears welling in her eyes.

'No, not here. These people were our neighbours, our friends. They know our friends. I can't think of anyone here.'

'Then what about somewhere else? Do you have anyone nearby but outside the city?' Maria asked.

'There's my sister Lena. She lives with her husband Frank in Dreieich, with their children. They have a big house. Frank is a builder. It's about three hours' walk south of here.'

'That's perfect. Get together the things you need. Take us to Klara, then Bridgette,' Maria instructed.

'Then we'll go to Dreieich?' Gertrude asked. 'How will we get out of the city?'

'We'll get you out, somehow,' Maria said, stroking her chin. 'We're going to all have to go together. Give me a moment with Antonio.'

'Would you like some beer? There's a fresh barrel opened.'

'Yes please,' Maria replied, as Gertrude went to the kitchen. 'Do you think they'll have posted sentries at the city gates?'

'Probably. But they're merchants, not soldiers. They won't be well disciplined. We should escape after nightfall.'

'Yes, but I'm not going without Manuel. We'll have to wait until he's ready to go. What do we do until then?'

'Why not wait in the synagogue? That's where Manuel is,' Antonio suggested. Maria thought for a moment.

'I'm sorry. Maybe you aren't as stupid as I thought. That's not a bad idea. It's the last place they'll look. They seem to think the Jews carry some sort of disease. They'll assume that their friends and neighbours all think the same. If the Jews have fled the city, why would they look for Gertrude, and the other wives, in the synagogue? We might be able to help with the wounded. At least we'd be doing something useful, rather than just waiting.'

They waited with Gertrude until dusk. Then they went first to Klara Schulz, then Bridgette Köhler. The Schulz children were ten and eleven. They thought it was quite an adventure. Bridgette refused to leave, not while Frederick was still in hospital. She said that she would take her baby with her to the convent and plead for admission. It was near the monastery hospital where her Frederick was. She felt sure they would be safe there. Maria and Antonio were reluctant, but Gertrude thought it was for the best, and that the sisters at the convent would protect her. Maria, Antonio, Gertrude, Klara, and the boys Heinrich junior and Ralph arrived at the synagogue a little after dark. The boys sniggered and the others smiled as Manuel and Maria kissed. Eventually, Maria pulled away.

'When will you be ready to leave, darling?'

'By the morning. We will have completed all the essential surgery. The two over there have fever, an infection from their burns. I expect the crises to come tonight. They will either recover or die, but there may be something I can do. I'll need to gather some things from the house. Just some clothes, my savings, and the Janssenscope. Heinrich is buying all the other medical items and furniture. His son will need them.' Heinrich Schulz junior looked up at his name, but quickly realised he wasn't being called. He was proud to share his father's name, but sometimes it caused confusion.

'When will he give you the money for your house?' Maria asked. 'We can't wait for long.'

'There's no need. I can trust him. I'll let him know where to send the bill of exchange by post once we're settled.'

'Oh, yes. Shall I get your things?'

'Why? Your wagon is at my house. We can just load everything, and everyone on board, and go.'

One of the fever patients survived the night, and the other didn't. In the dawn twilight, they all made their way to Manuel's house. He packed up his things and loaded them onto the wagon. They left the Janssenscope until the last minute, as it kept the boys amused. They enjoyed examining his specimens and examined the mould from the stale bread in the house too. Manuel had found some turnips and made a pottage of what remained edible in the house. At dusk, Antonio hitched Allegro and Bellezza to the wagon. Everyone except him and Maria got into the back of the wagon. Then Antonio and Maria tied a canvas sheet over the wagon. Maria opened the stable doors, and Antonio drove out onto the street. There was the sound of some shouting and the occasional gunshot from the market square. Maria climbed up beside Antonio and they set off around the backstreets to the South Gate. Maria jumped down as they approached the gate and followed the wagon. There were two of the rebels at the gate. They both held short infantry swords. Antonio explained he was a trader who had attended the fair and got delayed by the rebellion. One rebel stepped forward and demanded to search the wagon. The other rebel lingered by the gate. Anthony kept talking to the rebel by the wagon as he untied the canvas cover. Maria slinked along the wall towards the guard, who remained by the gate. He didn't see her coming, or the butt of her pistol as it struck his skull. As the rebel guard at the wagon looked around, Antonio landed an uppercut under his chin. Antonio dragged his victim to the gatehouse, where he and Maria trussed the rebels up with some rope they had on the wagon. They gagged them for good measure, wanting to get as many miles under their wheels as possible, before the alarm was raised.

They dropped Gertrude and the Schulz's off at Gertrude's sister in Dreieich. Lena insisted on feeding them before they continued their journey, and none of them could resist. Manuel had eaten nothing but the odd cup of chicken soup between tending the wounded. Neither Antonio nor Maria could remember their last decent meal. For sure, it hadn't been in the cells. Lena laid on an excellent spread. Manuel avoided the cured pork sausage, and Maria followed his example. Eventually, Antonio, Maria, and Manuel boarded their wagon. Gertrude and Klara waved as they trundled their way south.

'How long will it take to reach Frascati?' Manuel asked.

'About a month,' Maria replied. 'But we're not going directly to Frascati. We need to stop awhile near Turin. Don't worry, it's on the way.'

'Why do we need to stop in Turin?'

'So that Antonio can make up with his girlfriend, Greta.'

'How long will that take?'

'I don't know. But one way or the other, not long is my guess.' Maria glanced at Antonio, who scowled back at her. 'Don't worry, Greta's father is a doctor. You can talk shop, when I don't have other uses for you.'

# CHAPTER TWENTY-SEVEN

They had crossed the Alps, and were driving along a track with a long lake to their right. Boats were out fishing, the sun was shining, Maria was holding hands with Manuel and Antonio was staring blankly at the road ahead. They passed through a bustling small town into a forested section. Maria studied Antonio's face.

'There's a junction ahead, in about a mile,' Maria said. 'If we turn left, it will take us south. If we continue straight, it will take us to Turin. Which is it to be?'

'South. Greta won't have me back now. You saw how angry she was. I blew it completely. I didn't mean to, but you were right. I never asked her what she wanted. It didn't occur to me. I don't even deserve her, she's too good for me. She's a doctor now, curing people, like Manuel, and I just make wine. South, I can't face her.'

'It's probably none of my business,' Manuel said, 'but I think you have a very bad case of love sickness, with a large portion of melancholy on the side. I would prescribe continuing straight on. If you don't, it may never leave you. Do you want to live your whole life feeling as you do now?'

'He's right, Antonio. You have to fight for love. We all make mistakes, God knows I did. How is your arm, Manuel?'

'Much better.'

'What's the worst that can happen? She turns us away,

and we spend a few more days driving through this beautiful landscape. If we head south, you'll never know what might have been.'

'What can I say to make up for my stupidity?'

'I'm not sure you'll need to. She must have known how stupid you are for ages,' Maria saw the slightest hint of a smile, which quickly reverted to a scowl. 'Here it is, this is the junction.' Antonio reined Bellezza and Allegro in. The cart stopped. Antonio took a deep breath, then flicked the reins and they trundled straight ahead towards Turin.

# CHAPTER TWENTY EIGHT

In the town of Nichelino, near Turin, a debate about blood was taking place over dinner. Greta's studies had come to an end, at least as far as Bologna University was concerned. She wasn't sure what she would do next. She had invited Joseph to stay. She thought he'd be a useful distraction, but it wasn't working. She couldn't stop comparing him to Antonio. Joseph was serious, and in some areas, dogmatic. He was handsome, but she was not attracted to him. Antonio, on the other hand, worked hard on the vineyard, but was also dashing and adventurous. He could be funny, especially when recounting the exploits of his father and sister. Some of it seemed far-fetched, but having met Maria, she believed every word. He drew her like a moth to a flame. If only he had initiated his proposal, rather than his mother. Joseph and Antonio had one thing in common. They were both loyal.

'Have you really not read Servetus, Doctor Ferrero?' Joseph asked his host.

'Who?' Doctor Gino Ferrero asked.

'Michael Servetus. He was a quite brilliant man. Galileo lent me his book, Christianismi Restitutio. He says that blood flows from the right to the left chambers of the heart via the lungs. It is there that air enters the blood and gives it a bright red colour. So there aren't two separate bloods, the venous and the arterial, there is only one blood.'

'Is that what they're teaching you in Bologna, Greta?' Gino asked.

'No, Papa. There are three distinct physiological fluids. There is the arterial blood, the venous blood and the nervous fluid,' Greta replied.

'Good, I don't need to go back to school again then,' her father smiled.

'No, Papa. There have to be three fluids. It's the natural order of things. There are three bodily systems. The vegetative system deals with nourishment and growth. It is controlled by the liver and fed by the dark venous blood. The muscular system is controlled by the heart and fed by the bright arterial blood. The nervous function of sensitivity and irritability is controlled by the brain and fed by the nervous fluid. There are always three of everything: animals of the air, the sea, and the land. There are men of labour, men of prayer, and men of war.'

'But I'm sure he's right. All the dissections I've made corroborate his theory,' Joseph argued.

'Perhaps we could avoid talking about dissections over dinner?' Suggested Hilda Ferrero, Greta's mother. They finished dinner with talk of the weather and alpine flowers. 'Would you help me clear away please, Greta?' Hilda asked.

'Greta, why did you invite that Joseph boy to stay?'

'I'm wondering that too, Mama. He's a friend, and I thought he'd take my mind off things.'

'What things, dear? Has something happened between you and Antonio?'

'Don't mention him, Mama. He's dead to me now,' Greta said, scrubbing the plates in the bowl, vigorously. 'I never want to see him again.'

'What happened, dear?'

'Antonio came to see me in Bologna. They were on their way to Frankfurt. He told me that his father had bought a neighbouring farm, because his mother wanted me to marry him and move there, and that she'd be there to help with our children.'

'I see.'

'His mother has it all worked out. He's just a mother's boy. I think I'll marry a man, if I marry anybody.'

'Joseph perhaps?'

'Absolutely not.'

'He seems very clever.'

'He's wrong about blood, though. Everyone says the arterial and venous bloods are separate.'

'Everyone can be wrong, Greta.'

Greta was becoming increasingly irritated by Joseph. His arguments were persuasive, but ran contrary to almost everything she had spent years assiduously learning. Her father had asked Joseph what he was going to do now that they had finished their degrees. He was planning to go to Cairo in search of new books for his library. She didn't know what she would do, but it wouldn't be looking for more books. She'd read enough books in the last five years to last a lifetime. Greta's mother knocked on the bedroom door, then opened it.

'Are you coming down? Breakfast is ready.'

'I'm not hungry, Mama.' Hilda came and sat on the bed, and put her arm around Greta.

'Tell me about it.'

'Oh, what is there to tell? Joseph seems to have everything planned. He's going to Cairo to buy books. Then there are dozens of scholars he wants to visit. He plans to write books, telling everyone how wrong they are.'

'What are your plans, dear?'

'I don't know. For the last five years, I've studied medicine. I want to cure people, help people, like Papa.'

'You could help your father here, although his practice suffered when the crops failed. It's been a struggle to pay for your education. Of course we'd love to have you here with us.'

'Thank you, Mama.'

'I can't help noticing there's something missing. There's a sparkle that's left you. I hesitate to bring it up again, but both you and Antonio seemed so happy together.'

'So why couldn't he just ask me to marry him, rather than going on about what his mother wanted?'

'Men are strange, clumsy creatures. They rarely know what to say or how to say it. Your father certainly doesn't, a lot of the time. Of course, Antonio's mother would like to keep her family around her, so do I. But mothers also want what's best for their children. Birds have to fly the nest. I just think you seemed so right together, happy together. You aren't happy now, are you?'

'No, Mama.'

Greta felt confused and angry. Joseph was getting on her nerves. She felt very mortal, afraid, and bereft. She got up and walked over to the window. A cart was approaching the house, and Antonio was driving. His sister was with him, and a handsome young man. She wanted to run to the door. She wanted to fling it open. Her head told her to wait, to let him come to her. She backed away from the window. There was a knock at the door. It was Antonio's knock. She heard her mother's footsteps, then the door open.

'Antonio, it's good to see you again, and you must be Maria. You're obviously twins.'

'Mrs Ferrero, this is Doctor Manuel Nuñez, Maria's fiancé,' Antonio explained.

'Well come in. You're all very welcome. Greta's in the front room with a friend from university. I think he's getting on her nerves, he's certainly getting on mine. Why don't the rest of you follow me to the kitchen?' Hilda led Maria and Manuel to the kitchen. Antonio knocked on the door to the front room.

'Come in,' Greta said. He opened the door. She was standing by the window, looking outside. Joseph was sitting at the table writing. Anthony stood in the doorway. Joseph looked up.

'Hello, Antonio,' Joseph said.

'What the hell is he doing here?'

'Joseph is just staying for a few days, on his way to Cairo.' Greta explained.

'Turin is a funny place to be staying if you're on your way from Bologna to Cairo.'

'It's not very far out of my way, and Greta has needed cheering up. You upset her terribly, you know.' Antonio became aware of his fists clenching and unclenching. He wanted to take Joseph outside and beat him senseless.

'I don't think that is any of your business.'

'Joseph, would you leave us alone for a while? Papa is very keen to hear more about blood,' Greta lied. Joseph smiled, stood up, and left the room, closing the door behind him.

Antonio breathed deeply. He had to control himself. Part of him knew that if he messed this up he would regret it for the rest of his life. It would be so terribly easy to tip the wrong way. He took more breaths. His face was burning. If I upset her terribly, she must still love me. Why else would she be so upset? Think Antonio! Don't mess this up.

'Greta, I'm sorry. It all came out wrong. What I meant to say was that I love you, and I want to spend the rest of my life with you. It doesn't matter if that's here, or on the vineyard. What matters is being with you.'

'Is your mother happy with that?'

'I don't know. I haven't seen her for months. But I don't care, you're all that matters.'

Greta turned to look at Antonio. She held the power of happiness over him. She could see that. Yet the power she held had a twin, of sorts. It was the reciprocal power he held over her. She had been a fool to deny it. She ran to him and flung her arms around him. Her eyes bored into his soul.

'You can ask me again, if you want to.'

'Greta, will you marry me?'

'Yes. Yes I will.'

Gino opened several flagons of wine. It wasn't often they had seven around the table. Joseph was talking to Manuel about physiology and blood. Maria was asking Hilda about Greta, and Antonio was telling Greta about their adventures in Frankfurt.

'Have you really not read Servetus, Manuel?' Joseph asked.

'Who?'

'Michael Servetus. He was a quite brilliant man. Galileo lent me his book, Christianismi Restitutio. He says that blood flows from the right to the left chambers of the heart via the lungs. It is there that air enters the blood and gives it a bright red colour. So there aren't two separate bloods, the venous and the arterial, there is only one blood.'

'No, I haven't come across that idea. I'll give it some thought,' Manuel replied.

'We don't have to go over all that nonsense again, Joseph, do we?' Greta's father asked. 'Why can't you just accept what you're taught?'

'If my eyes, and my brain tell me the teaching is wrong, I have to go with my brain,' Joseph replied.

'So where are you going to have the wedding?' Greta's father asked.

'Wherever Greta wants it,' Antonio replied. 'It can't be soon enough for me.'

'We could speak to the priest here,' Greta said. 'See how soon he could arrange the wedding'

'But won't you want your family with you?' Hilda asked Antonio.

'Yes, but Greta's happiness is the main thing. I'm happy to marry her here tomorrow.'

'Why not marry twice? Here and in Frascati?' Maria suggested. 'We're going to marry in Frascati and

Amsterdam.'

'That seems unusual, Maria,' Hilda observed.

'Well, it's about a four or five day' ride from here to Frascati, but it would be two weeks from Frascati to Amsterdam. We'll marry for my family in the cathedral in Frascati, and for Manuel's family in the synagogue in Amsterdam.'

'Why a synagogue?' Gino asked.

'Manuel is Jewish, and it's important to him, and to his mother. We will raise any children that we are blessed with in both faiths. Why not, Jesus was a Jew.'

Everyone seemed to reach for their goblets at the same time. It was a while before anyone spoke.

'This is an excellent wine, Doctor Ferrero. It's Sangiovese, like ours, isn't it?'

'Yes. The soil here is poor, which makes the yield low, but the quality is excellent. So will you have two weddings as well?'

'Whatever Greta wants. I'd be happy to marry her on every day of my life.'

'Where will you make your home, dear?' Hilda asked.

'I've been giving it a lot of thought. Antonio's business is the vineyard, when he's not solving crimes with Maria. What would he do here? He has a vineyard in Frascati, and Rome needs more doctors. So I think it'll be Frascati.'

'Why don't we come with you then? We want to meet Antonio's family. It will be good to get to know each other before the wedding. You can get a locum to look after the practice while we're away, can't you, Gino?' Hilda asked.

'Yes, of course, Hilda.'

# CHAPTER TWENTY-NINE

William was playing outside when he saw the cart turn into their lane. Immediately, he recognised it. He didn't know whether to run and greet his elder siblings, or run inside and tell his parents. William decided that this was far too good news to pass up being the bringer of, and ran inside.

'Papa, Mama, it's Antonio and Maria. They're coming up the lane. There are others with them, too.' Francesca put down her sewing, and Antonio put down his quill. They ran outside, followed by Anna and Charlotte. Antonio reined in Bellezza and Allegro. Maria jumped down and hugged Francesca, then Anthony. Gino, Hilda and Greta climbed down from the back of the cart, followed by Manuel.

'Papa, Mama, may I introduce Doctor Manuel Nuñez, my fiancé.'

'If you will permit me, Sir Anthony, I beg your beautiful daughter's hand in wedlock?' Manuel asked.

'Formalities be damned. I haven't seen such unbridled happiness in her eyes, well, ever.' Anthony shook Manuel's hand, then hugged him. Antonio introduced Greta and her parents. For a few minutes, they stood outside introducing themselves.

'Mama, Papa, Greta and I have some good news too. We are also going to be married. We hope to ask the bishop and be married here. That's why Gino and Hilda have come with us,' Antonio announced.

'Oh my Lord, the spare bedrooms, and the dinner. Anthony, we'll need another chicken. Would you kill and gut one, please? William, Anna, come and help me get the spare bedrooms ready. Antonio, serve our guests some wine and settle them in the front room,' Francesca commanded, as she rushed back into the house, followed by William and Anna.

When Anthony had finished gutting the chicken, he washed his hands and returned to the front room. His guests were all standing and drinking his wine.

'Wouldn't you all like to sit down?' he asked.

'Papa, it's been a long ride. I don't think anyone could sit down yet, even if we wanted to.' Antonio said.

'What kept you so long? I've been out of my mind with worry. The letter came from Thomas Berry weeks ago. I sorted out a contract for bottles and sent the first delivery off to London. How did it take you so long to get back?'

'We've had a bit of an adventure. Manuel's aunt and uncle were murdered. It was his uncle, Daniel, who sorted out the contract for us, and the bill of exchange. We got involved in tracking down the murderer.'

'Did you find him?'

'Yes, but not before he'd started a riot and massacred dozens of Jews. The rifles came in useful. Maria used hers saving Manuel's life, and I saved the sergeant of the city guard.'

'Good Lord, I want to hear all about it later, but not now. Here comes your mother.'

'Antonio, Maria, would you take the bags up to the spare rooms and show Gino, Hilda, Greta and Manuel their rooms? I'll put some water on to boil in case anyone wants a bath. Oh my Lord, two weddings. I couldn't be happier,' Francesca beamed.

'Actually, Mama, three weddings.' Maria said.

'Whatever do you mean, three weddings? Who else is

getting married?'

'Nobody else but Manuel and I will be married twice. A Christian wedding here, and a Jewish wedding in Amsterdam,' Maria explained.

'A Jewish wedding, whatever do you mean, dear?'

'Manuel is Jewish. It's important to him, and it's important to his mother.' There was a long pause. 'We both know, better than you, the dangers of being Jewish. Any children we have, we will raise in both faiths. We will school them carefully in secrecy. Manuel is a master at the art.'

Anthony lay awake in bed. Francesca rolled over, then propped herself up on her elbows and kissed him.

'You can't sleep either, then?'

'No, I'm worried about Maria. It's a terrible risk marrying a Jew,' Francesca whispered.

'Yes it is. But he seems like a very nice man. I know you had delusions about her marrying a duke, but we'd both come to think she'd never marry anyone. Then in Paris I found out why. I've never seen her so happy, have you?'

'No, I haven't. I said she'd have to follow her heart wherever it took her, and she has. That's all that matters. I dare say a duke would have had countless mistresses and made her terribly unhappy. We can have odd notions of what would be perfect, and we're hardly ever right. Good night my love.'

'Hey, why waste a sleepless night, when love is all around?'

Over dinner, the story of Antonio and Maria's adventures were teased out of them. Manuel promised to show Anthony his Janssenscope the next day. The full horrors of Daniel and Edith's murders and the subsequent uprising they left until the children had gone to bed.

'But I don't understand why people hate the Jews so much. Why?' Francesca asked.

'It's a good question, dear,' Anthony replied. 'I think there are several related questions. Why do a group of people hate another group of people? Why should the hated group so often be the Jews? And why does an individual hate?'

'But we are talking about Jews, dear,' Francesca said, puzzled.

'I know, but I have lived my life against the backdrop of wars between Catholics and Protestants. Each group has been driven into a frenzy of hatred for the other. They'll burn a "heretic" to death without a moment's hesitation. It's often political, but sometimes genuine, religious, dogmatical lunacy. Jews are not always the target of this fanatical hatred. It can happen to others. As Maria said earlier, they encountered many witch burnings on their journey. But let's look at the Jews. Maria told us of Daniel's views, and I think he was right. The Jews were exiled from their land by the crusades and the Moors. The Easter story has been used to demonise them. I really must let myself into the papal library one day, and find out what all the other rejected gospels had to say. I wonder if they told the same story about the Jews asking for Barabbas rather than Jesus to be released. They have had their freedom to work restricted and been channelled into moneylending. That's not a popular profession, necessary as it is.'

'Darling, you should teach Manuel to wrestle, like you taught the children. He should be able to defend himself against these hateful people,' Francesca suggested.

'I think Maria is perfectly able to teach him. I'm sure they'll enjoy rolling around, grappling with each other in the straw. But I'm happy to assist when required.'

'Defending myself from Maria might be quite useful. She nearly tore my arm from its socket,' Manuel said, rubbing his shoulder. When the laughter died down, Gino spoke.

'Anthony, I'm not sure I grasped your point about political motives,'

'I'm sorry, Gino. It's simply that if things aren't going well for your group, let's call it a kingdom, then the way to unite your people is to blame their troubles on another group, be that witches, Catholics, or Jews.'

'Have you met many Jews?' Manuel asked.

'I've met a few. When I was in Constantinople, a Jew by the name of Joseph taught me Arabic. He was a delightful fellow. Then, although I didn't actually meet him, there was the case of Queen Elizabeth's physician. He was a Jew. Doctor Lopez, if I remember correctly. I was working for the Earl of Essex. Essex had fallen out of favour with the queen. Essex came up with the idea that the doctor was involved in a plot to kill the queen. Lopez confessed under torture, then retracted it. They executed him, of course. The prosecutor described him as "a Jewish doctor worse than Judas himself, not a new Christian, but a very Jew." I think Essex either invented the plot or believed gossip too readily. He was desperate for something to get him back in the queen's good favour. It didn't work. I think the queen was sorry to lose her doctor.

'Why do people believe that their troubles are because of the Jews?' Maria asked. 'I follow that you can try to unite your group by blaming its problems on a scapegoat, but why do people believe it? Are they all that gullible?'

'Most of them are, I'm afraid,' Anthony replied. 'We're pack animals. We follow the leader. The smallest difference marks a person as not part of the pack. If a child is fatter than the rest, or has a squint say, the bullies will persecute him, or her.'

'You make a good point, Anthony,' Manuel observed. 'To look at, you couldn't tell that I'm a Jew. I have attended both Catholic and Lutheran churches, and passed myself off as a Christian. It has been unfortunate, but beneficial for me. Jews who have converted have been accepted in the main. So the difference that turns a well-liked family doctor into a despised demon may be invisible, a simple decision, by the hated and the hater.'

'That's right,' Anthony said. 'What was my other question? Oh yes, it was why does an individual hate? Let's take the most loving person I know, Francesca. She hates Cardinal Aldobrandini. She hates him because she loves me, and Aldobrandini almost got me killed. If she didn't love me, she wouldn't hate him. They're connected, love and hate. It comes back to my theory of credit and debt. I believe that in the beginning, there was nothing. Then nothing exploded into a credit universe and a debt universe. An explorer that Maria and I met in Paris told us about Taoism. Taoists believe everything is derived from opposites, yin and yang. It's the same idea. Everything is connected somehow. I don't believe that love could exist without hate.'

'But that's absurd, dear,' Francesca objected.

'No, the more I think about it, the more certain I am.'

'We'll the more certain you are, the more doubtful I become,' Francesca replied.

# AFTERWORD

The Fettmilch uprising actually lasted for longer than I could spare Maria and Antonio. Accounts differ, but it seems to have lasted from 1612 to 1616. Fettmilch and thirty-eight of his supporters were arrested in September 1614, and in February 1616, Fettmilch and six others were executed. Commentators differ on whether the uprising was primarily aimed at the Jews, or at the patriarchal city governance. The likelihood is that it was both.

I hope you have enjoyed my story. If you have, then please post a review on Amazon. It's always good to hear what people have liked, and educational to learn what they haven't. Called to Account is the fourth book in the series. The first book is The Spy who Sank the Armada. It is a fictionalised biography of Sir Anthony Standen, who was Sir Francis Walsingham's principal spy providing him with all the intelligence on the Armada that he needed. It was only after publishing it that I completed my family history research and discovered that he was my 10th great-granduncle. The subsequent books, Fire and Earth, and The Suggested Assassin are fictional, regarding the family Standen, but set on a historical stage that I have made as authentic as I can. You can follow my latest news on my website davidvswest.co.uk

# ABOUT THE AUTHOR

David V.S. West was educated at St. Edmund Hall, Oxford, where he took a B.A. in Engineering Science. During a career in engineering and project management he was commissioned by Gower Publishing to write a book on Project Sponsorship. This led him to study creative writing with the Open University, and a new career as a writer. The Spy who Sank the Armada is the first novel in the series The Sir Anthony Standen Adventures. The second is Fire and Earth, and the third is The Suggested Assassin. He lives in Wiltshire.